She was lying on a canopied bed. A pink satin comforter with silver butterflies was turned back under her, and a frilly white pillow was behind her head. Her hair was braided and wrapped around her head in a crown, and the rouge on her cheeks and lips stood out against the blue-white pallor of her skin. Her eyes bulged, and there were purple marks on her throat.

"All right, you son of a bitch," said a cold voice behind me, "straighten up real slow and keep your hands where I can see them, or you're a dead man, so help me God."

DEATH'S BRIGHT ARROW

DEATH'S BRIGHT ARROW

A Paddy Moretti Mystery

James Sherburne

FAWCETT GOLD MEDAL • NEW YORK

A Fawcett Gold Medal Book
Published by Ballantine Books
Copyright © 1989 by James Sherburne

Library of Congress Catalog Card Number: 89-91165

ISBN 0-449-13434-2

Manufactured in the United States of America

First Edition: August 1989

To
JOAN SMITH
A Valuable Person

Contents

1

The Turnpike Takes Its Toll

My opinion of Jack Farringay, based on an adequate amount of personal experience, was that he had the idealism of a pawnbroker, the probity of a politician, and the morality of a pimp, all concealed by a facade of good fellowship that made him doubly dangerous to the uninstructed. When I saw him studying a scratch sheet by the paddock rail, my first impulse was to turn away and beat a quick retreat into the crowd. And then I recognized the man he was with. It was Sandy Braddock, stepbrother of the Squire of Kirkargyle.

It was May of 1894, and I was in Lexington, Kentucky, to cover the Spring Meet at the Fair Grounds for *The Spirit of the Times*, the sporting paper that employed me. In addition to reporting the races, I also made it a point to meet and interview as many of the local horse breeders as possible. Most of the stable owners were happy to oblige the readers of the country's premier sporting paper, but not Caleb McAuliffe, owner of the two-hundred-odd acres of rolling bluegrass pasture, immaculate stables, and porticoed mansion that constituted Kirkargyle. McAuliffe hated the press, local, state, and national, and was not prepared to grant an exception in my case.

This would have been perfectly agreeable to me, but it

stuck in the craw of my editor, Otto Hochmuth, who indicated by telegraph that he would consider my failure to provide such an interview as a dereliction of duty calling for severe redress. In matters such as this, Hochmuth's word was as good as his bond, and I had already given considerable thought to the problem.

Now, seeing the opportunity of meeting the man who had been pointed out to me as Caleb McAuliffe's stepbrother, I did not hesitate. Extending my right hand and grinning with bogus bonhomie, I cried, "Jack, you old rascal, give me the grip of your good right hand, for it's been two years since I saw you last!"

Farringay didn't pale—he was too experienced a confidence man for that—but for a moment his eyes narrowed and his lips whitened under pressure. Then he smiled vaguely and said in an apologetic voice, "I'm sorry, old man, but I'm afraid you have the better of me."

I caught his hand and squeezed it, while getting a grasp on his elbow with my other hand and drawing him away from his companion. "Ah, Jack, you wouldn't be denyin' your bosom crony, would you? You wouldn't be forgetting your old pal Paddy Moretti, would you, Jack?"

By now we were six or eight feet away from Sandy Braddock, who was watching us curiously. Farringay turned his face away from him and said in a low, intense voice, "Stop talking in that unspeakable brogue—it wouldn't take in a four-year-old. What the hell do you want, Moretti?"

"A bit of companionship in the name of auld lang syne, Jack. Is that too much to ask—from a notorious grifter with a criminal record as long as my arm, who would no doubt be making a quick trip to the calaboose which is his home away from home if I was to raise my voice to the local constabulary?"

Farringay's smile broadened, revealing gleaming, regular teeth, and he clapped an arm around my shoulders. "Don't blow my cover, Paddy—I swear I'll make it worth your while," he said tightly. "We've been good friends—

remember how I helped save your bacon at that fight-store dust-up in Kansas? Why, if I hadn't pulled that pigeon drop on old What's-his-name, you'd never have found out who killed Kid Slaughter.''

"I remember it well, Jack—especially the sight of your big brown eyes looking at me along the barrel of that pepperpot revolver of yours.''

"Bygones, bygones, Paddy! It's always been a source of considerable amusement to me that for a few moments there in Cogswell we actually thought of ourselves as being on opposite sides of the fence, so to speak. Incredible! I can't wait to kick around old times with you, Paddy— we'll get together for a real gabfest soon. But right now—'' He tugged with quiet desperation against my grip on his elbow, his handsome features set in an expression of forced geniality.

I put my face close to his. "You introduce me to Sandy Braddock, and I'll try not to blow the whistle, Jack. Tell him we're the dearest of friends, and insist the three of us have a drink together after the races, and you'll have a fighting chance of spending the night outside of jail.''

He wasted no more than an instant glaring at me in helpless frustration. Then, with a convincing whoop of joy he turned toward Braddock and called, "Sandy, would you believe it? Here's my old friend Paddy Moretti, come to write about us in his famous newspaper column! Paddy. I'd like you to meet Sandy Braddock, from Kirkargyle.''

Braddock stepped toward us and extended his left hand. I checked my instinctive right-handed response and met him with my own left hand, as I glanced down his right arm to the hand that hung, black-gloved and open, against his thigh.

"Glad to know you, Moretti," he said in a deep, slightly harsh voice. "I've read some of your stuff. Not that I'm that much of a horseman—I leave the bloodlines and such to my stepbrother. Two-dollar bets are more my speed.''

I told him that the two-dollar bettor was the rock upon which the church was built. Jack Farringay produced a silver hip flask and proposed a drink all around, and then the bugle signaled the next race.

As the horses took their position at the starting gate I studied Sandy Braddock and remembered what I had heard about Kirkargyle Stables. One of the two or three outstanding horse farms in the region during the seventies and eighties, it had fallen on leaner days in the last few years, due partly, gossip maintained, to errors and indecision by the owner, Caleb McAuliffe. McAuliffe's hostility toward the press had prevented confirmation of this, however, which was the reason for Hochmuth's insistence on a personal interview.

Braddock was a sturdy, broad-shouldered man of slightly below normal height, thick-necked and firm-jawed, with wiry dark brown hair and surprising blue eyes. His features seemed set in an expression of frowning concentration, but when he smiled his demeanor became almost boyish. My eyes went back to his right hand, which lay without movement, fingers half-curled, against his leg. Obviously the hand was either paralyzed or artificial.

We watched the race. Neither Braddock nor Farringay had the winner, and Jack passed his flask again for mutual solace while I jotted down notes in my notebook. Then we put our heads together and picked our favorites for the next race, and Jack went in search of a bookmaker with our bets. I took the opportunity to ask Braddock about some of the better-known Kirkargyle horses—Uranus, Sebastian, and Actaeon—and he answered curtly, "Actaeon's dead."

"The devil he is! When did that happen?"

"Last week. Damn fool accident. He was out in the field alone, late in the afternoon, and a pack of wild dogs pulled him down. They tore his throat out."

"I've never heard of anything like that in my life!"

"Neither have I. Neither has anybody. But it happened." He shook his head. "Just the kind of thing you expect at Kirkargyle—disasters made to order."

"You mean there have been other accidents like that?"

"You might say so," he said dryly. "But how many times do accidents have to happen before they become so predictable they're not accidents anymore?" I raised my eyebrows questioningly, and he started to answer, then stopped himself. "You'll have to ask my stepbrother that," he said curtly. "He's the one who knows about the horse business."

I would have pursued the subject, but Jack Farringay came back to the box with our markers, and the conversation turned to the odds on the next race.

During the rest of the afternoon I divided my time between the McAuliffe box and my normal round of clubhouse, paddock, and betting ring. I jotted down descriptions of each race, added bits of local color, and interviewed owners, officials, and jockeys who had the time and the inclination to be interviewed, while returning at frequent intervals to maintain contact with Sandy Braddock and with Farringay's flask. When the last race ended both men were money ahead, and the flask was empty. I looked significantly at Farringay and said, "Well, I'm afraid that all good things must come to an end, so I guess I'll be bidding the two of you an affectionate farewell."

Farringay said, with as good grace as he could muster, "Why, don't rush off, Paddy. Why don't we go somewhere for a drink?"

Before I had to pretend a polite reluctance to presume further on our brief acquaintanceship, Sandy Braddock said, "Come along, Moretti. We'll adjourn to the taproom of the Leland Hotel. I've shown the barman there how to make the best toddy in Lexington."

We caught a cab outside the Fair Grounds entrance on South Broadway and clattered along through bustling traffic to the center of town. The Leland was a new hotel with *moderne* furnishings and paintings of French peasants instead of the racehorses and politicians one expected to see in Bluegrass hostelries. The taproom was small, rather dark, and smelled of beer and good tobacco. We seated ourselves at a table, and Sandy gave our order of three cold toddies to the white-jacketed waiter. When they arrived, he drained his glass, set it on the table with a satisfied thump, and ordered another round.

Jack and I kept pace with him, and within a few minutes we were as free and easy with one another as old messmates from a man o' war. The only problem was that Braddock didn't want to talk about Kirkargyle, not its owner, not its horses, not its problems. He talked about politics and art and music and women, about whether President Cleveland should recognize the provisional government in Hawaii and allow the free coining of silver, whether Winslow Homer was one of the great artists of the Western world—but nothing about the problems of his stepbrother's stable. Farringay was no help to me; he was obviously trying to ingratiate himself with Braddock, and showed no interest in any subjects except those initiated by him.

Once when Sandy left the table I said sternly to the handsome confidence man, "Come on, Jack. It wouldn't hurt you to help me turn the subject to the business at hand at least once during the evening, now would it?"

"The business at hand? Whose business do you mean, Moretti? My business has nothing to do with sporting newspapers, and I'm sure that Sandy's doesn't either. What's more, if you keep pushing him, he just may get the idea there's more than good fellowship behind your somewhat suffocating attentions. So why don't you just keep cadging your free drinks and relax?"

I studied the cleft in his square chin, wondering whether a fifty-cent piece pressed into it sideways would remain there indefinitely. "What's your angle, Jack? If you're trying to rope him into a bunco game, you may have your work cut out for you—I'd put him down for a very smooth article."

Jack raised his hands in protest. "My interests here extend in a different direction entirely. I give you my word of honor, I'm not working any grift on him. That's not to say there aren't a number of chickens ready for the plucking around here, but Braddock isn't one of them. Believe me.''

''Then what are you hanging around for? Merely indulging your appetite for horseraces and twelve-year-old bourbon whiskey?''

Farringay didn't answer, but Sandy Braddock, returning from the washroom, answered for him a few moments later. ''Better slow down on the hooch if you're figuring to see the fair Dorcas tonight, Jack. She doesn't fancy having her admirers pass out in front of her.'' He grinned at me. ''Your friend here has added himself to a hapless group, Moretti—the suitors of Dorcas McAuliffe. Give him your condolences. From what I've seen, his chance for success is small, and his chance for getting off the hook is nil.''

Farringay lowered his head and replied, either in embarrassment or an excellent imitation of it, ''Oh, come off it, Sandy. She's a wonderful girl, that's all. And we seem to find a lot to talk about. But as for being one of her suitors—well, that's a good ways down the pike, as you Kentuckians say.''

Braddock raised his glass in a toast. ''I give you my stepniece, gentlemen. To fire and ice. If the one don't get you, the other one will.''

''To your stepniece,'' Farringay echoed with fervor. I glanced at him quizzically and repeated the toast, and we all emptied our glasses.

''Honorable intentions from you, Jack?'' I asked. ''Isn't that on a par with leopards changing their spots? Don't tell me you've finally succumbed to the lure of domesticity. I don't believe I could stand the shock.''

Farringay regarded me coolly. ''I won't tell you anything, Moretti. And if you don't mind, let's drop the subject. I'm not comfortable discussing ladies in a saloon.''

I was so startled by this pious platitude from the lips of a unmitigated villain like Farringay that I let the statement go unchallenged.

We drank for another two hours. Braddock became more

outgoing with each toddy he consumed; his laugh became louder, his jokes broader, his opinions more absolute. His gestures also became more sweeping—but they were made with his left hand only. His right hand, half-curled and gloved, rested against his thigh throughout the evening, not appearing above the tabletop. Farringay was affable and amusing, but directed his efforts toward ingratiating himself with Braddock, paying as little attention to me as he could without appearing impolite.

I had no luck at all in eliciting any information about the prospects and problems of Kirkargyle and its owner.

At nine o'clock we ordered Welsh rarebit and black coffee. Sandy Braddock looked at me over a forkful of melted cheddar cheese and asked, "Where are you bunking, Moretti?" I told him I had engaged a room at the Phoenix Hotel. "That'll never do. How you gonna get the goods on my stepbrother there? You want to do some Kirkargyle keyhole peeping, you better do it from inside the old homestead. Come along with us."

I protested politely that I wouldn't dream of intruding on the McAuliffe family without an invitation. "Hell, I'm a McAuliffe, ain't I?" he demanded. "In everything but name, I am. And I'm inviting you. So that's that. And don't worry about putting the family out. Farringay's been sleeping at the farm more nights than he's stayed in town. Since you boys are old friends, you can bunk together."

I didn't protest anymore. Braddock called for the check, and paid it in spite of Jack's and my remonstrances. Then, walking none too steadily, we made our way out of the hotel and down Short Street to Smiley's Livery Stable, where Braddock put up his buggy when he came into Lexington, pausing en route to secure a quart of whiskey from a storefront entrepreneur whom Sandy addressed as Joe Bubbling-Over. A few minutes later we were crowded together behind a handsome chestnut mare, singing as we clipclopped over the cobblestones along the Frankfort pike.

It was a beautiful spring night in the Bluegrass: the air was cool and moist, and smelled of freshly turned sod and young vegetation. A low-riding quarter moon gave light enough to reveal the blossoming dogwood trees and forsythia bushes that lined the road. The chestnut mare obviously knew her way home, and we three roisterers were free to concentrate on our singing. Braddock seemed to have a predilection for Scottish songs, and offered "Lord Randall," "Loch Lomond," and "The Bonny Earl of Moray" in a pleasing, if somewhat hoarse, baritone. Farringay showed a preference for comic and sentimental favorites, including a version of "A Froggie Did a Wooing Go" that lasted through thirty verses. When my turn came around, I obliged with "McCann, He Was a Diver," "A Horse Named Bill," and the jewel of my repertoire, "God Damn the Lane Hotel."

As I was finishing the last bravura chorus, the chestnut mare turned from the Frankfort road and headed down a side lane. Almost immediately she halted before a thick wooden pole that had once been connected to a turnstile at the side of the road, but now lay in the dirt across our path.

Braddock leaned forward. "What the—" he began.

"You're back again, ye bastards? Then have another!" cried a voice from the small house behind the turnstile, and a shot boomed out in the quiet night. The whiskey bottle, half-elevated to my lips, disintegrated in a sudden cloud of broken glass and bourbon spray.

"It's Sean Carmody!" Braddock cried. "Get down!"

Farringay and I hadn't waited for his suggestion. Farringay was hunkered down behind the buggy's off rear wheel, and I was hugging the ground behind the near front one. Braddock, doubled up behind the splashboard, called out, "Carmody! It's Sandy Braddock! What the hell are you doing, man?"

Another shot crashed out, accompanied by an orange tongue of flame from the black mass of the tollhouse, and the sibilant whistle of the passing bullet. After a moment's silence, the voice behind the gun shouted, "So it's wanting to kill us all, you are? Then come on, ye scuts! Come and finish the job!''

A third shot banged out, and then a fourth. I buried my face in the dirt and tried to think of something to say that would have a pacific effect on the aroused marksman, but failed. Apparently Jack Farringay was likewise unsuccessful.

Then, instead of the expected fifth shot, we heard the metallic click of a hammer striking an empty cartridge case, followed by a muttered curse and a second click. Braddock raised his head and called, "Carmody! We're unarmed! Nobody wants to hurt you! Put the gun down and talk to me!"

There was a moment of silence, and then a pale shape appeared in the window of the house. As my eyes readjusted to the darkness, I saw it was a slightly built man wearing a light-colored shirt and dark trousers. He held one arm across his chest, with a revolver clenched in his fist. His face was a featureless blur.

"Braddock?" he said dully. "So now you're riding with the Regulators too? Have ye come to see if Fugate's done the job your brother pays him for? Ah, ye bastards!" he cried, his voice suddenly rising to a scream as he drew back his arm and flung the pistol toward us, "you've killed my Molly, goddamn you!"

The pistol thudded against the side of the buggy, and Braddock straightened up and jumped to the ground. He moved rapidly toward the tollhouse door as Farringay and I scrambled to our feet and followed him. Inside, the house was in complete darkness except for the pale moonlight that silhouetted the slight form of Carmody against a rectangle of window.

"Get us a light, man!" Braddock ordered. He crossed the room and seized Carmody by the arm and shook him. "We can't do anything till you get us a light!" After a moment the other man seemed to rouse himself and stepped away from the window into darkness. A few sec-

onds later a match flared, a lamp wick was lit, and the
room was suddenly filled with yellow light.

I gasped at what I saw.

On a double bed in the rear corner of the room lay a
woman in a gray dress that was wadded up around her
hips and thighs, revealing heavy legs in coarse woolen
stockings. Her eyes were closed, and her head rolled from
side to side on the pillow. The left side of her face, from
hairline to below her cheekbone, was swollen and pulpy
looking, and on her temple was an evil abrasion the size
and color of a ripe plum. Two dried trickles of blood ran
down her upper lip, and I saw they had stained her teeth.
She could have been in her late thirties, but the face of the
colleen she had been was still evident under the toneless
flesh.

A baby lay on the mattress beside her, and four pairs of
eyes gazed out from the darkness under the bed.

Sandy Braddock swore and stepped to the injured woman's side. "Molly, what's happened?" he demanded in a
shaken voice. "Can you hear me? My God, who did this
to you?"

The woman's eyes opened, and she stared up with an
unfocused gaze. "Oh, not the children! Don't hurt the
children! Please God, it ain't their fault!" Her face dis-
torted with terror, she struggled to pull herself to a sitting
position, then collapsed back onto the pillow with a shuddering groan.

"It was a rock they threw. It come in through the window and hit her right where she was standing," Carmody
said.

Braddock wheeled to face him. "She's badly hurt, Carmody. Has a doctor been called?"

"And who would have gone for a doctor, with your
murdering friends outside shooting at everything that
moves?"

Braddock stooped down to peer under the bed and began to drag out small bodies. "Come out now, and let me

look at you! Everybody all right? Nobody hurt? Speak up now!''

Four children, two boys and two girls ranging from three to eight years old, stared back at him unblinkingly. The eldest, a scrawny girl with her black hair plaited into a braid that reached her waist, shook her head. ''Ain't nobody hurt but Ma,'' she said in a small, flat voice.

Farringay broke his silence to ask what was going on, but Braddock didn't answer. Instead he turned to Carmody and brusquely ordered him to take the buggy outside and ride for the doctor. ''We'll be here till you get back—but you better make it fast.''

Carmody hesitated a moment, his face belligerent and desperate, then made his decision and ran from the house; a moment later we heard his voice urging the chestnut mare into a canter as the buggy spun away down the road.

Farringay and I exchanged glances, and Farringay touched Braddock on the arm. ''I don't know what the devil is going on here, but is there anything you want us to do, Sandy?''

Braddock stood a moment without answering, his powerful shoulders bent, and an expression of pain or sadness on his face. I noticed his left hand was held against his side, the fingers pressing into the flesh. Then he shook himself. ''Help me make Molly as comfortable as we can. See if you can find any clean cloths for bandages, Jack. Moretti, hunt up some fresh water. At least we can clean her up while we're waiting.''

It took Carmody twenty minutes to return with the doctor. During that time, as Braddock gently tended the injured woman, washing the ugly wound and covering it with a folded towel while the children stood in a row against the wall and watched in round-eyed silence, Farringay and I moved out onto the tiny front porch. He produced a cigar case and offered it to me, and we both lit up and smoked in silence for a while.

''You seem to have a gift, Moretti,'' he said at last, ''for carrying disaster with you wherever you go. It hangs around your neck like an albatross. In another age it would be the subject of an epic poem.''

"It's myself that's responsible for that poor woman in there with a hole in her forehead? Come on, Jack, you're the well-connected man in these parts. And what do you make of this business, anyway? Did you ever hear of these 'Regulators,' or this Fugate that Carmody was talking about?''

Farringay frowned at the smoldering tip of his *claro*. "Fugate works at Kirkargyle. The Regulators have something to do with the toll-road squabble that's going on down here—I don't know what, and I don't care. My interests lie in a different area entirely. And I would be happy to keep it that way, if you don't mind.''

"I don't mind at all—as long as one hand keeps washing the other, and I get the story I'm looking for. Now this Fugate fellow—does he have anything to do with McAuliffe's stable?''

"He does, yes. Manages it, as a matter of fact.''

"And these Regulator fellows—does he manage them, too?''

Farringay shook his head irritably. "I said I don't know anything about this toll-road business, Moretti. Can't see how it's any business of yours, either, but if you think it is, I suggest you address your questions to Sandy Braddock.''

I nodded agreeably. "Or maybe to the lady in the picture, Jack. Dorcas—wasn't that her name?''

"She has nothing to do with this,'' he snapped.

"And did I say she did? I'm just trying to get people's names straight before I meet them. This Dorcas—a woman of captivating assets, I gather.''

"Goddamn it—'' Farringay began, then stopped and cocked his head to one side. "Listen, there's a buggy coming. That must be Carmody with the doctor.''

And so it was. The chestnut mare, now gleaming with sweat, pounded up the lane and came to a panting stop beside the broken turnstile. Carmody threw himself from the seat on the left side as a heavyset bearded man in a wrinkled white suit alit more deliberately from the right. Carrying his black satchel in his hand, he stepped up on the porch. "Good evening, gentlemen. A bad business. Excuse me." He pushed past us and entered the house, with Carmody following, and the door slammed shut.

Jack and I waited another five minutes on the porch, and then Sandy Braddock emerged to join us. "Hell of a damn thing," he said heavily. "The liquor's dying in me, and our reserves are gone."

"How's the woman?" Jack asked.

"Not good. Doc doesn't think she'll make it. And Carmody with five kids on his hands. So much for the luck of the Irish."

"What about the law?" I asked. "Shouldn't somebody be getting the word to the sheriff?"

Braddock sighed. "I told Doc Foley we'd put in a call from Kirkargyle. Sheriff'll have men over here in half an hour, and he and Doc will see to Molly Carmody and find some place to put the kids. There's nothing keeping us here any longer, lads. Let's go find a drink."

The three of us climbed back into the buggy, and Sandy Braddock flicked the reins. The chestnut mare moved into a reluctant trot, and five minutes later we turned into a drive between two fieldstone pillars. The moon was gone from the sky, and the great colonnaded house stood out against the stars as unreally two-dimensional as a painted flat upon a stage. Sandy circled the house and stopped beside a small stable in the rear. "A horseman takes care of his mount before he thinks of himself," he said dryly, and proceeded to unharness the chestnut mare and lead her to her stall. Then he put one arm over Farringay's shoulders and drew him toward the house as I followed. "Now it's our turn," he said.

He led us through a dark hallway that opened into a dark room of indeterminate purpose, through that into another short, dark hall, and thence into a lighted study with paintings of thoroughbreds on the walls and bearskin rugs on the floor. He went directly to a bookcase, the bottom two shelves of which were lined with bottles and glasses. He poured himself a stiff drink and gestured toward the shelves with his gloved hand. "Help yourselves while I inform the sheriff of the situation, gentlemen." He took a step toward the door, and then paused and added with a half smile, "And, before I forget—welcome to Kirkargyle."

2

Reflections on Poetic
Inevitability

Farringay and I each carried a glass up to the bedroom we were to share, and I stretched out on the brightly quilted bed and sipped my bourbon as Jack fastidiously hung his coat and trousers over a wooden hanger. "Well, here we are again," I said. "It seems like only yesterday."

Farringay hung his shirt, collar, and tie over his coat, took off his shoes, polishing them with his stockinged feet, and stripped off his socks and garters. Then, clad only in his underwear, he reversed an armless chair and sat down with his forearms resting on its back. He regarded me gravely, his chiseled features set in an expression that conveyed trustworthiness and candor.

"Paddy, old comrade, it's important that we understand each other and guard against any possible *faux pas* that might cause inadvertent embarrassment. Now, this bizarre situation tonight has nothing to do with either of our objectives, and it would be a great mistake to involve ourselves in it in any way."

"It would?"

"Of course it would. It's purely a local issue, and has nothing to do with either of us. Your interest is writing a story on the McAuliffe stable, and mine is, as I'm afraid Sandy made only too clear, the young lady of the house. I suggest we emulate the shoemaker and stick to our lasts.''

"How do I know whether or not I'm interested in this Carmody business until I know about its connection to Kirkargyle?" I asked, sipping my whiskey pensively.

Farringay sighed. "You know Walt Whitman's poem 'The Song of the Open Road'? Well, he never would have written it about the Kentucky Bluegrass, because most of the roads around here aren't open at all. They're toll roads, privately owned, and they're closed to anybody who doesn't pay the price to travel on them—so much per horse, so much per wagon. Some of them even charge you to walk on the shoulder.''

"Is that legal?"

"According to the courts it is. But there are plenty of people who are damn tired of paying for the privilege of traveling to and from their own homes. Particularly people with businesses in the country, like horse farms. You can understand a man not wanting to pay hundreds of dollars a month just to bring a few wagon loads of feed to his stable.''

"So that's what the Regulators are doing—indicating the displeasure of the local gentry with the toll roads.''

"You could say that, yes.''

"The latest example of which is the unpleasantness tonight, involving a certain Fugate, who hails from right here at Kirkargyle?''

Farringay felt for the cleft in his chin as if to reassure himself it was still there. "That's what Carmody said—it may not even be true. Look, Moretti, the important thing is, it's not going to do either of us any good to get involved in this business. It's not going to help you get a story, and it's certainly not going to do me any good with Dorcas McAuliffe.''

I looked at him thoughtfully. "Tell me about Dorcas McAuliffe, Jack. Somehow, I've never thought of you as such an impassioned suitor. Or are there certain gross financial aspects involved?''

He straightened his shoulders and tilted up his chin manfully. ''I don't expect you to give it immediate credence, but I am seriously, deeply attracted to Dorcas McAuliffe. She is a woman who could give new meaning to my life. I have no greater ambition than to persuade her to share my future years.''

''Share and share alike,'' I said agreeably.

''I know what you're thinking, old friend. You question whether my motives are disinterested. Remembering the old Jack Farringay, it's difficult for you to believe in the new. You suspect an ulterior motive.''

''The profit motive, I believe it's called.''

He waved his hand in dismissal. ''You can't imagine how unimportant mere material considerations become when compared to the treasures of the heart. Ah, Paddy, try to understand—it's like being born again!''

''With a silver spoon in your mouth. If you're going to undergo the pains of redelivery, that's sure the way to do it.'' I sipped my bourbon, which was as authoritative as a bishop's blessing. ''It's all right, Jack. I won't cramp your style. If you can marry yourself an heiress and make yourself the Squire of Kirkargyle, why, more power to you. Live and let live. I hold no grudge for that Kansas business, even if you would have left me dead and buried in a hole in the prairie if you'd had your way. So put your mind at ease. I wouldn't dream of mentioning your unsavory past to anyone, under any conditions, unless forced into it by circumstances beyond my control.'' I paused to admire the way the whiskey beaded on the glass. ''So let's talk some more about the problems of the McAuliffes.''

Farringay compressed his lips as if he had bitten into a green persimmon. ''I think Caleb McAuliffe is behind the Regulators. His man Fugate is the local leader, and he wouldn't do it without the boss's okay.''

''All right, what about the stable? What did Sandy mean

when he said that when accidents happen so often they're predictable, then they're not accidents anymore?''

"There's been a run of bad luck. Two of Caleb's most promising horses have been killed in the last month— Actaeon, the colt Sandy mentioned who was pulled down by dogs last week, and a filly called Nile Queen who managed to step on a copperhead, if you can imagine it.''

"In the Bluegrass?''

"Oh, they have them here. Or at least they had one, which is all it takes. And besides that, there's been a procession of pulled ligaments, bruised fetlocks, damaged pasterns, split hooves, and all the other ills that horseflesh is heir to, up to and including the blind staggers. A very disheartening period for Kirkargyle, you may be sure.''

"Enough to jeopardize the future of the stable?''

"Oh, I wouldn't think so. No, nowhere near that serious. Kirkargyle is a rock. But enough to ruin a lot of dispositions.''

"Such as Caleb's.''

"Caleb's was ruined long before that.'' Farringay smiled sourly, suggesting that his relationship with his prospective father-in-law offered room for improvement. He drained his glass abruptly and rose. "This has been charming, but I think it's time for a little shut-eye, Bunky. Tomorrow we can pursue our disparate goals, but for now shall we knit the raveled sleeve of care?'' He pulled back the quilt and the sheet under it and climbed into bed. "Get the light, will you, old man?''

I finished my drink slowly, and by the time I joined him in the canopied walnut bed he was breathing in a deep, measured cadence. I lay with my hands behind my head, staring at the ceiling and considering the ramifications of my present position. After a few moments I turned to gaze at the face on the pillow beside me. The eyes were closed, and in the dim light the profile might have been that of a handsome warrior, a young hero lying in state in his coffin.

"Farringay, you son of a bitch,'' I whispered, so as not

to wake him, "for pure brass-bound effrontery, you win the Bible."

His eyes remained closed as he answered, in a normal voice, "The respect of my peers is reward enough. Good night, Moretti."

The next morning we were awakened by an elderly black man with a ring of white hair around a gleaming bald pate, who introduced himself as 'Lijah and announced that breakfast was served in the morning room. Jack made a decent toilette, due to the fact that he kept shaving gear and a change of linen at Kirkargyle, but I descended the stairs feeling noticeably the worse for wear.

The morning room, decorated in toast brown, rust, and two shades of green, was at the back of the main wing of the house, and faced east. French doors opened onto a terrace, which overlooked rolling fields crisscrossed at wide intervals by whitewashed fences. A fresh breeze ruffled the mesh curtains and mingled fresh field odors with the smell of coffee, fried ham, and fresh-baked bread. A long table with a snowy linen cloth paralleled the French doors, and behind it stood the diminutive 'Lijah, tending to an array of covered plates and chafing dishes.

Jack Farringay, with the aplomb of a corporation lawyer, introduced me to the persons seated around a second, circular table. "Judge McAuliffe . . . Miss Rhoda . . . Miss Dorcas . . . allow me to present my old friend Paddy Moretti, who is in Lexington to cover the Spring Meet. Paddy is associated with the sporting paper *The Spirit of the Times.*"

Caleb McAuliffe rose and extended his hand, and then almost withdrew it when he heard my occupation. I grasped it before it got away and said, "I look forward to the privilege of a bit of conversation with the dean of Kentucky breeders!"

He frowned and disengaged himself as rapidly as civility allowed. "I don't give interviews, Mr. Moretti. Perhaps Jack brought you here under a misapprehension."

"Oh, you mustn't blame Jack for that, Judge McAuliffe.

It was Sandy Braddock as suggested you might be generous enough to satisfy the curiosity of thousands of dedicated followers of the sport of kings.''

"Sandy, hey? Damn his eyes," Caleb McAuliffe growled. He was a tall, narrow-shouldered man with a lofty brow, deep-set hazel eyes under angry white tufts, and a long, fleshy nose from the sides of which deep grooves bracketed a narrow, purple-lipped mouth. He turned half away in irritation, then remembered his manners. "Well, have some breakfast while you're here, anyway.''

"Goodness, I should hope so!" cried the white-haired woman seated next to him. She extended a fragile, blue-veined hand to me. "Never let it be said a pilgrim was turned away hungry from Kirkargyle, Mr. Moretti. Especially one who comes in search of our own especial truth.'' Her fingers lay as still and weightless in my palm as a dead bird.

"Whatever that truth turns out to be, eh, Aunt Rhoda? Welcome, Mr. Moretti. Eat hearty and give the house a good name. And if Daddy won't talk to you about the stable, then *I* will!" Dorcas McAuliffe smiled at me with frank, chocolate-brown eyes and a deliciously formed mouth; her strawberry lips were parted to show gleaming white teeth, and her lustrous auburn hair fell loosely to her shoulders. She was tall and slender, although in no way unfeminine—the curves of breast and hip were drawn in long, firm lines. The combination of direct intelligence and cool sensuality she seemed to offer had an immediate effect on me; I have always had a weakness for bluestockings, although more often than not it has remained unreciprocated. I took her hand and bowed over it.

"Better yet, maybe you both will," I said. "I look forward to it.''

Farringay was helping himself at the buffet, and I followed him from dish to gleaming dish, filling a Wedgwood plate with thin slices of old ham and red-eye gravy, cheese grits, turkey hash, and buttermilk biscuits with honey and blackberry preserves. When I ran out of space on my plate, I carried it to the circular table and sat down between Jack and Miss Rhoda. For the next few minutes my mouth was too full to talk, which was just as well, since Farringay was lying enough for the two of us.

The identity he had invented for himself, I quickly discovered, was that of the younger son of a Maryland squire and breeder of thoroughbreds who had served the Confederacy as a cavalry raider during the War Between the States. (Farringay, like most champion liars, included a grain of truth in his most imaginative concoctions.) To Caleb McAuliffe he presented the face of a knowledgeable yet deferential professional horseman; to Miss Rhoda, that of an attentive young man who combined common sense with a touch of the poet; and to Dorcas, that of a strong-minded swain who has been totally captivated by the most enchanting woman in the world. He was like a juggler with three balls in the air, each moving through a precise independent arc which nonetheless meshed perfectly with the others. It was a virtuoso performance. I hated it.

As I was washing down the last of the old ham with my second cup of coffee, Dorcas politely included me in the conversation. "Does your friendship with Jack go back a number of years, Mr. Moretti, or are you more recent acquaintances?"

"I'm sorry to say I only met the lad two years ago," I answered. "Who knows what exhilarating experiences I've been deprived of?"

"Our time together has made up in intensity what it has lacked in duration," Farringay said with a bland smile.

I was considering a further ambiguous comment when Sandy Braddock entered the room. His face was pale, and there were dark circles under his eyes—he looked as though he had slept poorly in spite of the amount of whiskey he had drunk the night before. He was in his shirtsleeves and hadn't bothered to shave. Ignoring the buffet, he walked directly to the sideboard and poured himself a stiff drink.

When he had downed half of it, he turned to face the circular table.

Grinning crookedly, he said to his stepbrother, "Your bullyboys had themselves a night last night, Caleb. Tried to bash Molly Carmody's brains out. Damn near succeeded."

"Shut up, Braddock," McAuliffe snapped, his voice rising in pitch. "We have guests."

"Hell, I know that. Who do you think brought them here?" He drank the rest of his drink. "Did you give Fugate his marching orders, or did he dream them up himself?" He put his glass down, picked up the decanter, and splashed out another two inches of bourbon. "Not that it makes much difference to Molly or her five kids, of course."

Dorcas sat straight in her chair, her napkin crumpled in her hand. "Did something happen to the Carmodys last night, Sandy?" she asked in a tight voice.

"Yes, something. Something terrible." Setting his glass down, he folded his left hand under his right elbow, and began to narrate the events of the previous night. As he described Carmody firing on us Dorcas's eyes widened in alarm, and when he mentioned the children hiding under their injured mother's bed, she dropped the napkin on the table in front of her and rose to her feet.

"Wait a minute!" Braddock snapped. "Where do you think you're going?"

"Why, we can't just sit here eating breakfast while those poor children are out there with their mother at death's door!" She started around the table. Braddock intercepted her.

"Dorcas, there's nothing you can do. The sheriff's taking care of the legal end, and Doc Foley's seeing to Molly and finding some place for the kids to go. Most likely there's nobody left at the tollhouse, and if there is you'd only be in the way. So sit back down and have another cup of coffee."

"He's right, of course," Judge Caleb said.

"Certainly he is, dear," Rhoda agreed. "I'm sure everybody's doing everything possible, and the best thing we can do is let them get on with their jobs."

Farringay and I nodded to show our agreement. Dorcas looked from one to another of us and compressed her lips into a firm line. "Very well. As long as it's understood that we at Kirkargyle will do everything in our power to help those unfortunate people, and to see that this kind of thing doesn't happen again."

"Of course, dear," Miss Rhoda said. "I'm sure we'll do everything that mortal man can do against the force of poetic inevitability."

Dorcas made an exasperated sound like a creaking hinge and pushed past Sandy Braddock. Her cheeks were flushed with anger. "You all enjoy your breakfast, you hear?" she cried with sharp sarcasm, and raising her chin and stiffening her back, she marched from the room.

Caleb McAuliffe slapped the table explosively and glared at his stepbrother. "I have been in contact with the sheriff this morning, and he informs me that an investigation is under way on last night's unpleasantness. Incidentally, he'd like you to stop by his office and make a statement, if you can stop drinking long enough. I trust you won't find it necessary to blurt out any of your half-baked theories."

I looked expectantly from one family member to another, but Caleb and Sandy turned their faces away from each other. Aunt Rhoda looked at me over her biscuit. "All families have these little currents and eddies, Mr. Moretti. No doubt your own family has small areas of disagreement from time to time."

"With a mother from Ireland and a father from Italy and both of them positive they were sitting on the left hand of God Himself, there were some little currents and eddies, indeed there were. But I was interested in what you said about 'poetic inevitability' just now, Miss McAuliffe. What did you have in mind?"

The old lady frowned. "Why, think, Mr. Moretti. When a Cleopatra dies, it is poetically inevitable she die by the bite of a serpent. When an Actaeon dies, he must inevitably be torn apart by hounds. You don't think these things are coincidences, I hope. The mythographers know there are no coincidences. There are only the threads of life, to be spun, woven, and snipped at their appointed time and in their appointed way.''

''I see what you mean about people, but I don't think I've ever heard the principle applied to horses before. I mean, it's easy enough to imagine a man who was named for Julius Caesar conducting his life in such a way that he ended by being stabbed to death by his friends—but it's a bit harder to imagine a horse conducting his life the same way.''

She cocked her head and peered at me quizzically. I couldn't tell if there was amusement in her look or not. ''Not even the Emperor Caligula's horse? Even after he was appointed by his master to the consulship, the same office that Julius Caesar held?''

I blinked. ''Caligula's horse. Hmmm. Well—well, wouldn't he have to be stabbed to death by other horses who were senators?''

She looked at me as if I were crazy. ''Horses who were senators? That's the silliest thing I ever heard of!'' She terminated the conversation by breaking another biscuit, spreading it with honey, and popping it decisively into her mouth.

I glanced quickly around the room. Caleb and Sandy were both continuing to avoid each other's eyes. Caleb finished his coffee, dabbed at his compressed lips with a napkin, and rose from the table. He gave a courtly nod to the ladies and a cold glare to Jack and me, and left the room. Sandy emptied his glass, looked at the whiskey decanter indecisively, and then poured himself a cup of coffee and stood by the French doors, staring out across the tiled terrace. I joined him.

''Will you be driving into Lexington this morning?'' I asked.

"I thought you came out here to get a story," he said belligerently. "You scared off already?"

"I wouldn't put it that way. It does seem that I have as much chance of getting a story from Judge McAuliffe as I would from Queen Victoria. To tell you the truth, I'm not so sure it's a good day for personal interviews."

Braddock glared at me. "*I'll* give you an interview, if that's what you want. The decline and fall of Kirkargyle, chapter and verse. How power corrupts—all the dirty and discreditable details. A success story in reverse; failure snatched from the jaws of success, because certain people weren't willing to take yes for an answer. Would that fill the bill?"

I wasn't sure how to respond, and Miss Rhoda saved me the trouble. Turning to Braddock, she suggested sympathetically, "Sandy, why don't you get 'Lijah to fix you a nice hot bath? I just know it'll improve your outlook on life one hundred percent."

"It'll take more than a damn bath—" Braddock began hotly, and then stopped as two newcomers entered the room. Although both were well dressed, they were hardly a matched pair. The younger man, in his middle twenties, was tall and slender, with long blond hair brushed casually back from a narrow brow, and an expression on his pleasantly regular features that seemed both diffident and mocking. The other, heavyset, fortyish, and six inches shorter, looked like a man who has never considered taking himself lightly. He had receding black hair and heavy black eyebrows and, judging by the shadow on his meaty cheeks, could have had a heavy black beard if he had wanted one. He had the thick lips of a sensualist, but they were pressed tightly together in a way that suggested considerable self-discipline.

"What will take more than a damn bath, Sandy?" the younger man asked cheerfully. "Putting the roses back in your cheeks again? You're right, but if you spike that coffee you won't notice."

The older man pushed past him and demanded, "Where's Caleb?"

Miss Rhoda straightened in her chair and nodded formally. "Good morning, Mr. Lawler. Good morning, Carroll. How nice of you to drop by. Have you met our guest, Mr. Moretti? Mr. Moretti is a newspaperman from New York." She included me in her smile. "These are our neighbors, Mr. Emmett Lawler and Mr. Carroll Glass, Mr. Moretti."

I said I was pleased to meet them. Glass shook hands civilly, but Lawler couldn't wait to turn away from me and demand again, "Where's Caleb?"

"Probably giving the troops their new instructions," Sandy rasped. "You heard about last night's derring-do, I trust? Or were you there to see for yourself, leading the battalion from Folly Hill in the Battle of the Tollhouse? A brilliant victory—it must be a source of considerable pride to you."

Ignoring him, Lawler turned to Miss Rhoda. "I'd like to see your brother right away, Miss McAuliffe."

"Why, you're free to look for him, Mr. Lawler. I'm sure you know your way around the house." She nodded in dismissal and said to the younger man, "Won't you have some breakfast, Carroll? I believe there's still some ham and grits there, or 'Lijah can bring you some eggs, if you'd like."

"Oh, just a cup of coffee, I believe, Miss Rhoda, thank you kindly." He poured himself a cup at the sideboard. "Has Miss Dorcas finished already, or hasn't she come down yet?"

"Come and gone, Glass," Farringay said with satisfaction. *"C'est la vie."*

"Indeed. Fortunately she's taken barely fifty percent of the feminine charm with her." He smiled gallantly at Miss Rhoda and, carrying his coffee cup, took a seat beside her and began an archly flirtatious conversation. Lawler left the room in search of Caleb, and Sandy stared out the French doors with his back to us, the fingers of his left

hand pressed into his side. Shortly Miss Rhoda finished
her biscuit and made her exit, and Carroll Glass and Farringay somewhat unwillingly exchanged a few remarks on
some kind of contest or exhibition apparently scheduled in
the near future—exactly what kind, I couldn't make out.
Then Farringay rose to leave, and I rose with him.

Outside the breakfast room I suggested that we take a
walk together. He considered the proposal a moment and
nodded his head in agreement. We left the house from a
side door and sauntered back toward the livery barn, and
the two large horse barns beyond it.

"Bargains between honorable men are sacred," I mused
aloud, "and surely it's distasteful for gentlemen even to
mention them. But unfortunately, Jack, I'm afraid I have
no alternative. The agreement was for a certain amount of
forgetfulness in exchange for a story—and I don't seem to
be getting the story."

"Ah, Bunky, you can't blame me for that. We're equally
victims of circumstance."

"No doubt that's true, but it doesn't alter the situation.
I need information. Judge McAuliffe won't talk to me, and
I don't even know the right questions to ask Sandy. There's
so much going on around here you need a program to
figure it out. So I think you better be my program."

His expression was blank for a moment as he thought
about what attitude to assume. Then he smiled genially
and put one arm around my shoulders. "If I can clarify
any questions for you, I'll be most gratified. Fire away,
old friend."

"All right. First off, tell me about the Regulators."

He shrugged. "You know as much as I know now. The
local landowners are trying to force the private toll roads
out of business, either legally or otherwise. They're working to pass a bill in Frankfort, and they're also sending
out armed bands to harass the turnpike operators. Which-
ever way works is all right."

"And Caleb McAuliffe gives the orders?"

"For one group, anyway. At least that's what Sandy says."

"All right. Tell me about these accidents that are getting to be predictable—the 'poetic inevitability' business the old lady was talking about."

"I don't know any more than I told you last night. Two good horses have died accidentally in the last month." He frowned. "They have to be accidents—there's no way they could be anything else. The first one was a very promising colt by the name of Actaeon. Have you ever heard the name Actaeon before?"

"It's out of Greek mythology, isn't it?"

"Right, although I don't think anybody recognized it except Miss Rhoda. Seems that Actaeon was a famous huntsman. One day, when he was out hunting with his dogs, he happened to catch sight of the goddess Artemis taking a bath in some sylvan nook. He probably gave an appreciative whistle, as any gentleman would, and that blew the gaff to the lady, who unfortunately took considerable pride in her virginal status. She promptly turned him into a stag, whereupon all his hounds attacked him and tore him limb from limb." He glanced at me severely. "A cautionary tale, Moretti."

"Indeed it is. And the same thing happened to this colt?"

"Well, I don't know if he watched any goddess take a bath, but he sure as hell got himself torn to pieces by dogs."

"How could that happen?"

"It was late in the afternoon, around dusk, and he was off by himself in the back pasture, cut off from the other horses by a stand of trees. He was too far away from the stables for anybody to hear anything. By the time they found him the body was cold."

"Any reason to believe it wasn't on the up-and-up?"

"None at all. Wild dogs have always been a problem hereabouts. Some farmers who raise sheep have been ruined by them. They don't often attack a horse, but it's been known to happen." He shook his head. "If it wasn't for the horse's name, nobody would give it a second thought."

We were approaching the livery barn. I angled to one side to go around it, and we continued toward the first of the two horse barns a hundred yards beyond. "About the other horse, the one that was snake-bit," I suggested.

"Nile Queen. One of the prettiest little fillies you've ever seen. Dorcas loved her; it just about broke her heart when she heard what happened."

"You said it was a copperhead? She stepped on it? Out in the field?" He nodded, an expression of sadness on his handsome features. We walked in silence for a moment. Then I said, "That's stretching the poetic inevitability business a bit. Actaeon being killed by hounds is one thing—it's exact—but a horse named Nile Queen being bitten by a copperhead is something else. If she had been named Cleopatra—or if the snake had been an asp—but the way it was, it doesn't quite fit."

"Close enough," Farringay said.

"Yes, I guess it is." We walked through the lush grass, already knee-high in early May. A meadowlark gave its penetrating skirl, and a pair of red-tailed hawks sailed through the cloudless sky in great unhurried circles. The rolling bluegrass land spread out around us like a vast and very expensive carpet.

"I need to know about the family, Jack. Caleb and Sandy and Miss Rhoda—and Dorcas, too. Tell me about them."

He nodded resignedly. "Caleb and Sandy are stepbrothers. The old squire, Caleb and Rhoda's father, married Sandy's mother just before the war. The old Judge died in sixty or sixty-one, and Caleb stayed home and managed the farm. Sandy took off and joined the Confederacy—he and Rhoda's fiancé, Amory Glass, were both in Morgan's Raiders."

"Amory Glass—would he be kin to Carroll Glass?"

Farringay's nostrils flared. "He would. Amory Glass was his uncle. The family owned Windemere, down the road. Still does, what's left of it," he added with malicious satisfaction. "Anyway, after Morgan cashed in his chips Sandy and Glass transferred to Joe Wheeler's outfit. In the fighting after Atlanta Glass was killed and Sandy lost his right arm. It probably would have been better if he had died, too."

"How so?"

"Sandy was a painter. Apparently a damn good one. He was just beginning to make a reputation for himself when the war came. Unfortunately, he painted with his right arm."

"You mean he stopped painting for good? What did he do after Appomattox, take up the life of the gentleman horse farmer?"

"No, Caleb was doing all of that that needed to be done. Sandy gave most of his attention to the other pursuits of the gentry—cards and whiskey and women. The only interest he had in horses was betting on them."

"He never married?"

"Not that I know of. I gather that Belle Breezing's exemplary establishment on Megowan Street has served as a substitute. By the by, Paddy, that's a name you might want to paste in your own memory book. I recommend it highly."

"Thank you," I said. "I gather, then, that Dorcas is the heir to Kirkargyle. The sole heir?"

"That's right. Her mother died two years after she was born, and the Judge never married again. She grew up as an only child, mostly raised by servants, and I guess you could say spoiled by them. And spoiled by the stablehands, too—she grew up loving horses like only rich little girls ever do. She showed them, raced them, jumped them, hunted them, helped with the stallions when they were at stud and the mares when they foaled—they say she'd rather spend a night in a stall than in her own bed. When the Judge sent her east to school, she couldn't stand it; she was back at Kirkargyle in a month."

"Sounds like the right equipment for somebody who expects to inherit a horse farm."

He cleared his throat. "She's steadied down a good deal since then. As a matter of fact, the only riding she does anymore is an occasional morning turn around the farm."

"Oh? What happened?"

He turned to me with sudden anger. "Now listen, Moretti, I'm prepared to go a certain distance with you for old time's sake. But I think we've talked about Miss McAuliffe as much as we're going to."

I raised my hands. "Far be it from me to intrude in the delicate areas of the heart, Jack. I have as much respect for your finer feelings as you have for mine."

The nearer of the two horse barns was before us, and Farringay led the way inside. "Let's look at some horses, Moretti." The first stall on the left was unoccupied. "That was Nile Queen's," he said.

"Who's the well-endowed gentleman next door?" I asked, nodding at the big roan stallion in the second stall.

"Uranus. He was a big stakes winner for years, and Caleb's finally decided to put him out at stud. He's probably the most valuable animal on the place. With any luck he'll be cranking out foals till well into the twentieth century."

"I can believe it," I said admiringly. Uranus tossed his handsome head and rolled his eye as if he knew what was being discussed. "Not the worst life in the world, is it, old man?" I asked him.

We walked down the wide aisle and Jack identified the horses in turn. He knew them all, and a number of them seemed to recognize him, nuzzling his hand and whickering in greeting. "Hello, Thunderer, are you behaving yourself? . . . Oh, Bonne Jeanne, *ma belle amie*, have you been true to me? . . . Ah, Sebastian, you glutton, the only thing you care about is food! . . . This is Saladin, Moretti—with all the Arab blood you'd expect. . . ." We were nearly at the far end of the barn when a man came out of the tack room and stood facing us with his hands on his hips.

"What are you doing here?" he asked unpleasantly.

"Why, just checking on the stock, Brother Fugate. And how are you this morning? A little tired out from the night's activities? I think it's a shame the way you fellows put in a full day's work and then have to spend half the night out regulatin', and all."

Lomas Fugate appeared to be almost as broad as he was tall. He was a little under average height, with shoulders that would hardly pass through a doorway. His arms and thighs bulged with muscle, and the cords on his neck stood out like cables. His wide, flat face was weathered to the color of saddle leather. He glanced at me and returned his glare to Farringay. "Judge McAuliffe know you're out here sticking your nose in things that don't concern you?"

"Why don't you ask him, next time you see him?" He put one hand on my arm. "Fugate, this is Mr. Moretti. He's a writer for *The Spirit of the Times*, getting material for an article about Kirkargyle, and it would be nice if you would try to be civil to him while he's here."

I extended my hand. "I'm sure there's not much going on that you don't know about, Mr. Fugate. I'll be grateful for any help you give me."

He folded his arms and looked at me speculatively. "You would, would you? I bet you would."

I made some complimentary comments about the appearance of the horses and asked his opinion about an upcoming race, and in a few minutes his belligerence began to abate. When I suggested that I might want to mention him in my story, he became almost congenial.

Jack assumed an air of boredom, leaning against a stall door and covering a yawn with his hand. When Fugate and I reached a conversational hiatus, he asked abruptly, "When's the next match, Lomas?"

Fugate frowned warningly and glanced at me. Jack shook his head. "Moretti's all right, you don't need to worry about him. What's the setup this time?"

Although we were alone in the barn, Fugate lowered his voice to answer. "Tomorrow night, eight o'clock. Kimbro's barn. You know where that is?"

Jack nodded. "Who's on the card? General Grant?"

"Umm-hmm. Him and Glass's Tusker. And a likely youngun Jim Foushee's bringing over from Owen County. And some others I disremember." Suddenly ill at ease, he drew away from us. "Well, I got work to do. See you fellers later."

When he had maneuvered his shoulders through the tack-room door I asked Farringay, "What was that about? More bare-knuckle fighting?"

"No, something a bit more exciting than that. Something a little harder to come by, too." He smiled. "Something that gives a betting man a real run for his money. Something I bet a famous sports reporter like you has never seen in his life!"

"Ah, you've captured my attention for a fact. What is it, Jack?"

His smile became wolfish. "How would you like to be my guest for an unequaled exhibition of pugnacity and fortitude? Make wagers on the issue of life or death itself? Watch your favorites struggle for survival as the very air itself becomes incarnadined?"

"What are you talking about—Gettysburg?"

He threw back his head and laughed. "The next thing to it, Moretti. Tomorrow night you're going to see a dogfight."

3
Something—Unpleasant

Nobody at Kirkargyle wanted to go into Lexington that day, and it seemed pushy to ask for a horse or a buggy for my own use, so I made plans to spend my time on interviews. I tried for Caleb McAuliffe first. He was in a room in the back of the house that Farringay identified as the armory, apparently because, instead of pictures, its decorations consisted of obsolete weapons such as flintlock pistols and muzzle-loading rifles, sabers, dirks, and even an ash bow and a quiver of arrows.

"I thought I indicated that I have nothing to say to the press, Mr. Moretti," he said. "I trust you don't intend to abuse my hospitality, sir."

I assured him such a breach of manners was the furthest thing from my mind, but that both he and I, as professionals in the world of horse racing, had a responsibility to the enthusiasts who ultimately paid our bills. We owed them the facts they needed to arrive at the decisions they acted upon.

"I owe them nothing. I owe you nothing, beyond the ordinary civility which you are transgressing." His fleshy nose was white at the tip, and his purple lips were compressed to the size of a buttonhole. He held a letter opener in his hands and bent the blade into an arc. "Please leave me, Mr. Moretti. I would prefer that any further communication we have be at mealtimes, if you should happen to be here then.''

So much for the Squire of Kirkargyle. I returned to the front of the house, where the sound of music led me to the drawing room. Dorcas McAuliffe was seated at the keyboard of a gleaming ebony grand piano, performing for her admirers. Judging by the expression of determination on her lovely face, she wasn't enjoying it. She was playing ''I Dreamt I Dwelt in Marble Halls'' with accuracy but little verve; her brows were knitted, and her front teeth pressed into her lower lip. Jack Farringay, Carroll Glass, and the man named Lawler formed a semicircle around the piano, all wearing expressions of rapt attention.

I passed through the drawing room and entered the billiard room beyond, where Sandy Braddock was running balls along the side cushion. He was shooting left-handed, with the cue stick resting on the back of his gloved right hand. There was an awkwardness about his movements, but his eye was excellent.

''Billiards, Moretti?'' he asked, and cocked his head toward a rack of cues in the corner. I selected a cue and chalked its tip, and we lagged for break. He won easily, and proceeded to score five three-cushion combinations before missing a shot. I barely made my first shot and missed the next by three inches. ''I assume, Moretti,'' he said dryly, ''that you're not a billiard shark out to make a killing.''

''To tell you the truth, rotation pool is more my game.'' I hesitated. ''But what I'd rather do is talk about Kirkargyle. I'd like to have that interview you promised me a bit ago.''

He sighed. ''I'm afraid I have to renege on that. I spoke in anger, and it's not my place to comment on the operation of the farm.'' He placed his cue on the green felt in front of him and rolled it gently to and fro. ''My brother Caleb has complete control of Kirkargyle and all its business affairs, and it would be an intrusion into his area for me to discuss them with you. It's one of the things I have accepted. So, I'm sorry." He spoke evenly, but looked as if the words had left a bad taste in his mouth.

"I won't ask you to speak for publication if you don't want to—but off the record, what did you mean this morning when you said those things about failure snatched from the jaws of success, and certain people not being willing to take yes for an answer?"

He looked down at his cue. His heavy jaw rested on his barrel chest and his lower lip jutted forward an inch. Then he looked up, and his piercing blue eyes gleamed beneath his overhanging brows. "I have no idea what I meant, Moretti. I often say things that puzzle me later. It's a foible my friends must forgive me for." His eyes told me he didn't expect me to believe him.

I tried again. "It's a sad thing about all the accidents. With the rumors and all. Nothing like a good honest newspaper story to dispel rumors."

"Let it alone. I've told you—anything you get about Kirkargyle, you get from Caleb McAuliffe. Understood?" He picked up his cue and laid it across the back of his right hand. "How does a quarter a shot sound to you? Otherwise I won't be able to keep my mind on the game."

I nodded glumly, and he immediately ran seven combinations. I had mentally earmarked ten dollars for my losses, and it took me that same number of minutes to lose it all.

Leaving Braddock at the table, I walked back through the drawing room. Dorcas was now playing the "Fantaisie Impromptu," with less success than she had enjoyed with "Marble Halls"—the tempo was mechanical, and occasional wrong notes jarred the harmonies. Her three swains all seemed to be trying to conceal a lessening of their musical enthusiasm: Carroll Glass's fingers tapped a nervous arhythmic tattoo on the top of the piano, Lawler's beefy face wore a preoccupied expression, and Jack Farringay's eyes brightened with unmistakable relief when I entered the room. He stepped briskly around the baby grand, clapped me on the back, and pantomimed a wordless greeting.

As though equally glad of the interruption, Dorcas stopped in midmeasure and rose from the bench. "Joining us, Mr. Moretti? Then for heaven's sake let's call a halt to this musical moment and go play croquet or something. I can only take so much culture at a time or my head will burst." She swept around the piano past her three admirers, took my arm, and led me into the side yard, where a croquet court was set up.

We played croquet for two hours, first playing singles because we were an odd number, and then, after Lawler crossly retired from the game, forming teams—Farringay and Glass against Dorcas and me. There was much good-natured banter and simulated anger, and an underlying edge of real hostility between Jack and Carroll Glass. I was glad when Emmett Lawler left the game; he was a man whose disposition was bullying even when he assumed a jocose manner. He seemed the least likely of the three suitors to prevail, and yet there was a scornful condescension in the way he treated Glass and Farringay that hinted at his confidence in the final outcome. But if he had any reason for it, Dorcas herself gave no indication. She showed a fine impartiality to the three of them, and to me as well, laughing and scolding and pretending despair or elation as the game required.

I picked up a good deal of information during the course of the game. Lawler owned Folly Hill, the farm that abutted Kirkargyle on the west, and his fortunes in the racing business seemed to be rising as fast as Kirkargyle's were falling. I gathered he had never married, had channeled all his energies into the acquisition of land, horses, and money.

Carroll Glass also owned a neighboring horse farm, although apparently he spent a considerably smaller part of his time on its management than Lawler devoted to Folly Hill. Glass, it seemed, preferred to spend his days—or nights—in more entertaining ways, and the estate he had inherited paid the price. Lawler had purchased a twenty-acre parcel from him within the last month.

Of the three suitors, I found Jack Farringay the most adept. Although he was acting out a bogus role in front of a very demanding audience, which included one person who knew for a fact he was a confidence man wanted in half a dozen states, his nonchalant grace never faltered. He played the gallant with Dorcas, joked easily with his two rivals, and exchanged fabricated reminiscences with me, while at the same time displaying a diabolical accuracy with mallet and ball. It was hard to remember that once he would have cheerfully left me dead in a Kansas wheat field.

After three games Dorcas pleaded fatigue, and Lawler by this time having left, the four of us returned to the drawing room. We chatted for a few minutes over glasses of sherry, and Dorcas excused herself for a nap before dinner. When she had left the room, Farringay stretched out his legs, folded his hands, popped his knuckles, and said to Glass, "So you're going to try your Tusker against General Grant, are you? Do you have a ready market for fresh dog meat?"

Glass yawned and tapped his fingers against his open mouth. "I don't think I'll need one. But if you disagree, and want to put your money where your mouth is, I'll attempt to accommodate you." He glanced at me, and then back at Farringay. "Is Brother Moretti in on our local diversion?"

"He's a sportswriter—everything is grist to his mill." He grinned at me. "Don't worry. Paddy's discretion is legendary, and he's a champion source of new money—he never wins a bet."

"Jack mentioned you were planning a little contest for tomorrow night," I said. "I can't say I approve of the sport, but I'll withhold my opinion till I've seen it for myself. He's wrong about the money part, though. I'm one of the born winners of the Western world."

"Thanks for warning me." He stood up and shook out the sharp creases in his trousers. "Well, back to the galleys. I'll see you gentlemen at Kimbro's barn tomorrow night, if not before." He waved indolently and bobbed his head. "Good day, gentlemen."

I spent the time until dinner watching horses. Most of the Kirkargyle stable were now out in the fields, the mares and their foals in one pasture, the stallions, colts, and geldings in another. Leaning on a whitewashed fence, I was able to identify most of the animals I'd seen that morning—Uranus, the mighty stallion; Sebastian, rangy and hungry looking; Bonne Jeanne, who moved so delicately her hooves barely touched the grass; Saladin the dashing Arab; Thunderer, the long-legged sorrel yearling; Marse Henry and Templar and Anne Boleyn. . . .

Ah, the effortless elegance of you, I thought, *the unquestioning acceptance of superiority and its privileges. Never a thought of the sway-backed nag pulling the ice wagon, never a tear for the poor wreck waiting for the knacker's hammer.* I felt again the fascination for the thoroughbred horse that had seized me like an infection when I was a boy in Corbo County, Ohio, and had drawn me inescapably into my life as a racing writer.

Then I remembered the other two horses who should have been with their stable mates in the field. *Actaeon, Nile Queen,* I thought. *There has been a sufficiency of accidents here. Let's be done with poetic inevitability, whatever that may be.*

It was a wish not destined to be fulfilled.

Dinner was a constrained affair. Caleb McAuliffe barely spoke, his stepbrother was logy with drink, and his sister alternated between silences and bursts of cryptic mythological observation. Farringay, as the only suitor present, pressed the opportunity to charm Dorcas, but she was subdued in her responses. My conversational sorties met with little success.

It was obvious to me that I had overstayed my welcome, assuming I had ever had a welcome to overstay. I was making no headway whatever on a story about the fortunes of Kirkargyle, and I determined to return to Lexington early the next morning.

Miss Rhoda, Dorcas, Farringay, and I spent two hours at a card table as Dorcas attempted to instruct the rest of us in the new fad of bridge whist. I admitted defeat a bit after eleven o'clock, excused myself, and went to breathe the cool, moist night air on the porch. A few minutes later I retired to my room. Farringay wasn't there yet. During the few minutes it took me to fall asleep I thought about ways to explain to my editor, Otto Hochmuth, that no reporter in the world could have gotten an interview with Judge Caleb McAuliffe.

I awoke in the early hours of the morning, suddenly and with a feeling of anxiety. It was as if I had received a strong sensory signal, a sound or smell or flash of light, but when I opened my eyes it was to empty darkness. I sat up and put out my hand. "Jack, what was that?" There was no reply. I felt the pillow next to mine. No head rested upon it. I was alone in the bed.

I got up and turned up the light. Farringay's clothes were neatly hung over their wooden hanger. I crossed to the window and stood listening, but all I heard was the faraway moan of a railroad locomotive and the rustling of the wind in the trees. I peered out into the darkness, but there was nothing to be seen but shades of black.

Even though there seemed to be no reason for it, my sense of dread increased. I stood for half a minute by the window, barely breathing, all my senses sharpened, my heart pounding.

Something's happened. Something so bad I don't even want to know about it.

But I have to know, I told myself. *That's what I'm here for.*

I turned away from the window and found my trousers. I had pulled them on and was cinching my belt when the bedroom door opened and Jack Farringay entered. He was wearing a robe over his underclothes and soft leather slippers on his feet. He paused as he saw me, an expression of surprise on his handsome face. "Hello! What are you doing out of bed?" he asked.

"There's something—I don't know. Jack, did you hear a noise just now? What's happened?"

"Happened? Nothing's happened, as far as I know. At least nothing between here and the bathroom. I wouldn't know beyond that." He stepped closer and peered into my face. "What's the matter, Paddy? Have a brush with the bogeyman?"

"Something woke me up, something—" I shook my head. "I don't know. But I'm worried, Jack. I think we better take a look around."

"You do have the wind up, don't you? What do you think it was, something inside or outside?" He stepped aside and held open the door to the dark hallway. I reluctantly stepped through it, with him at my heels.

"Outside, I think," I whispered.

The house was deathly still. We made our way along the hall, past bedroom doors on either side, to the broad staircase.

"Nobody shrieking in their beds," Farringay observed softly.

I led the way downstairs. The hall, faintly lit by moonlight that filtered through the fanlight over the double door, stretched wide and empty on both sides of us. We paused, listening, but heard nothing. Nonetheless, my feeling of apprehension was growing.

I carefully turned the front doorknob and opened the door, and we stepped out onto the porch. The breeze touched my face, chilling the drops of perspiration on it. Clouds scudded across the half-moon riding above the treetops. A night bird cried.

I took a step toward the left end of the porch. At that moment a gruff voice from behind me said, "What the devil are you boys doing out here?" and the front door closed behind us with a clap.

I turned to see the stocky shape of Sandy Braddock

standing in the shadow. He was wearing boots, trousers, and a shirt open at the neck and with the cuffs turned back. He took a step toward us and emerged into the moonlight, which edged his wiry hair with silver. "What is it?" he repeated. "What brings you out at this time of night?"

I began to tell him about my feeling of disquiet, and he interrupted, "I know. I think I heard the same thing—or sensed it, or felt it, or whatever it was." He shook his head. "Something—unpleasant."

Farringay continued to the end of the porch and looked along the side of the house toward the stables. "Sandy, should there be a light back there?" he asked.

"No. Is there one?"

"There is. Looks like a lantern. Back about where the first stable is, I think."

Sandy and I joined him. A lantern glowed in the blackness, a yellow pinpoint of light that seemed to move as we watched it. Sandy swore. "Nobody's got any business back there in the middle of the night! Let's see what's going on!"

He jumped from the porch and started trotting toward the stable, with Farringay and me at his heels. Stumbling across the irregular ground as we passed the dark mass of the livery barn, I almost fell, only recovering by grabbing Jack's arm. The moon disappeared behind the clouds, and the growing dot of lantern light became as big as a penny, as big as a half-dollar.

As we neared the stable I could see that the door was open and the lantern was inside, hanging from a post and illuminating the first stalls. Sandy pulled the door wide, and we burst inside.

It was a scene of unforgettable horror.

The great stallion, Uranus, was sprawled on his back in his stall, rear legs spread, front legs bent as his hooves pawed feebly at the air, neck stretched, eyes bulging and unfocused, lips pulled back from his fierce grinning teeth. His breath came in shuddering gasps.

He was a stallion no more.

Dark red blood gleamed across his belly, pooled in the creases where his legs joined his body, streaked in rivulets down his sides.

A bloody sickle lay on the dirt floor beside him. Next to it was something that looked like a sodden, hairy pouch.

A sick-sweet stink of ether poisoned the familiar smells of hay, manure, and urine. Ether—and blood.

Braddock, Farringay, and I stood frozen in the doorway, for a long instant unable to move. Then sudden, violent movement beyond the stall drew our eyes to a struggle on the barn floor, and we made out two bodies locked together. The man on top had his hands on the other's throat, and was both strangling his opponent and banging his head against the floor, regardless of the other's ineffectual resistance.

Braddock was the first to react. "Fugate!" he cried, leaping toward the struggling men. "For God's sake, what are you doing?" He straddled them, grasping the collar of the man on top with his left hand and smashing his right arm down against his wrists. A moment later Farringay and I joined him, and after a brief but intense battle we separated the two contestants and dragged Lomas Fugate to his feet. The other man remained on the floor, propped weakly on an elbow and rubbing his throat.

Fugate glared wildly from one to the other of us, and with a sudden groan pulled away and stumbled into Uranus's stall. "Quick, before he bleeds to death!" he cried. "Got to cauterize it! Braddock, get the alcohol! Farringay, get a fire started! Get that sickle blade hot! You, newspaper fella, hold his head—keep him calmed down if he starts to come out of it!"

For the next ten minutes the four of us were very busy indeed.

When the immediate work was done, when the great horse, still fortunately half-drugged, lay quiet except for his heaving flanks and bulging eyes, Braddock turned to Fugate for an explanation. Fugate said woodenly, "Some-

thing woke me up. I guess it was maybe a horse screaming—I don't know, I just heard it once. Couldn't get back
to sleep. After a while I come over here to look around.
Combs, there''—he gestured contemptuously toward his
erstwhile opponent on the floor— ''him that was supposed
to be watching the horses tonight, he was passed out,
stinking drunk with an empty bottle beside him. And Uranus—'' He made a despairing gesture in lieu of words.
''All I wanted to do was kill the son of a bitch!''

''I wasn't drunk!'' protested the man on the floor in a
shaken voice. ''I didn't have but a couple of swallows!
You didn't have no call to try to kill me, goddamn it.
Somebody musta doped me, like they did the horse.''

Fugate started for him again, but Braddock grabbed his
arm. ''That's enough of that now. Let's start using a little
common sense. Combs, come here. And bring that bottle
of yours.'' The stablehand got to his feet, scooped up an
empty pint bottle from the floor, and brought it to Braddock, who sniffed it and handed it to Farringay. ''Smells
like ether to me,'' he said. Farringay nodded. I took the
bottle from his hand and smelled it. There was no doubt—
mixed with the odor of bourbon whiskey was the same
sickly stench we had smelled when we entered the barn.

''All right, Combs, do something useful,'' Sandy said.
''Go wake up Judge McAuliffe and tell him to get out
here. And try not to wake up the rest of the house while
you're doin' it.''

Combs disappeared, and the rest of us looked bleakly
at one another. Fugate knelt down beside the laboring
Uranus and stroked his neck with rough compassion.
''Why?'' he burst out. ''Just tell me why? Why would
anybody do a thing like this?''

Sandy Braddock shook his head. Farringay looked at
me, raising his eyebrows. I nodded slowly and cleared
my throat. ''It might be—I mean there's no sense to it,
but—'' I hesitated, hoping Jack would take over. When
he didn't, I went on awkwardly, ''—but it looks like some
more of what Miss Rhoda calls 'poetic inevitability.' ''

Sandy stared from me to Jack and back to me. Uranus whickered, and Fugate muttered soothing, inaudible words. From beyond the range of the lantern, a dozen other horses breathed and shifted their weight nervously.

"He's right, Sandy," Jack said. "I don't like to say it, but he's right."

"What are you talking about?" Sandy cried.

"I remember reading *The Wonder Book* and *Tanglewood Tales* when I was a boy," I said. "In Greek mythology Uranus was the husband of Mother Earth. His son was Cronus. Cronus wanted to rule in his father's place, and his mother decided to help him. She gave him a sickle—"

Instinctively all our eyes went to the curved steel blade on the floor of the stall, a blade that had been used twice tonight, for widely different purposes.

"—and he gelded him," I finished rapidly. "His own father. Uranus. That's the story." I spread my hands. "I don't like it any better than you do, Sandy, but that's what mythology says."

Braddock shook his head unbelievingly. "But—somebody *did* it! I mean, some real person came in and *did* it! This wasn't an accident, like Actaeon or Nile Queen! This was intentional! Why in the name of heaven would anybody do a thing like this?"

Farringay and I exchanged glances. Farringay said, "The horse's name was Uranus, wasn't it?" And I thought, *What was it Miss Rhoda said? Mythographers know there are no coincidences*.

4
Prevailing Rates

If you castrate a horse named Uranus, do you do it because he's a horse, or because he's named Uranus? Or neither? Or both?

There wasn't much more sleeping done at Kirkargyle that night. In a matter of minutes Judge McAuliffe and Dorcas arrived at the stable, followed shortly by the local veterinarian and his assistant. A full complement of farm- and stablehands milled about until Lomas Fugate bullied them into a semblance of order. About dawn the sheriff appeared and questioned Fugate, Combs, Sandy Braddock, Farringay, and me, to no apparent result. Then we straggled back to the house.

Breakfast was waiting in the morning room, Miss Rhoda presiding. With the hard, angular morning light behind her, her fine white hair floated around her head like mist, and her skin seemed to fit her skull too tightly to wrinkle. She was wearing a pale green robe of Chinese appearance that buttoned to the neck. She gestured toward the sideboard as Jack and I entered the room. "Good morning, gentlemen. Please help yourselves, if you can find the appetite for it."

'Lijah helped me to scrambled eggs, sausage, and muffins, and I carried my plate to the table, where Sandy

Braddock was sitting beside his stepsister. He regarded me
dourly through red-rimmed eyes, over the edge of a coffee
cup half-filled with something that wasn't coffee. When
Farringay, carrying a plate as well stocked as mine, took
a seat beside us, Braddock growled, "Keeping your
strength up, boys?"

"I should hope you are," Miss Rhoda said firmly. "At
times like these, when we find ourselves under the shadow
of dark powers, we owe it to ourselves to maintain our
physical vigor and adopt a positive mental attitude, no
matter how difficult it seems."

Sandy snorted. "Gives you something to print in your
paper, Moretti. Why aren't you hightailing it back to Lexington to send off a telegram? Thought you reporters never
let grass grow under your feet."

"I'm not sure there's a story in it for us at all," I said.
"It's a terrible thing, but whether it's news or not, that's
something else." I tasted a muffin and washed it down
with a swallow of coffee. "But you're right—I will be
getting back to Lexington this morning, if I can borrow a
horse."

"We can go in together," Farringay said. "That way
we can take a buggy and travel in style. We can leave it
at Smiley's." He raised his eyebrows inquiringly, and
Braddock gave a brusque nod.

We three men ate—or in Braddock's case, drank—our
breakfasts in silence, as Miss Rhoda played hostess. She
made no further reference to the shadow of dark powers.
Her monologue dealt with spring in the Bluegrass, past
and present—the parade of wildflowers and budding trees,
the social whirl of hunts and balls, barbecues and boating
parties, the excitement of yearling auctions and racing and
breeding seasons. She commented on girls making their
debuts, boys returning from colleges, engagements made
and broken, marriages solemnized. There was nothing
more serious in her observations than you would find on
the social page of the morning newspaper, until she said,
with no change of tone or expression, "Of course, it's very

difficult to do any social planning under these conditions. One hopes the goal will be achieved soon, whatever it may be—of course, assuming that goal is not the destruction of Kirkargyle and all it stands for, which I fear is very possible.''

Farringay touched his lips with his napkin. ''The goal, madame?''

''The purpose of the sobering examples of poetic inevitability which have been shown us, Mr. Farringay. While it is impossible to predict coming events, the attitude of the Fates toward *hubris* is well known. It is invariably punished by death.'' She smiled solicitously at me and asked, ''Another muffin, Mr. Moretti?''

As my mouth was full, I shook my head. Sandy Braddock set his cup down with a clatter. ''Rhoda,'' he demanded, ''do you have the slightest damn idea what you're talking about?''

''It has never been my place to criticize the operation of this farm, Alexander. Perhaps, if things had worked out differently, I might have brought my influence to bear in a positive way, but as it is I have been content to stand on the sidelines and watch the men of the family administer Kirkargyle's affairs as they saw fit. Or,'' she continued, with a sharp glance, ''refusing to accept any administrative responsibility at all.''

''Comment noted and filed, sister dear,'' Braddock said sourly. ''I took all the responsibility I ever needed when I was with Fighting Joe in Georgia.'' He slid his right hand quickly from the tabletop into his lap.

''Perhaps just not *quite* enough responsibility,'' Miss Rhoda said.

''Oh? What do you mean? That I didn't keep your precious Amory Glass alive to come back and marry you? I'm sorry about that, Rhodie, but I was thinking about something else at the time. Like getting the hell out of there in one piece—which I didn't quite succeed in doing, as you may have noticed.'' He grinned savagely. ''Us

Cavaliers of the Lost Cause had a different priority for our responsibilities than you Home Folks, I'm afraid.''

"I've never judged you for your behavior during the war, Alexander. I wouldn't presume to. I was referring to your refusal to carry out your duties here at Kirkargyle since your return."

"Duties?" Braddock cried. "What duties? Mucking out the horse stalls? I suppose I could do that, if I asked Fugate politely, and if brother Caleb said it was all right."

I felt acutely uncomfortable. Glancing at Farringay, I saw that he was staring at his breakfast plate. Miss Rhoda continued in a calm conversational voice, "The duties of a caring and supportive family member, Alexander. I'm afraid your refusal to play this role is one of the causes of the disastrous sequence of events that has befallen us."

"Don't talk to me about caring and supportive family members," Braddock snapped. "How much support have you been to anybody in this family? How about poor Elizabeth, when she needed you? Or Dorcas, after the hunting accident? Or even Caleb, when Elizabeth was dying—even the Great Stone Face might have used a bit of sisterly sympathy then! God almighty damn, all of us got more support from the Man in the Moon!"

"We have guests, Alexander," Miss Rhoda said coolly.

"Oh, you don't say! From the way you've been going on, I thought we were alone in the house!" He stood up and flung his wadded napkin down beside his cup. "I don't know much about poetry and mythology, Rhodie—is there anything in it about chickens coming home to roost?"

At that moment one of the French doors to the terrace opened, and Emmett Lawler thrust his chunky body into the room. "Good morning—I hope I'm not interrupting," he said bruskly. "Walked across the fields from Folly Hill. Heard you had some trouble last night. Sorry. Is Miss Dorcas about?"

Sandy Braddock stamped out of the room without answering. Miss Rhoda nodded to acknowledge his presence and said, "I doubt if she's feeling up to a social call, Mr.

Lawler. But please take a plate from 'Lijah and have some breakfast, if you like."

"Why, thanks, I think I will." He turned to Farringay and me. "Join me for a second cup of coffee, gentlemen?"

We rose to our feet simultaneously and excused ourselves. Miss Rhoda smiled graciously, and Lawler expressed his feelings with a shrug of his burly shoulders.

" 'I do not like thee, Dr. Fell—' " Farringay quoted as we walked down the hall.

"I share the feeling, and I'm not even the man's rival in love. When do you want to go into Lexington?"

"Oh, an hour or so. Care to shoot some billiards?"

"No thanks. I think I'll stretch my legs and work off some breakfast."

Farringay went upstairs and I walked around the house and back toward the horse barns. Two men were cleaning bloody straw out of Uranus's stall as the gelded stallion stood dumbly between them, head hanging almost to the floor. A girl of sixteen or so leaned against the doorframe watching the scene. She stood provocatively, her weight on one bare foot and the other foot against the boards behind her, her maturely curved belly and breasts pressing against her folded arms. Her long, braided hair was carrot red, and her eyes were green. When she saw me she straightened her back and smiled. "Howdy," she said. "I reckon you're the newspaper fella from up north."

I said I was and asked who she might be.

"Marybee Fugate. My daddy's the farm manager. Do you go to those big theaters, and wait at the stage door for the stars to come out, and take them to fancy restaurants, and drink champagne wine out of their slippers, and all that stuff?"

"Not every night, no. But if you were working at one of the theaters, maybe I would."

"Yeah?" She uncrossed her arms and began to toy with one of her braids. "You think I'm good enough looking to be on the stage?"

"I haven't the shadow of a doubt." I sniffed the air. The smell of ether, though less overpowering than before, was still strong enough to irritate the throat. I took a step backward, out into the fresh air. "That stink is enough to sicken a man."

"That ain't the half of what's bothering old Uranus now," the girl said, grinning. "I bet he's trying to get use to what he don't have no more. Thinking about all the mares he ain't never going to do any good. Wishing he was dead, I reckon."

I looked in vain for a trace of sympathy in her expression. Her pug nose was wrinkled and her eyes were dancing, and she had refolded her arms behind her back, thrusting her breasts forward. "I wouldn't think a thing like that would improve a man's disposition, for a fact," I said.

She tossed her head, glancing past me at the stablehands working in the barn. "Some menfolks deserve a little of the same thing, if you know what I mean," she said archly. "Carrying on like they was all stud horses—if they was to get cut up like Uranus, there wouldn't be nothing left of them at all!"

One of the stablehands swore under his breath, and Marybee laughed aloud. "If the shoe fits, Willis Shumway!" she cried merrily. Then, as if tired of the game, she turned back to me. "Them chorus girls—how do they get a job in a play? Do they have to be friendly with the man that owns the theater, or the top star, or can they just walk in and show what they can do? I mean, if I was to go to New York, could I just go out and get me a job? I mean, if I was good enough, and all?"

My eyes traveled down her precocious body and up to her eager face again. "To a large extent it's a matter of contacts, Miss Fugate. *Personal* contacts. It depends on who you know. Now take me, for instance. I happen to know a vast number of influential theater people. A lot of them would be very happy to do me a favor, for such is the power of the press. And of course I'd be delighted to exercise my influence to help a deserving friend. It's a world where one hand washes the other, so to speak.''

Her eyes narrowed. ''Does that mean I could get me a job?''

''With a certain amount of sympathetic help, it's not the most impossible thing in the world.''

Her smile returned, revealing large, flawless white teeth. ''I like the way you talk, with all them big words. I bet you could just sweep a girl off her feet, if you was to try.''

''Wouldn't take much trying, with you,'' growled a voice behind us. ''A wink and a squeeze would do it.'' There was the sound of a slap, and Marybee jumped three inches in the air. ''Now stop hanging around the barns and get the hell back to the house. Your mother needs you.''

''The way you talk, Papa,'' the girl said primly. She shot a parting glance at me, said, ''Good-bye, Mr. New York,'' and began a hip-swaying walk toward home. Lomas Fugate watched her for a moment, his expression a mixture of anger and indulgence. Then he spat on the barn floor.

''Girl's twice too pretty and not half smart enough,'' he grumbled. ''She's looking to get herself in trouble if she ain't careful. But nobody can tell her nothing.''

''A darling little girl. She'll be a fine-looking woman when she grows up,'' I said innocently.

Fugate shot a hard glance at me. ''There's some that thinks she's just about growed up already. Sniffin' around her like dogs around a—'' He paused, disliking the simile on the edge of his tongue. ''Turning her head with fancy talk about things that ain't never going to happen,'' he substituted. I shook my head to indicate sympathy with a father's lot.

We watched as one of the stablehands spread fresh straw on the floor of Uranus's stall. The big horse continued to stand with his head nearly touching the floor, oblivious to the movement around him. The skin on his shoulder twitched, and a disgruntled horsefly buzzed a circle around him before alighting again. He expelled a breath in what sounded disconcertingly like a human sigh. I felt a sudden pang of sadness.

"Who the devil could do such a thing?" I wondered aloud.

Fugate didn't answer. Instead, he raised a clenched fist in the air, held it poised for a moment, then smashed it against the doorframe. It was a gesture of such violence that it would have broken bones in the hand of a punier man. The two workmen looked up in surprise, and even poor Uranus shifted his weight uneasily.

Then Fugate's lips parted in a grimace attempting to be a sociable smile. "You still interested in seeing the match tonight, Mr. Moretti? It's going to be a corker."

"The match? Oh, you mean the dogfight you and Jack were talking about. Well, I don't know—I'll have to come out from Lexington. You think it'll be worth it?"

His smile grew wolfish. "Oh, it'll be worth it, all right. To me it will be. To some other people, well, maybe they'll wish they'd stayed at home." I raised my eyebrows and he continued, "Young smart alecks with more money than sense—and them damn shanty Irish from the toll roads—and a local boy or two that ought to know better—maybe they'll be sorry they came. But anybody with brains enough to know a winner when he sees him, he'll think it's worth it. You bet he will!"

I said I'd take him at his word. He repeated the instructions about getting to Kimbro's barn, where the evening's canine competition was to be held. I tried without success to return the conversation to the mutilation of Uranus; Fugate simply shook his head and refused to answer. After a few moments I left the barn and returned to the house.

A buggy was drawn up by the front steps, and Jack Farringay and Dorcas McAuliffe stood together on the porch. From the closeness of their bodies and the warm expression on Dorcas's face I deduced that my roommate was improving the shining hour. When he saw me he squeezed her hand and said, "Until the next time, then.

No matter how soon it is, and it will be soon, it will seem like ages to me.'' She breathed her farewell in a voice too low for me to hear, and Jack climbed onto the buggy seat and waited for me to follow him. I made a brief adieu to Dorcas, asking her to be sure to express my sympathy and gratitude to the other members of her family, and a few moments later Farringay and I were trotting along on the road to Lexington.

"You didn't mention that you were planning to come back this evening for a little recreational dogfighting,'' I said.

"I didn't think it was something she'd want to hear,'' he said blandly.

We passed the tollhouse. Its broken windows were dark, and the wooden turnstile pole still lay across the road. A broken rocking chair leaned crookedly against the porch railing, and a child's shoe lay in the road by the steps. I felt a chill at the desolation of the scene. "I hope the poor woman's getting good medical attention and the kids have a decent place to stay,'' I said. Farringay shrugged, not bothering to answer. Our wheels bumped over the pole and we continued through the rolling bluegrass meadows, between the whitewashed fences that bordered the Lexington pike.

In town we left the horse and buggy at Smiley's Livery Stable and separated, after agreeing to meet again at seven o'clock that evening. I went to my room at the Phoenix Hotel to change my linen and prepare for an afternoon at the track, stopping at the desk to check for messages from my editor, Otto Hochmuth. Fortunately there were none.

After shedding my jacket, shirt, and tie and sponging myself from the waist up, I mixed myself a drink from the bottle of excellent bourbon my bellboy had supplied me with, and stretched out on my bed to think about the state of things at Kirkargyle. It was odd, I thought—although a great deal had happened since I had ridden with Farringay and Sandy Braddock toward the McAuliffe farm two nights ago, I was still as far from a publishable story as I had been then. It seemed that a pattern of destructive violence had developed there, but only the third case—the gelding of Uranus—was clearly an act of human mischief; the deaths of Actaeon and Nile Queen were apparently tragic but accidental coincidences. There was no doubt that Kirkargyle was in decline financially, but whether that decline was due to Caleb McAuliffe's bad luck or failing powers, or to some outside agency, had so far been impossible for me to ascertain, and would probably continue to remain so.

Jack Farringay's role was that of a simple fortune hunter, it seemed, although as I well knew, nothing in his character would prevent him playing a more sinister part if the opportunity presented itself. The toll-road brouhaha could hardly have any connection with the problem of "poetic inevitability" at the Kirkargyle stables.

No, I thought as I took a sip from the glass balanced on my chest, there was no way I could pull together a brilliant exposé from the bits and pieces of information and innuendo at my disposal.

I sighed, rolled off the bed, and found myself a nearly clean shirt and collar.

The track was crowded, and the combination of blue skies, brisk May weather, and a slate of excellent horses in three of the afternoon's races created a festival air. I arrived with ample time before the first race and scouted the paddock and betting ring for a familiar journalistic face. In due time I found one; it belonged to Harry Cocanougher, once a sports reporter for the *New York Herald*, and now reduced, through a combination of drink and domestic difficulties, to a berth on the Lexington paper of the same name. He greeted me with a spark of hope in his rheumy eyes. "If it isn't the Moretti, with his hip pocket abulge with a bottle of the best, or else the tiger has changed his stripes, the serpent has lost his sting, and the millennium has arrived while I was otherwise engaged," he said, trying for a light touch.

"I'm sorry to say the only thing that bulges my hip

pocket is me. But I'll tell you, Harry, if you're hoarding any little journalistic tidbits about today's program, I'll be glad to consider an exchange at prevailing rates." Prevailing rates meant one or more drinks at a nearby saloon after the last race.

"Let me think about it." He licked his lips and wrinkled his brow as he ran down his mental card file. "No, no—no, not that—no, not that either—oh, I couldn't give that away—"

"While you're agonizing, tell me this. What's going on at Kirkargyle?"

His eyes popped wide. "Ah, you mean that business with Uranus last night. The story's all over town, but nobody really knows anything. The newest example of the famous McAuliffe jinx, apparently. I don't know how you can make a newspaper story out of it."

"Tell me about the jinx."

He shrugged. "To begin with, it was just rumors about some not-smart dealing by Judge Caleb—paying too much for this horse, selling that one too cheap, entering some over their heads, and putting others in claiming races when they were starting to show promise—just a number of cases of poor judgment. But then the accidents started."

"Actaeon and Nile Queen?"

"Yeah. And there may have been others. Anyway, that's when the jinx talk got started. Now, with this Uranus thing, it's starting to look like the McAuliffes are on a sinking ship." He cocked his head and studied me shrewdly. "From one McSorley's alumnus to another—do you think there's a story here we can use?"

" 'We,' Cocanougher?" I echoed. "I have no idea what story 'we' can use. I have heard it said that the only individuals who should be permitted the first person plural are royalty, editors, and people with tapeworms. As a matter of fact," I continued, in a kinder tone, "I have no idea if it's a story *I* can use. If it turns out to be, you will find it out in the pages of *The Spirit of the Times*, where I hope you will read it in good health.

"And now to less theoretical matters. For prevailing rates—who do you like in the first race, and why?"

We spent the remaining minutes until post time analyzing the entries and trying to steal information from each other. After the race we separated, agreeing to meet later at a neighboring saloon called Dingley Dell, and I circulated through the grandstand in search of other acquaintances.

When the fifth race came around, I noticed that one of the entries was named Prince Hal, and the owner listed was Emmett Lawler of Folly Hill Farm. I happened to be in the clubhouse as the horses filed onto the track, and was interested in some of the comments I heard. One red-faced sportsman whose nose was veined like a maple leaf in autumn said, "Here's another one for that bastard Lawler to win, I reckon. Odds are five to three. Goddamn. Miserable."

"You don't have to bet on him," said his companion, a portly specimen in a hairy tweed jacket with leather patches.

" 'Course I have to bet on him. I don't want to lose, do I?"

As the horses drew up to the starting line, a beanpole on the other side, studying the entrants through binoculars, grumbled, "Prince Hal's a shoo-in, curse it. Too bad young Glass doesn't still own him, instead of that Lawler fella. The boy could use the money."

"Pshaw," snorted the mustached country squire type beside him. "If Carroll had ever paid attention to business, he wouldn't have to sell off half his property. Besides, if he still owned Prince Hal, the odd's *wouldn't* be five to three, they'd be fifty to one. That's one boy that just can't never win for losing."

"Maybe he's lucky in love," the beanpole said. "He ain't in anything else, that's for sure."

"And that means dogs, too," said the squire, lowering his voice.

"That's what they tell me," agreed the beanpole.

The race was as cut-and-dried as the clubhouse consensus had predicted; Prince Hal took the lead at the half-mile pole and increased it to seven lengths by the finish. It was obvious that Emmett Lawler had himself a valuable piece of horseflesh.

No Kirkargyle horses were running that day, and the McAuliffe box remained empty all afternoon. I kept an ear cocked for references to Uranus and the Kirkargyle jinx, but failed to acquire any publishable information. At five-thirty I was bellied up to the bar at Dingley Dell, waiting for Harry Cocanougher.

When he appeared, he looked as though the struggle to get through the afternoon without a drink had just about done him in. He ordered a double whiskey and, raising the glass to his lips with both hands, still managed to spill a third of it on the bar. He set the empty glass down and rolled gummy eyes at me. "You did say prevailing rates?" I nodded, and he ordered and drank another double, this time without spilling a drop. Then he let out a long sigh. "I don't suppose—" he began.

I shook my head. "Conversation between friends can also be intoxicating, Harry."

He smiled mournfully. "As long as it doesn't have to do the whole job itself, Paddy. It's a long time since I've been able to get plastered on puns and paradoxes."

We talked for twenty minutes before I bought him another drink. He told me everything he knew about the McAuliffes and Kirkargyle: the family, the horses, the business and sporting rivalries, the neighbors, the employees, the public and private gossip. We had visited the free lunch counter and carried plates of pigs' knuckles and hard-boiled eggs to a corner table, and I had ordered a double whiskey for my informant and a stein of beer for myself when Cocanougher said, "The girl still won't get on a horse, I understand—and it's almost two years since the business with the kid."

"You mean Dorcas? What business with the kid?"

"It was a rough thing that happened at Kirkargyle year

before last—I guess you might call it part of the McAuliffe jinx, too. It was during a hunt. Dorcas was a great one for hunting in those days, a hell of a horsewoman, who would have spent twelve hours a day out with the hounds if she could have found anybody to keep her company.'' He paused to rap an egg on the edge of the table and began peeling it carefully.

"Go on."

"Well, one day she was out front of the hunt, going hell-for-leather, and she took a blind jump. When the horse came down there was this kid underneath. Little six-year-old girl who'd been having herself a picnic in the woods. Broke her neck, killed her instantly. The horse went down, and Dorcas damn near got pinned—just barely got her leg out from under in time. Horse had to be destroyed. A hell of a thing." He peeled the last bit of shell from his egg, sprinkled it with salt, and bit off half of it.

"I should think," I said. "Enough to turn anybody against hunting, especially a young woman right out of boarding school. Who was the kid?"

He swallowed and cleared his mouth with a gulp of whiskey. "One of the tenant families that live on the farm—I don't remember the name. I suppose Judge Caleb paid them a couple of hundred dollars to fix it."

"Tell me about Judge Caleb. Has he always been the warm, lovable fellow he is today?"

"I guess everything started to go to pot when his wife died four years ago. She was the former Elizabeth Aldean, of the Sevenoak Aldeans. She and Caleb ran Kirkargyle as a partnership, and people thought she represented sixty percent of the brains in the business. It was she who got Caleb appointed a judge, and she made most of the buying and selling decisions for the stable. After she died, it was all downhill."

"How did she die?"

"Some kind of growth, I think. Nobody ever said specifically. But it took a long while. She was in bed for the last six months, in pain and drugged most of the time. It was hard on Caleb. He may be a son of a bitch, but he loved her, and when she was dying he didn't have the heart to mind the store like he should have. You can't blame him—but he didn't let anybody else mind it either, and that's when the trouble started.'' He glanced at the empty glass in front of him. ''This endless exposition is thirsty work, Moretti.''

''We're through with prevailing rates, Harry. We're now engaged in idle conversation, just two old friends passing the time of day. Actually, I was wondering when *you* were going to buy *me* a drink.''

It took him two or three seconds to react, but when he did he immediately rose and gave me a formal nod. ''I fear the press of business requires my presence elsewhere. But it's always a pleasure to chat with you, Paddy, and if my casual remarks have been of any value to you, please don't embarrass me with any expressions of gratitude.'' I promised I wouldn't, and he headed for the door, leaving the saloon with considerably more bounce in his stride than he had shown when entering.

Half an hour later I met Jack Farringay at Smiley's Livery Stable, where he was waiting with our horse and buggy. Again we stopped at Joe Bubbling-Over's liquor store on our way out of town, and then continued west along the pike toward Frankfort. We rode in silence. I turned my jacket collar up against the evening chill.

It was just after eight o'clock when we reached Kimbro's barn.

5

The Dog It Was That Died

I have always liked dogs. Not with the carefully unsentimental stiff-upper-lip kind of comradeship shown them by elderly widowers—certainly not with the sugary possessiveness of maiden ladies who substitute pekes and poodles for the sons and lovers they never knew. I could take them or leave them alone, and most of the time I left them alone. But, on balance, I have liked them.

So it was with mixed feelings that I followed Jack Farringay into the hot, smoky clamor of Kimbro's barn. My anticipation of a new sporting sensation to enjoy, a new discipline to analyze and catalog, was balanced by the uneasy fear that what I was about to see would be hard to cope with. Was I ready to watch dogs tear each other apart in the name of sport? Surely I was a better man than that. Or wasn't I pretending to a fastidiousness I didn't really possess, and in the process denying the honest lust for blood and violence that motivates every true male animal? My mouth tasted brassy and my sinuses were uncomfortably dry.

Charlie Kimbro, the owner of the barn, was standing just inside the door talking to three men, one in homespun, one in overalls, and one in a beautifully cut linen suit. They were passing a fruit jar full of moonshine back and forth. We each handed Kimbro a five-dollar bill, which he pocketed absently. Farringay introduced me, and Kimbro smiled and offered a flabby hand; his eyes gazed, unfocused, over my shoulder. "Proud you come. Make y'self comfortable. Have a drink?" I refused with thanks, and he turned back to his cronies, swaying as he grabbed for the jar.

There were close to a hundred people in the barn, mostly men, although here and there were women's faces, hot-eyed with excitement. Ages varied from the teens to the seventies or eighties, toothless gaffers next to acned schoolboys, one grandmother alongside two women who must have been her daughter and her granddaughter, all three grinning expectantly, the granddaughter holding a baby in her arms. Most of the men were drinking, smoking, and shouting, and the noise and smell combined in an atmosphere so dense one almost had to wade through it. Accents ranged from the harsh twang of the mountains through the semisouthern drawl of the Bluegrass to the crisp staccato of the northern cities; educational levels from illiterate to college laureate; economic status from poverty to affluence. Except for the aura of recklessness that was as tangible as the smell of corn whiskey, it might have been a testimonial to democracy in action.

The aura worked immediately on Jack Farringay—his eyes glittered as he gripped my elbow and said huskily, "Let's get some money down before the claret flows, Moretti." He drew me through the jostling crowd until we reached the edge of the pit at the center of the barn, where a dozen gesticulating men were thrusting handfuls of currency at a slack-jawed young man with a clipboard; as he accepted each handful, he scrawled a mark with a stubby pencil before stuffing the greenbacks into his overall pocket. "That's Kimbro's son Lonnie," Farringay said as he elbowed his way through the clot of bettors. "He holds all the money—if you don't bet with him, you don't bet at all." He pushed out a wad of currency. "Hey, Lonnie—two hundred on General Grant. Farringay's the name."

Lonnie nodded and made a mark on the clipboard, then looked up questioningly. Immediately one of the men next to him cried, "I'll take it! Put me down!" and began hurriedly to count bills from a thick roll. Lonnie looked at me expectantly until I shook my head, then gave his attention to the new bettor.

"I think I'll wait till I know a little more about the game," I told Farringay.

He shrugged. "Let's take a look at the General," he said.

Lomas Fugate and his dog were surrounded by a crowd of onlookers on the other side of the barn. Fugate was on his knees, and the dog sat in front of him, head resting against his owner's thighs. He was an American Staffordshire bull terrier, or pit bull, as they are generally called—a short, bandy-legged dog weighing perhaps forty-five pounds, with a white, smooth coat and a black ring around one eye. His muzzle was long and wedge-shaped, with the mouth extending far back. His ears, which had presumably once been three inches long, erect and pointed, were now merely lumps of chewed flesh curving around the earholes in the skull. His sinewy tail whipped back and forth as he regarded his master with silent adoration.

Fugate seemed oblivious to the crowd around him as he talked to his dog. His words were inaudible, but his intonation was soft and musical, and the expression on his brutal features was rapt. As he talked, his hands moved over the dog's body, squeezing his paws, scratching his head, tugging gently on the folds of his skin. My sudden thought was that they seemed as close as lovers alone together.

"Look at those jaws," Farringay said to me. "Marvelous! I've seen Fugate let him swing from a rope; the brute can hang on, swinging in the air, for half an hour—more, if Fugate would let him. He loves it!" He licked his lips. "Wait till you see him clamp down and start pulling. He'll peel a face like you'd peel a banana. That's what the General is, Moretti—a face dog."

"A face dog?" I asked unwillingly.

"A dog that always goes for the face. Different dogs fight in different ways. Throat dogs always go for the throat, stomach dogs always go for the stomach, leg dogs always go for the big artery in the hind leg. You see one of them hit, and there'll be claret spraying for twenty feet. You don't want to stand too close when a leg dog's fighting."

I made a mental note. "What kind of dog will General Grant be fighting today?" I asked.

"A rider, I think. That's what they call a dog that tries for a position on the other dog's back, so he can get a good grip on the nape of his neck and wear him down. Friar Tuck's supposed to be the best rider around. He's whipped a half-dozen dogs in the last year." He grinned. "But mark my words, Moretti—he's trying for one too many tonight!"

"I believe it," I said.

"Hey, Moretti, I thought you were a follower of the sport of kings," shouted a voice in my ear. "What are you doing at a lowlife redneck affair like this?"

I turned to see Sandy Braddock grinning over the lip of a jar of corn liquor. There was a fixity to his gaze and a looseness to his lips that told how far he was into the bottle. I answered pleasantly that sports reporters, like other beggars, could ill afford to be choosers. He shook his head. "No, that's not what you're supposed to say. I'm disappointed in you. What you're supposed to say is that there's not all that much difference between killing dogs and cutting the nuts off horses. As high-class sporting events, that is." His grin widened as he turned to Farringay. "As a Maryland gentleman born and raised, wouldn't you agree, Jack?"

"If you say so, Sandy," Farringay answered smoothly. "Although personally I've never had any experience with mutilating valuable horseflesh." He gestured toward Fugate and General Grant. "I presume you're planning to win a little money on the Kirkargyle entry here."

Braddock stared at the fighting dog and took a sip of whiskey. His grin disappeared, and a look of sadness took its place. "Damn fool animal's about to get maimed if he's lucky and killed if he's not, and look at him. How he loves the man that's doing it to him!"

"It's their nature, Sandy," Farringay said. "They live to fight. If you took that away from them, they'd just as soon be dead."

"Oh? You're sure about that, are you?" He shot a mocking glance at Jack, then turned back to General Grant, and recited softly to himself,

> " 'Still thou art blest, compared wi' me!
> The present only toucheth thee:
> But och! I backward cast my e'e,
>   On prospects drear!
> And forward, tho' I canna see,
>   I guess an' fear!' "

I recognized the Scots dialect, if not the verse. "Burns?" I asked.

"Aye, Bobbie Burns, nane ither," Braddock said, rolling his *r*'s. " 'The best laid schemes o' mice and men gang aft a-gley, an' lea'e us nought but grief an' pain for promis'd joy.' " He stared at his liquor jar. "Bobbie knew. Bobbie knew it a'."

"Sandy's a devotee of Burns," Farringay said with the slightest hint of scorn. "He prefers his Scotch from a book and his bourbon from a bottle."

"And neither of them's much help in a place like this," said Braddock. "So put your money down on the General, Moretti. When there's stupidity and blood on both sides, you might as well make a profit from it. There's no honor to be won, God knows."

Glancing across the crowded barn, I saw the elegant figure of Carroll Glass moving toward the pit. He was carrying a dog in his arms, and a half-dozen shouting and laughing men accompanied him. "There's a familiar face," I said.

Farringay followed my eyes, and his body tensed; his face twisted into an expression of rage, his lips formed an obscenity, and his fists clenched at his sides. Then in a moment he was under perfect control again. "Ah, yes, the unlucky Squire of Windemere, with one of his last remaining pieces of livestock under his arm," he drawled. "Be sure to save out some money to bet against his cur, Paddy."

Glass stopped near the edge of the pit and set his dog on the ground. In the brief interval before he was surrounded by his hangers-on, his glance found us, and he inclined his head in a formal nod.

I asked Jack about the evening's card. He told me there were three fights scheduled—the first between General Grant and Friar Tuck, the second between two dogs from outside the area, one from Cynthiana and the other from Bowling Green, and the third between Carroll Glass's Tusker and a local dog named Brian Boru, owned by a toll road employee named Gallagher. "That'll be a blood match, for sure," he said cheerfully. "The harps are here in force tonight to see their dog take revenge on the Regulators for what happened to the Carmodys."

"Is Glass a Regulator?"

He laughed in delight. "Not as far as I know. But Fugate is, and rumor has it that Judge Caleb is one of their backers, and for an ignorant bog-trotter that's close enough. I'm glad I don't place my bets for emotional reasons. If I did, I'd never be able to decide which of their dogs to bet against."

I was adding the phrase "ignorant bog-trotter" to my mental inventory of Farringay's personal liabilities when Charlie Kimbro, the evening's master of ceremonies, stumbled over the foot-high board that formed the edge of the pit and took his place in the center, his son Lonnie by his side. "Ladies and gentlemen," he called, and the noise level dipped by a third. Impressed by the result, he grinned foolishly and repeated, "Ladies and gentlemen."

"The hell you say. Show me one," cried a ringside wit.

Kimbro took the shout of laughter that followed as a tribute to his oratorical skills; beaming, he bowed from the waist, and would have fallen if his son hadn't steadied him. "First event of the evening," he continued after regaining his balance. "Favorite of the Bluegrass . . . courageous champion of a dozen hard-won battles . . . Lomas Fugate's GENERAL GRANT!" He waved a hand at Lomas, who was squatting beside the General at the rim of the pit, as the crowd roared its approval. Then, with a much less expansive gesture in the other direction, he continued, "And from Owen County, leading contender"— he paused for a whispered exchange with his son, then continued—"FRIAR TUCK, owned by Jim Foushee of Owenton!" A few cheers were mixed with the general groans and catcalls. The man gentling his dog at the other edge of the pit grinned sardonically and gave a mock salute. "Ladies and gentlemen," Kimbro concluded, "let the festivities begin." He took a gulp of whiskey from the fruit jar in his hand, now almost empty, and stumbled out of the pit.

Final preparations for the fight began. The referee, a big-bellied man in red suspenders and sleeve garters, stood in the center of the ring frowning magisterially as each dog owner approached his rival's dog and was offered a bucket and a sponge by the dog's second.

"What are they doing?" I asked Farringay.

"Each breeder washes the other's dog. That way he can be sure its coat hasn't been treated with anything that would poison his own dog or make it refuse to fight."

"Is there much of that kind of thing?"

"It's been known to happen," he said dryly.

Lomas Fugate and the Owen County man washed down the dogs as the seconds squatted beside them keeping them calm. Fugate was slow and painstaking, drawing the cloth along the animal's body as gently as if it were his own

General Grant, instead of the General's mortal enemy. The Owen County man was equally solicitous. They reminded me of two acolytes preparing for Mass.

Similtaneously they finished the washing, toweled the dogs dry, and returned to their own sides of the pit. Fugate picked up General Grant and, holding him against his chest, stepped over the edge into the pit. The Owen County man did likewise. The big-bellied referee took his position in the center of the ring and placed his fists on his hips. The susurration of a hundred indrawn breaths filled the barn.

"Pit 'em!" the referee shouted.

Each owner released his dog, and instantly the two animals came together with an audible thud, their bodies blurred as they twisted and spun in the air, seeking favorable position. Friar Tuck, whose brown coat and purple gums suggested a touch of chow in his ancestry, maneuvered with Oriental subtlety to achieve his desired place on the General's back, and the General attacked with the directness of Nelson at Trafalgar. Each dog clamped on to the best hold he could find and abandoned it only when he could move to a better spot, the General moving toward Friar Tuck's eyes and muzzle, Friar Tuck hoping to shield his face until he could reach his antagonist's neck.

Dogfighting, I soon discovered, is more like wrestling than boxing, more like baseball than soccer. It is a sport of swift motion and long stillnesses, lightning jabs too swift for the eye to follow, separated by what seems like interminable intervals of stasis. But the drama builds during the stillnesses, as the audience senses the pain each animal feels in each new configuration, and prays for any change that may bring even an instant of relief. As the temperature in the barn rises, the smells of sour sweat, harsh tobacco, and whiskey mix in an almost visible miasma.

And of course there is the blood.

The General moved his adamantine jaws two or three inches at a time, at intervals of a minute or more, as Friar

Tuck struggled to slide around his enemy's shoulder and lock his teeth in his neck. At one point Friar Tuck's muzzle was buried at least four inches in the General's side, and I was sure that his next move would put his teeth through a vital organ. But instead of penetrating deeper he moved up the ribs toward the neck, and the opportunity was lost.

Ten minutes into the fight both dogs missed their grip and fell apart. Instantly Fugate and the Owen County man scooped up their champions and carried them to their corners, each shielding his dog from the sight of the other as he ministered to him for a few precious seconds before the fight resumed. Fugate literally licked the General's wounds, his tongue reaching places the dog couldn't reach himself. He sucked blood from the hole in the General's side and spat it on floor, licked mucus from the eyes and muzzle, filled his own mouth with water and spouted it between the animal's iron jaws. General Grant stared up at him with trust and consuming gratitude.

The crowd seized the opportunity to reopen the betting, and Lonnie Kimbro worked over his clipboard furiously. Most of the bets from the spectators favored General Grant, and the Owen County man's second nodded to Lonnie in acceptance of each one.

"How do you like it so far?" Farringay asked.

"More fun than a tooth extraction," I replied. "What do you think—is the General going to tear Tuck's face off?"

In answer, Farringay caught Lonnie Kimbro's eye and called, "Another hundred on General Grant!" The bookmaker glanced at Friar Tuck's second for confirmation, then noted the bet. Farringay rubbed his hands together and licked his lips.

"Pit 'em!" the referee bawled, and the battle resumed.

If there was any diminution of strength or savagery when the two dogs thudded together for the second time, I couldn't detect it. Each resumed his characteristic attack, Friar Tuck maneuvering for back position while General

Grant tried for a face hold. For ten more minutes they seemed equally remorseless, equally indefatigable.

Then Friar Tuck started to run out of time. The General's teeth were locked in his cheek, while his own muzzle was still six inches from the knot of neck muscles toward which he was maneuvering. He seemed to realize he had to change his style if he hoped to remain in the game. He began to squirm, twist, and kick, struggling to break loose, snapping his jaws in quick bites as if to inflict the sudden pain that could effect his release. But to no avail; General Grant was now in command and knew it. He used the struggles of his antagonist against him; when Friar Tuck tugged one way, the General jerked the other. And since his grip never weakened, the result was predictable.

"By God, he's peeling him!" Farringay cried. "If Friar Tuck doesn't cur out, he'll be a bare skull in two minutes!" Friar Tuck reached the same conclusion simultaneously; his body seemed to soften, his jaws opened, and an audible whine testified to his pacifistic desires. General Grant maintained his grip for a few moments to prove his absolute control, then released it with a contemptuous shake of his head and sauntered bandy-legged back to his corner, where Lomas Fugate swept him up in a hero's welcome. Friar Tuck slunk backward, face shredded, belly almost dragging the floor.

In the ensuing confusion Farringay went to collect his bet and I made my way through the shouting crowd to the outside door. The night air smelled startlingly fresh and cool. I walked around the corner of the barn, where the noise was muted, and stood with my back against the boards, filling my lungs. *Jesus, Mary, and Joseph,* I thought, *half an hour in that place is like a day in the stockyards.*

I watched the clouds that scudded across the low-hanging moon and thought about bad things happening to animals. For most of my life I had been making my living in a business that could be thought of as the exploitation of horses for financial gain, without ever feeling any guilt toward the source of my salary. I was fully aware that sometimes they were doped, sometimes forced to run with torn muscles and broken bones, often beaten to make them run faster, or slower, as their owner demanded. Most of them ended their days at the knacker's, if they weren't destroyed for injuries first. More often than not it was a life that was, as Hobbes might have said, nasty, brutish, and short—and as a racetrack reporter, I had never been caused a moment's uneasiness.

But the buggers don't try to tear each other's heads off!

True. But apparently they're not immune to castration, or snakebite, or being drawn and quartered—not if they're Kirkargyle horses and run afoul of poetic inevitability.

All in all, I thought moodily, *our four-footed friends might be well advised to avoid the Bluegrass entirely this season.*

My ears, as well as my eyes, were becoming acclimated to the hushed darkness around me, and I became aware of voices a few feet away, beyond the next corner of the barn.

Or rather, *a* voice—for although I could sense that it represented half of a dialogue, the responding voice was inaudible. It was a woman's voice, plaintive and also smug, like a poker player poor-mouthing a powerful hand.

"Why, acourse I'm sure, wouldn't have told you if'n I wasn't. A woman knows these things." She paused to allow a murmured rejoinder, then continued, "Well, you're glad, ain't you? You want to do the right thing, don't you?" This time the answering murmur carried a sense of agitation. The woman was silent for a few moments, and when she spoke again, it was to cry, "Oh, it's cruel for you to talk that way! And it ain't true—you know it ain't true! Why, I haven't even looked at a boy since—" Her voice dropped to a whisper, which was interrupted by a rumbling response.

By now I had recognized the female voice as belonging to Marybee Fugate, Lomas's precociously endowed daughter. My curiosity aroused, I took a couple of stealthy steps toward the corner of the barn. Marybee's voice rose.

"Now, you just hold up a minute, Mr. Smartie. Maybe you better think twice 'fore you say anything you're going to be sorry for later. . . . No, I ain't threatening you, I'd never do nothing like that. . . . Aw, hon"—her voice became kittenishly provocative—"just being close to you makes me go all hot and funny inside. Hold me, hon." There was an angry grunt, and Marybee's voice snapped, "Well, you just better *learn* to like it again!"

I took three or four more steps toward the corner of the barn, but before I reached it I heard another voice, rough and male, shouting, "Marybee! MARYBEE FUGATE! Where the hell are you?"

"That's Daddy! He's looking for me! You skedaddle, now, 'less you want him to catch us out here!" The man muttered a few words in reply. By the time I reached the corner and stuck my head around it, all I could see of him was a shape disappearing among the black trees. Marybee stood alone, her back against the barn, smoothing the material of her dress against her proud young breasts.

Lomas came around the corner from the other direction. He leaned forward as he saw her, hunching his shoulders and clenching his fists. "You! What you doin' out here in the dark? You meetin' somebody? Don't lie, goddamn it! You're fixin' to fool around with some young shitass in the bushes!" He reached out his hands for her, and she drew away from him.

"It was so hot and smoky in there, Daddy! I felt real giddy, honest I did! I came out for a breath of air before I fainted away!"

He gripped her arms. "You didn't come out here to meet some boy?" She shook her head and denied the accusation reproachfully. He dropped his hands to his sides. "Well . . ." he said awkwardly, "well, I guess you didn't see the General win then."

"No, Daddy. I'm sorry."

He sighed. "Well, it was something to see, I tell you. That old fella, he just kept agoin' and agoin', and never let up for a minute. He hung on like he wasn't about to let loose in this life. I was proud of him, I tell you.''

''I dearly wish I'd seen it, Daddy.''

He raised his arms and reached his hands toward her, then froze as he saw me over her shoulder. ''You there—what the hell you think you're doing?'' he demanded.

I stepped toward them as I answered, ''The same thing as your daughter, Mr. Fugate—just getting myself a breath of fresh air. And may I take this opportunity to congratulate you and your magnificent animal for an unequaled demonstration of canine pugilism? I hope the redoubtable General didn't receive any serious injury in the process.''

He shook his head like a bull. ''What? What are you talking about? You been out here sniffing around this girl?'' I denied it and repeated my congratulations on the fight with less circumlocution. Mollified, he allowed himself a small grin. ''Yeah, the old boy done himself proud, all right. I give him a drink of beer and a hunk of steak, and he's sleeping like a baby.'' His grin widened. ''I don't reckon that Owen County fella's gonna do much bragging on his dogs for a while, not after tonight. You have yourself a few dollars down on the General, Moretti?''

''I'm sorry to say I didn't. I'll know better next time.'' *In the extremely unlikely event I ever find myself watching another dogfight,* I added mentally.

We exchanged a few more words, and then, as a roar from inside indicated that the next fight was about to begin, I started back. As I rounded the corner I met three boys carrying an open fruit jar and drawing fiercely on cigarettes. From the way they swaggered, they were impressing themselves and one another with their masculinity. They were dressed in overalls and dungarees, but didn't look like farm boys. I stepped to one side as they caught sight of Marybee.

''Ooh, I been struck blind!'' cried a towheaded lad with a face like a sheep, making groping gestures with his hands in front of his face. ''It's a face to take away a man's sight entirely!'' He stumbled toward Marybee, his hands extended. "Speak, fair maiden, so I can find you in the dark." Behind him his two companions followed, giggling. If any of the three recognized Fugate, or even noticed his presence, they didn't show it.

"You mind your manners, boy," Marybee said sharply.

"I hear her! It's the lady of my dreams!" the towhead crowed, reaching out his hands for her. "Ah, *macushla*, give us a little kiss and cure me poor eyes with the magic of you!"

"Get away, you dirty Irish hyena!" Marybee drew back against the barn, her hands suddenly clawlike. "Don't you dare come near me—none of you people, never!" Belatedly sensing the approach of an ugly scene, I took a step toward the towhead. Before I could do more than that, Lomas Fugate swung into action.

Moving as effortlessly as an acrobat, he stepped around his daughter and stood facing her teaser, his fists raised, knees bent, weight evenly distributed on both feet. He feinted with his left hand and drove a sledgehammer right against the Irish boy's cheekbone. The boy dropped to his knees, supporting himself on his hands. Fugate stepped closer and deliberately kicked him in the head. The boy collapsed in the dirt, and instantly Fugate turned on his two friends. He whipped a bowie knife with an eight-inch blade from inside his jacket and held it before him, its point weaving from one side to the other. His eyes glittered in the moonlight, and his teeth were bared in a savage grin. "Who's the next one?" he asked softly. "You?" He thrust the knife at the nearest of the boys, who leaped back with a yelp of terror. "Or you?" The knife blade flashed in a sudden arc a foot from the second lad's belly, causing him to stumble backward and sit down on the ground. "Say some more funny things to my daughter while I open you up and see what's inside you."

Since Marybee was standing with her arms folded, watching events with a delighted smile and obviously not about to intervene, it seemed to be up to me to prevent imminent bloodletting. With considerable misgiving I touched Fugate on the left, or unoccupied, arm. "Ach, man, would you be putting yourself in Death Row for the sake of spalpeens like these?" I asked. Unfortunately I fell into the brogue, as I sometimes do when in a wheedling mode, forgetting that it might be less than appropriate under the circumstances. I realized my error an instant later. Fugate's left arm whipped around my shoulders, and the edge of the bowie knife pressed firmly against my throat.

.   "So you're another one, are you? You're after her, too, you mick bastard!"

"Me? Mick? I'm Moretti, remember! Moretti, of the Naples Morettis!" I cried, pulling futilely against his iron grip.

His eyes showed no comprehension, and for a moment I thought I was a dead man. Then Marybee touched his arm and said, "You don't want to kill him, Daddy. He ain't one of them."

His eyes flickered toward her. "He ain't?"

"No. He never deviled me like them others did."

"Oh." The knife blade's pressure eased, and the mighty arm relaxed. "If you say so, hon." I exhaled and rubbed my throat gingerly as the two Irish lads picked up their towheaded associate and half carried him toward the barn entrance. Fugate shouted after them, "There's plenty more where that came from!" and replaced his knife under his jacket.

Another roar from the crowd inside the barn marked the progress of the second fight in the evening's card. Fugate looked sternly at his daughter. "I reckon you've had all the fresh air you need, so let's us get back inside." She nodded submissively. I followed them to the door. As they entered, past a half-dozen idlers eyeing her with interest, Marybee's carriage changed from modest to provocative; her back arched, her hips rolled, and her lips pouted in disdain. I paused to let them get well ahead of me and then followed them inside. Two new dogs were pitted, their jaws locked in one another's bodies, which were slimed with blood. My eyes found Jack Farringay, his mouth open as he shouted a bet to Lonnie Kimbro, and I decided I didn't want to resume my seat beside him. Continuing to search the crowd, I saw another familiar face—that of Emmett Lawler, the Squire of Folly Hill. Something about his expression of disinterest in the midst of the hysteria around him attracted me, and I made my way to a space next to him.

He answered my greeting with a cool stare. "Mr. Moretti, isn't it? Can we expect to read an account of tonight's event in *The Spirit of the Times*?"

"I'm afraid not, Mr. Lawler. It's not a subject my editor would approve of. Congratulations on Prince Hal in the fifth today—a superior horse indeed."

He nodded in agreement and selected a cigar from a handsome alligator pocket case, not bothering to offer me one; he clipped it and lit it carefully and drew in a luxurious lungful, and then regarded me with raised eyebrows, as if surprised I was still standing beside him. "Something?" he asked.

"Prince Hal used to belong to Carroll Glass, I understand. It must be hard on him, losing a winner like that."

His thick lips pressed together as if to prevent a smile. "I wouldn't know," he said in dismissal.

"Especially with you being the new owner. You and he being rivals for Miss McAuliffe, and all." His face darkened, but before he could speak I went on, "What a horse farm it would be if your Folly Hill was joined to Kirkargyle! Almost as big as the Alexanders' Woodburn! And with your Prince Hal, and those McAuliffe mares like Bonne Jeanne—"

"That's about enough, Moretti."

"A much handsomer proposition than merging Kirkargyle with Carroll Glass's Windemere. Although if that's what Miss Dorcas is planning, I guess she better do it soon—while there's still some of Windemere left."

Lawler's eyes were narrow slits under lowering brows. "Are you trying to antagonize me?" he asked softly.

"No, sir, just checking on a possible story. Are you a native of the Bluegrass, Mr. Lawler? Your accent sounds more eastern than southern."

"My accent is none of your business—and none of your friend Farringay's, either. And that's enough. I came here to watch a fight, and that's what I intend to do. I suggest you do your watching from somewhere else." Turning away from me, he took a half-dozen quick steps away and wedged himself between two yelling fans. I thought about following him, and decided against it. I made my way instead toward the pit and the grimly struggling dogs in it.

Farringay was watching with rapt attention. "No shortage of claret in this fight," I observed pleasantly. He grunted, not taking his eyes from the contest in front of him. "Any fine points you'd like to comment on? Length of fangs? Resistance of skin? Accessibility of vital organs?" He grunted again. I shrugged and settled down stoically to watch the fight.

It had its good side and its bad side. Its good side was that it was over in fifteen minutes. Its bad side was that one dog killed the other one very messily.

When it was finished I looked into Farringay's flushed face and said thoughtfully, "One thing I remember about you from Kansas, Jack—you like to mix business with pleasure. Another thing is, you always have to have more than one iron in the fire."

"So?"

"So I have a hunch about this dogfighting. It reminds me of the bare-knuckle fight store you and your friends were running out west—both of them blood sports, to appeal to your personal appetite, and both of them naturals for confidence swindles."

He turned to face me, his face a study in artless perplexity. "Confidence swindles, Paddy? I'm afraid I don't follow you. My presence at this event tonight is purely recreational, believe me. And as for the Kansas business, I can only assure you that I've learned my lesson. Nothing

could be further from my mind than sinking back into a
life of opportunism and deception.'' He leaned closer and
lowered his voice. ''Also, my hopes with regard to Miss
Dorcas occupy my attention completely.''

''Jack, you've never seen the day you didn't have a
backup plan. If you don't win the McAuliffe matrimonial
sweepstakes, you'll need something else to slide into, and
my guess is it will be a dog store.''

He grimaced as if attempting to solve a calculus problem in his head. ''A dog store?'' he repeated.

''A dog store. Like your fight store, or a footrace store
or a wrestle store. A con game where ropers bring their
marks to bet on an event which is supposedly fixed, but
which blows up in their faces when their money is down.
An illegal event, so they can't take their troubles to the
authorities. And a nice bloody event, so you can satisfy
your taste for claret.''

Farringay said patiently, ''But a *dog* store, Paddy—in
all my checkered career I've never heard of such a thing.''

''Neither has anybody else, which is what makes it so
good. It's a Farringay original. If you set it up right, you
could have marks coming in from all over the country.''

''And you've figured out how to set it up?''

''Oh, no. I don't have that kind of a mind. If I did, I'd
be in the business myself, instead of grubbing for small
change on a sporting paper. But *you* do, Jack. And that's
what you're doing—that's the second string for your bow,
in case Miss Dorcas gives you your walking papers. Fess
up, now. Ain't it the truth?''

Farringay's expression was so benign that I felt a twinge
of uneasiness. ''You're a marvel, Paddy. Your imagination
is one of the things I admire most about you. The other is
your discretion.'' He paused, his eyes holding mine for a
long moment. Then, glancing away, he said lightly, ''We'll
have to resume this later, I'm afraid. It's time for the fu-
neral service for Glass's cur.''

I saw that the leftovers from the last fight had been
cleared from the pit, and that now Carroll Glass and a

man I took to be his second were squatting beside a one-
eared brown-and-white pit bull at one side of the ring, and
two other men, one wearing a derby and the other a checkered cap, were ministering to a badly scarred black-and-
white veteran on the other side.

The crowd was louder and more unruly than before,
shouting encouragement or denigration, booing the officials, insulting and threatening one another. And while the
earlier disorder had been good-humored, this had an edge
of ugliness to it. For the audience was clearly divided into
two factions, the minority Irish, the majority anti-Irish.
There were perhaps twenty-five Irish adult males, a handful of wives, and ten or fifteen boys in their teens or
younger. They represented the toll road faction. The rest
of the crowd either were members of the Regulators or
sympathized with their goals.

Charlie Kimbro did little to ease the situation. By this
time he appeared to be too drunk to stand alone—his son
Lonnie supported him with one hand while clutching his
clipboard with the other—and chose to emphasize the po-
larizing characteristics of the contestants: ''—from the for-
eign fields of the Emeral' Isle—proud blood of champeens
coursing through his veins—victor of half a hunnerd hard-
fought contests—(what the hell is his name again, Lonnie?)—BRIAN BORU! An' in other corner, the toast o'
the Kentucky Bluegrass, the fearless defender of country,
church, and womanhood, Mr. Carroll Glass's jus'ly acclaimed—TUSKER! Ladies 'n gen'lmen, place your bets!''

The crowd responded so eagerly that Lonnie was kept
busy for five minutes scribbling on his clipboard while
Carroll Glass and the Irishman with the derby, whose name
was Gallagher, gave last-minute attention and support to
their animals. Farringay called in a fifty-dollar bet on Brian
Boru, and I glanced toward Emmett Lawler to see if he
was also betting against his matrimonial rival, but he stood
with his arms folded, smiling slightly, apparently aloof.
Across the barn I caught a glimpse of Sandy Braddock
with a pink jar raised to his lips, and at the back of the

crowd I thought I could make out Lomas Fugate, holding his daughter firmly by the arm.

During the delay before the fight the tension tightened like a cord stretched to the breaking point. Added to the aura of tobacco, whiskey, and unwashed bodies was a smell like tarnished brass, the foul stink of blood lust. I swallowed and spat to clear my mouth, but the bitter taste remained. Belatedly I wished that when I had been outside I had stayed there, but it was too late to beat a retreat through the densely packed bodies now.

"Pit 'em!" cried the big-bellied referee.

Glass and Gallagher released their dogs, who met with a bone-jarring impact in the center of the ring, erect on their back legs, twisting and snapping for advantage, their tails wagging furiously in a parody of friendliness. Glass's Tusker was a throat dog, and so was Brian Boru, so each was able to obtain a grip on the other almost immediately. From then on it was simply a question of which could sever the other's jugular first.

"Tear his throat out, you Irish bastard," Farringay called through his cupped hands. "Rip him apart! Let's see some blood!" His face was flushed and the cords of his neck stood out.

A spectator directly in front of us turned his head and cried, "Shut your fool mouth 'fore somebody shuts it for you!"

Farringay leaned forward until his face was almost touching the other's. "Want to try it, you ape?" he asked with a Satanic smile.

Before the man could decide to accept the proposal I seized my companion by the arm and pulled him back. "For God's sake, Jack, will you try to control yourself? There's enough bloodshed around here already, without you adding ours on top of it!"

The two dogs waltzed drunkenly around the pit, their snouts buried in each other's throats. Their two owners, forbidden to touch them as long as they had a grip on each other, were on their knees in the ring, each man leaning close to his dog and exhorting him to greater effort. Suddenly Tusker went over on his back, Brian Boru followed him, and the dogs shifted their grips simultaneously. In that instant Carroll Glass seized his dog and jerked him up into the air. Both dogs maintained their holds for a moment and then released them, and Glass stood upright, holding Tusker against his chest. Most of the audience gasped, and the Irish roared in outrage.

"Foul!" Farringay screamed. "He touched his dog while they were locked! The Irisher wins!" Gallagher scooped up Brian Boru and held him above his head as if acknowledging a victory.

Glass, his face twisted with anger, shouted to the referee, "They were separated, goddamn it! Tusker was free—I saw it! They were both free, or I wouldn't have touched them!"

"Cheat!" Farringay shouted through megaphoned hands. "Rotten cheat! The Irisher wins!"

The referee raised his hands above his head and called out, "The dogs is free. Thirty seconds' time out, and then pit 'em again!"

A groan rose from the Irish contingent. Farringay cupped his hands again and hollered, "Are you blind, you fat turd?"

The spectator in front of Jack spun around and drew back his fist. Jack opened one hand, placed it in the man's face, and pushed. The man sailed backward, flailing his arms wildly, and crashed into the backs of the two men standing ahead of him, who immediately turned and began to pummel him. In a moment their battle merged with others around them that had originated for equally confused reasons, and the barn exploded into violence. In the pit I saw Brian Boru's second hit the referee in the belly and double him up, whereupon Tusker's second clouted Brian Boru's second on the ear and lofted him five feet. Part of the Irish faction formed themselves into a flying wedge and charged toward the ring, either to protect their champion or punish the opposition. They were immediately met by superior forces, and the wedge dissolved into twenty separate engagements.

Then something hit me on the back of the head, and I was suddenly on my knees, surrounded by struggling bodies. *Got to get back on my feet, or I'll be stomped to death entirely,* I thought, grabbing someone's jacket to pull myself erect. Jack Farringay was beside me, grinning evilly while two men hung around his neck. He bent back one man's fingers until he released his hold, and I hit the other a solid blow on the temple, dislodging him as well. Jack's eyes danced. "Obliged, Bunky."

"*De nada.* Can we leave now, please?"

Then a pistol shot rang out, and for a split second everyone froze. It was one of the Irishmen, a scrawny fellow with a bushy red mustache, and he was holding a hogleg Colt revolver with both hands, pointed toward the ceiling. "Ye Protestant tinkers, I'll have your heart's blood!" he cried as the pistol barrel described a wavering ellipse.

The exodus began. Brawlers nearest the door reevaluated the situation and decided the pistol shot had changed the equation; they were followed out by successive waves of combatants, both Irish and non-Irish, until only a handful remained inside the barn. The scrawny gun-toter stared at his Colt in bemusement, as if unable to understand its catalytic capabilities. The referee sat in the middle of the ring, feeling his belly gingerly with both hands. Lomas Fugate and his daughter stood apart, his hand clutching her arm; the expression on his face was grim, and on hers, almost ecstatic. Emmett Lawler was engaged in conversation with another well-to-do-looking fellow, apparently unruffled by recent events. Charlie Kimbro was having a drink from Sandy Braddock's bottle as his son Lonnie frowned over his clipboard. Gallagher was inspecting Brian Boru's wounds—and Carroll Glass lay on his back in the center of the ring with Tusker cradled in his arms.

I felt a sudden chill of apprehension. I touched Jack on the arm and nodded toward the pit. His eyes narrowed, and he followed me. We bent over Glass, and Jack touched the carotid artery.

"Is he—" I began.

Jack turned to me, and his expression was unreadable. "He's just unconscious. Too bad his dog wasn't so lucky." He stood up, shot his cuffs, and touched the dog in Glass's arms with the toe of his gleaming shoe. "I'm afraid the redoubtable Tusker's fighting days are over. Somebody's cut the cur's throat from ear to ear."

6

Breakfast at Kirkargyle— or Ithaca?

"**D**amn it, Moretti, people who spend the night in my bed are generally willing to reach *some* kind of physical accommodation with me! If we're going to continue seeing each other like this, you simply must learn to restrict yourself to an absolute maximum of seventy-five percent of the area. Surely that's not asking too much!"

Farringay frowned at me from the mirror atop the dresser as he ran a comb through his wavy black hair. I propped myself up on an elbow and regarded him unsympathetically while I tasted the inside of my mouth. "It was all I could do to hold on to a four-inch strip of mattress with my rump hanging out in the air," I answered. "Anyway, it wasn't my idea to come back here. I would just have soon gone back to Lexington." I pulled myself into a sitting position. "What time is it?"

"About eleven-thirty. The McAuliffes left for church more than an hour ago. They should be back for breakfast in a few minutes."

I sat on the edge of the bed scratching myself and thought about the previous evening. After the free-for-all in Kimbro's barn, followed by the discovery of the unconscious Carroll Glass and his deceased dog, the few of us who remained at the arena and were in at least partial possession of our senses—Jack, Emmett Lawler and his well-dressed friend, Lomas and Marybee Fugate, Lonnie Kimbro—clustered around Glass and tried to bring him back to consciousness; Gallagher knelt with his back to us, tending his Brian Boru, and Sandy Braddock and Charlie Kimbro squatted beside the big-bellied referee and plied him with therapeutic moonshine.

Glass opened his eyes after a minute or two, groaned, started to sit up, and became aware of the inert weight he was cradling in his arms. "What—" he began, and then, as he realized what had happened to the dog, his expression changed to bewilderment, to incredulity, to horror, and finally to despair. He laid the small corpse on the ground beside him and rested his hand gently over its muzzle. "Old Tusker, even you," he said huskily. "Forgive me. The bastard."

"What happened, Glass?" Lomas Fugate demanded. "Who done it to you?"

Glass looked up slowly. His eyes moved from face to face in the circle above him. When he spoke, his voice was level and almost conversational. "Why, I'm sorry to say I don't know. Somebody who didn't like my dog, I reckon. I aim to find out, though." He touched the back of his head gingerly. "I heard that damn fool shoot off his pistol, and after that"—he grimaced—"the lights went out."

"No idea who it could have been?" Emmett Lawler asked.

Glass took his time answering, rising to his feet and brushing dirt from the back of his coat and trousers. Then he picked up the body of the pit bull and tucked it under one arm. He looked around the circle of faces again, smiled coldly, and said, "Not as I'd care to say." He took Lonnie Kimbro's arm with bloodstained fingers. "I think we've got some business to discuss, Lonnie."

But Glass received no support from the Kimbros, who, supported by the referee, insisted that Brian Boru had won through Tusker's disqualification. Since most of Brian Bo-

ru's supporters were absent Irishmen, it was obvious that
the bulk of the wagers recorded on Lonnie's clipboard
would remain in Lonnie's pocket. Glass did not argue;
when he saw the decision was against him, he shrugged
and strode from the barn, carrying his dead champion in
his arms.

The rest of us followed shortly. Jack and I were prepared to ride back to Lexington, but Sandy Braddock insisted that we come with him to Kirkargyle instead, and
we were glad to allow ourselves to be persuaded. Braddock rode ahead on a placid old mare, dozing and swaying
in the saddle, and we followed in our buggy.

After a few minutes of silence I said, "Not a very lucky
man, that Glass fellow."

"Not very, no."

"Emmett Lawler seems a good deal luckier."

"So he does."

"I wonder if he's luckier in love, too."

"You wonder that, do you?"

"Don't you?"

"I hadn't thought about it." He clucked his tongue to
the horse and flicked the reins. "In matters of the heart,
Bunky, it's my experience that luck has very little to do
with the outcome. Lawler may the luckiest man alive, and
it won't help him in the slightest with Miss McAuliffe. He
is, to put it simply, outclassed."

I turned to look into his impassive face. "Who do you
think killed Glass's dog?" I asked. "And why? It doesn't
make any sense to me." Farringay shrugged. "Where's
the poetic inevitability?" I went on. "Unless you want to
struggle with something like 'Dogs who live in Glass's
house shouldn't stow bones' "—Farringay groaned audi-
bly—"I don't see any pattern at all. I mean, show me
somebody named Tusker in the *Tanglewood Tales*. Or in
the *Encyclopaedia Britannica*, for that matter."

"You have a devious mind, Moretti. Maybe someone
just disliked the cur. Or his master."

"Hmmmpf." We rode on in silence. In front of us

Sandy Braddock lost one of his stirrups and inclined alarmingly to the side, saving himself at the last moment by clutching the pommel of his saddle. Muttering profanely, he recaptured the stirrup and settled back into the rocking-chair rhythm of the plodding mare.

I folded my arms and said casually, "That's a fascinating idea you have, Jack. It should go over like a house afire."

"Oh? What idea is that?"

"You know. The dog store. It's a natural, and you're just the fellow to put it across. You'll have marks coming in from everywhere east of the Mississippi. Brilliant!"

In the moonlight his eyeball gleamed as coldly as a frozen cod. "I've already congratulated you on your imagination—and your discretion. Between the two it's hard to say which is your more valuable characteristic."

"All right—if you want to be that way." We lapsed into a silence which lasted until we reached Kirkargyle, where, refusing Sandy's proposal for a nightcap, we bedded down in the same guest bedroom and on the same narrow bed we had shared before.

The next morning I watched as Jack completed his toilette before the mirror. He brushed his dark, lustrous hair with thirty strokes of a military brush and tilted his head to one side to inspect the result. It apparently pleased him, for his saturnine expression was transformed by a broad smile. He touched the cleft in his chin with one finger and said, "Your uncle Dudley's holding up rather well, wouldn't you agree?" He turned his profile to the glass, inspecting himself from the corner of his eye. "A clean mind in a healthy body. The Greeks were right."

"The Romans," I said sourly. *"Mens sana in corpore sano."*

"Them, too. You should act accordingly." He slipped on his jacket and gave his cravat a final touch. "Better get dressed. We'll be eating breakfast as soon as the family gets back."

Twenty minutes later the McAuliffes returned, and were

soon followed by a dozen guests. 'Lijah presided over an impressive spread in the morning room, and Sandy Braddock dispensed champagne and stronger waters from a side table. Caleb McAuliffe, the very model of a Kentucky country squire in frock coat, white trousers, and a string tie, greeted new arrivals with grave courtesy, while Miss Rhoda and Dorcas added their different versions of feminine charm.

I took a glass of champagne from Sandy. "Your very good health, sir," I toasted him. "You look very well this morning, considering."

He gave me what was intended for a debonair smile. " 'Inspiring, bold John Barleycorn, what dangers thou canst make us scorn!' "

"Burns?"

"The source of my strength." The glass he held in his black-gloved hand was filled with a liquid considerably darker than champagne. He drank, his bloodshot eyes regarding me over the edge of the goblet, and then asked, "I forgot to inquire how you did in Lonnie's handbook."

"I didn't bet—which is the nearest I've come to winning in months. How about you?"

"Oh, lost a bit. I seem to remember putting fifty on Tusker, there at the end. Remind me to tell Glass to keep his hands off his dogs when they're in the pit. That, or keep them the hell out of the fights. Tenderness ill becomes a dog breeder, makes him a menace to the betting public." His eyes left mine and moved nervously around the room; obviously our conversation was not commanding his attention.

"Have you had any thoughts about Tusker being killed?"

He shrugged. "Pointless. He'd lost anyway. 'Wee, sleekit, cow'rin, tim'rous beastie'—not so wee, but tim'rous enough, the damn cur went over on his back. Why would anybody bother killing him?"

"Poetic inevitability?" I asked hopefully, sipping my champagne.

He looked at me blankly. "How's that?"

I shook my head. "Nothing." Dorcas McAuliffe was standing a few feet away, and for a moment was between guests. Our eyes met, and she stepped toward me and hooked her arm through mine.

"Mr. Moretti, I'm delighted to see you at Kirkargyle again. Now maybe we'll have a chance to have that conversation we missed last time." I said I hoped so. "Are you finding lots of good stories to write about us here in the Bluegrass?"

"To tell you the truth, I've had luckier times, Miss Mc-Auliffe. For one thing, I have the definite impression your father takes a dim view of the sporting press."

Her chocolate-brown eyes crinkled delightfully at the corners. "Oh, Papa's just an old bear sometimes. You keep after him, and I bet he'll be talking your arm off in no time." She dismissed the subject with a wave of her graceful hand. "Did you know Mr. Farringay when he lived in Maryland?"

"No, it was after that. I met him in a professional capacity some distance west of there."

"Oh, while he was racing some of his horses? I know he traveled a great deal and left his brother to handle the day-to-day operations at the farm. It must have been an exciting life."

"I'd say so, yes." I sipped my champagne. She greeted a new breakfast arrival with a smile and then turned to me again. "I envy you your familiarity with him, Mr. Moretti," she said evenly.

"You're very frank, Miss McAuliffe."

"To a fault, I'm afraid, or at least some of my family think so. I hope you'll be as frank with me. I might as well say that I am attracted to Jack Farringay, but I'm perhaps a bit unsure of my own judgment. There are things about Jack I don't understand. That, combined with the way my father feels about him—"

"Judge McAuliffe takes a dim view of the lad?"

"He takes a dim view of every man I know except Emmett Lawler." She shook her head irritably, and her rich auburn hair swirled about her shoulders. "He doesn't believe Jack comes from Maryland at all. He doesn't think it's true about Jack's father being a Rebel raider during the war, or the family raising bloodstock on their farm, or Jack handling the racing end, or anything. He says Jack's nothing but a fortune hunter."

I inspected the champagne in my glass carefully, sniffing the bouquet and studying the little bubbles. "He says that, does he?"

"Yes, he does! But you're an old friend of Jack's—you said you've known him for two years, long before he came to Kentucky. So you know how wrong my father is!"

I glanced down at her slender fingers resting on my sleeve and answered lightly, "Why, I've never claimed to be an authority on him. Never visited the old homestead, or anything like that—our relationship was always in a sporting context, you might say. But I'm sure his father was a Confederate raider. I have reason to know that."

The smile that brightened her face showed she took my words for a blanket endorsement. "Why, of course he was! And their farm was in Anne Arundel County, and they went sailing in Chesapeake Bay in the summers, and used to ride into Washington and see the Senate when it was in session—"

"Well, of course I never knew anything about that," I said uneasily.

She gave me the affectionate look one reserves for the dear friend of a dear friend. "Tell me about the first time you met him. You said it was out west somewhere?"

"Yes, it was in—it was in Kansas, if I remember—or maybe it was Nebraska. It might have been either, as a matter of fact—" I took a swallow from my glass and looked around the room for some excuse to change the conversation. Nothing suggested itself as I stumbled on, "Is it Council Bluffs that's in Kansas, or is it Cedar Rapids? Or do I mean Cedar Falls? Ah, I never can get the lot of them straight!''

Her expression became puzzled. ''Are there racetracks in those towns?''

''Tracks? Did I say there were tracks?'' My searching gaze found Dorcas's father involved in an intense conversation with a man I didn't know, a slight, desiccated-looking fellow with a jaundiced complexion and thin hair buttered across a bony skull. From their expressions, it was apparent they were arguing. ''Say, your father's having quite a discussion there,'' I cried. ''Who's the turkey gobbler with him?''

She followed my eyes, frowning. ''Oh, that's Mr. Yates—Willis Yates. He's a lawyer. We've known him for years, but he and Daddy don't always get along anymore.''

She turned back to resume her interrogation, but was interrupted by Caleb McAuliffe's voice, raised in anger. ''That's enough, sir! I'll not be blackguarded in my own home by the paid agent of a pack of thieving jackals!''

In the sudden silence the other man's answer, although spoken in a soft and pleasantly flutelike voice, rang like a bell. ''Perhaps not in your own home, Caleb—but I guarantee you if Carmody's wife dies, you'll hear some things you don't like in a court of law!''

''Are you threatening me, Yates?'' McAuliffe shouted.

''Not threatening, prophesying. My God, how long do you think the state is going to allow the Regulators to take the law into their own hands while you and your friends sit back like country squires and pay their bills? You don't think for a moment that you're fooling anyone, do you? Everybody in central Kentucky knows where the money for your thugs comes from.''

''And what about *your* money? You're on retainer from the toll road! You've sold your Bluegrass birthright for a mess of pottage!''

''It's a legal business, Caleb, unlike the arming of mobs. There's nothin' wrong with the toll roads that the state legislature can't cure, all straightforward and aboveboard. All it needs is the people in Frankfort to write the laws.''

"Hell, most of them are on the toll-road payroll, like you!'' McAuliffe's face was dark red, and his voice trembled with rage. "You damned blackleg! You're a traitor to your class!''

Willis Yates stepped back and drew himself up to his full five feet five inches. The only sign of displeasure on his avian face was a twitching at one corner of his mouth. He nodded curtly. "Just hope that the Carmody woman doesn't die,'' he repeated.

Dorcas and her aunt Rhoda arrived simultaneously to make peace between the combatants. The older woman put her hand on McAuliffe's arm and said, "Now hush, Caleb. I declare, you sound like a wild man. Stop yelling at Willis and say you're sorry!'' Dorcas placed herself between her uncle and the lawyer, and took Yates's hand between hers. "Uncle Willis, you haven't eaten enough to keep a bird alive. You come with me, and we'll get you a glass of champagne and some of that good corn pudding and old ham.'' When he resisted, she put her arm around his waist and drew him with her. "You hear me? Come on now—we haven't had a chance to have a nice talk since I don't know when.''

Watching the lawyer being drawn toward the buffet, McAuliffe cleared his throat and called after him, "I apologize, Yates—lost my hospitality along with my good sense. Glad to have you here at Kirkargyle!'' The lawyer didn't look back, but acknowledged the sentiment with another nod.

Conversation became general again. I saw Farringay talking to Sandy Braddock and was making my way toward them when Carroll Glass entered the room.

His face, though pale, was composed, and his bearing was graceful almost to the point of arrogance. The only reminder of his experiences the night before was a bruise the size of a half-dollar on his left temple at the hairline. His eyes went immediately to Dorcas and Yates at the buffet, but he approached Judge McAuliffe and Miss Rhoda first.

From Judge McAuliffe's expression, he appeared to be nonplussed by Glass's arrival. He hesitated a moment before taking the younger man's hand, then gave it a perfunctory shake and dropped it. He cleared his throat, murmured an inaudible pleasantry, and turned away as if called by more pressing business. Miss Rhoda, on the other hand, stared at Glass wide-eyed, one blue-veined hand pressed against her breast. She took an unsteady step toward him and said, in a clear, high voice, "How delightful to see you again, Mr. Glass. Are you on leave from your regiment?"

Dorcas gasped and moved toward her aunt, and Caleb McAuliffe turned back to her with an exasperated grimace. Miss Rhoda continued, "I wish I had known your intentions, sir. Perhaps then we could have made plans to utilize your brief civilian hours to their best advantage."

Glass bowed, an ironical smile on his lips. Miss Rhoda turned to her brother. "See who's come to see us, Caleb. It's Amory Glass, from Windemere, on leave from General Wheeler's army in Georgia." She smiled coolly at Carroll Glass and flirted her fingers along the lace at her throat. "I do declare, I believe the military life agrees with you, Mr. Glass."

Dorcas put her arm protectively around her aunt's shoulders. Although she spoke to Miss Rhoda, her eyes were fixed disapprovingly on Glass. "You come with me, Auntie. I need your advice on a very important subject, and it simply will not wait."

"But child, our guest—" Miss Rhoda began.

"—will understand," Dorcas concluded, drawing the older woman firmly away.

Sandy Braddock appeared, glass in hand, looking from Rhoda to Caleb and back again, as though wanting to help and not knowing how. Receiving no encouragement from his brother, he moved toward me and said, "Old Amory just returned from the siege of Atlanta? If he had any sense, he'd stay put. Poor Rhoda—must apologize for her, Moretti. A source of considerable embarrassment.''

"Not at all. She's a lovely lady. I'm sure everyone understands and sympathizes.''

"Kind of you." Moodily he looked at Carroll Glass, who was now standing alone and gazing out the terrace windows. "What do you say, Glass?" he said abruptly. "Had any more of your livestock butchered since last night?"

Glass's smile broadened. "No, Braddock—nice of you to ask, though. It's the kind of warmhearted neighborliness I expect to find at Kirkargyle.''

Sandy waved his ungloved hand in dismissal. "Don't mention it. We're always flattered by your attentions to our womenfolk. *Our* women—plural. Notice the subtle use of the plural pronoun."

Glass's expression saddened. "I'm sorry about Miss Rhoda, I really am. But it's not my fault—"

"—that she's a mite peculiar? I didn't say it was." His voice was harsh and unforgiving as he went on, "But that ain't the plural I had in mind:"

The eyes of the two men locked. Carroll Glass opened his mouth and then, thinking better of it, closed it again.

At that moment a new breakfast guest arrived.

Emmett Lawler stood just inside the door, a broad smile splitting his beefy face as his eyes evaluated the scene before him. His suit, a beautifully cut powder-blue gabardine, was quietly assertive, his linen was snowy, and his shoes glowed like banked coals. The impression he created was one of easy yet unarguable mastery. After a moment he made his way across the room toward Caleb McAuliffe and put out his hand. "Good day, Judge. Another of the gala get-togethers Kirkargyle is famous for. Thank you for inviting me."

McAuliffe returned the greeting warmly, continuing the handshake while he patted Lawler's shoulder. As the two men stood together chatting, I observed expressions ranging from dislike to detestation on the faces of Glass, Brad-

dock, and Farringay, and Dorcas's lovely features
momentarily registered a look of extreme irritation.

As Lawler turned from McAuliffe and started toward
Dorcas, Miss Rhoda said distinctly, "So all the suitors are
gathered at Ithaca, waiting for Penelope to make her
choice. My! I wonder when Ulysses will come?"

Just·what we need, I thought as I mentally flipped
through the pages of Homer, *another exercise in poetic
inevitability.*

Everyone stared at the small white-haired figure in surprised silence for a moment, and then Sandy Braddock
gave a bark of laughter. "Better be prepared for an archery
lesson, boys. I reckon there are going to be a mess of
skewered suitors around."

Caleb McAuliffe's lips compressed into a thin blue line.
"I'm afraid you're fatigued from church, Rhoda. Wouldn't
you like to lie down?"

Miss Rhoda turned her penetrating eyes toward me.
"You know what I'm talking about, don't you, Mr. Moretti?"

Feeling the unwelcome cynosure of all attention, I said,
"I do? Are you sure? I mean, I wouldn't want to disagree—"

"We talked about it. Don't you remember?" She
frowned and continued with deliberate patience, like a
schoolmarm to a backward pupil: "About how mythographers know there are no coincidences. Look around the
room and what do you see? The circle of suitors is complete. Penelope has finished a day of weaving and unrav-
eling. Have Telemachus and his father armed themselves,
do you think, Mr. Moretti?"

Hoping to disassociate myself from the woman's mania
as much as possible, I explained to the room, "Just a little
lighthearted conversation Miss Rhoda and I had—finding
classical parallels for present-day happenings—something
like charades." Faced with the guests' collective disapproval, I turned back to the frail white-haired woman and
continued lightly, "But you're not playing fair, ma'am.

The point was that names could create their own destiny, that people named Caesar should beware the Ides of March, and Jonahs shouldn't hang around with whales. There isn't anybody named Ulysses or Penelope or Telemachus at Kirkargyle.''

"Don't be so literal," Miss Rhoda snapped. "There are suitors, aren't there? Sitting around the dining hall, consuming food and drink and waiting for the lady of the house to choose one of them.''

"And," interposed Sandy Braddock, "there's a quiver of arrows on the wall in Caleb's armory, just waiting to be put to good use. You reckon they'll be put to use today, Rhoda?''

"If they are," Jack Farringay said, "as one of those most directly concerned, I'd like a few minutes warning so I can adjust my schedule." He grinned at Dorcas, and received a frown in return.

Miss Rhoda's gaze remained sternly fixed upon me. "The interpretation of poetic inevitability, Mr. Moretti, is in itself a creative act. It is the response to nuances as well as to bald facts. The Fates do not reveal their plans to the literal-minded.''

"I couldn't agree with you more, ma'am," I said. "I only wish the nuances didn't keep changing.''

Judge McAuliffe took his sister's arm. "I don't think you heard me, Rhoda. I said it's time you took your nap." He began to draw her toward the door, but she resisted him by hooking her other arm to Sandy Braddock's.

"Caleb," she said, "you are named for the Jewish gentleman who was allowed to enter the Promised Land when Moses himself was kept waiting outside the door. I haven't figured out why somebody who has been favored like that should treat other people the way you do—but I don't think it's safe for you to rest on your laurels yet awhile.''

"Hear, hear," said Braddock. "Pour it on him, sis.''

Turning to face him, Miss Rhoda continued levelly, "Your name, on the other hand, tells us all we need to know. Alexander sat down and wept because he had no more worlds to conquer. Didn't you sit down and start to weep when you came back from the war—and haven't you been weeping ever since?''

Braddock jerked back as though he had been struck. His arm rose, and for a moment I thought he would hit her. Then he laughed shakily and stepped back. ''You don't play favorites, anyway. I wonder who Rhoda was in mythology—one of those women who ate their babies?'' He raised his glass to his lips and drank unsteadily. There were lines of pain around his eyes.

As if everyone had decided simultaneously to cover up an embarrassment, the room was suddenly abuzz with conversation. I fended off the overtures of a middle-aged matron who wanted to talk about her last visit to New York City and made my way toward the champagne. Taking a new glass from 'Lijah, I found myself standing next to the lawyer, Willis Yates, who was lighting a panatela. I introduced myself and we shook hands.

''Do I understand you represent the toll-road company here in the Bluegrass, Mr. Yates?''

''One of them—there are half a dozen.'' He looked up at me from wise and hooded eyes. ''What's your interest in the toll roads, Mr. Moretti?''

''Nothing, really. I'm interested in Kirkargyle, and I couldn't help overhearing your bit of a dust-up with Judge McAuliffe just now.'' I went on to mention witnessing the trouble at the Carmody tollhouse, and the hostility between the Irish and the Regulators at Kimbro's barn the night before. ''So, when I heard you say that the Judge is a supporter of the Regulators—''

''Hold your horses, son. Caleb McAuliffe and I go back a long ways. I've been a friend of the family for better than twenty years, and whatever difference of opinions we may have now, I expect that friendship to last another twenty, God willing. So I'm afraid I don't have any comment to make to the newspapers.''

''I'm only interested in this Regulator trouble insofar as it bears on the racing business, Mr. Yates. The paper I work for is a sporting sheet called *The Spirit of the Times*—"

"I know who you work for. I've seen your byline often enough." He smiled slightly. "You write a good column, even if it's never helped me pick a winner."

"Then you know the kind of thing I'm looking for. Just stuff that will help me write intelligently about the stable and the horses. Background, really."

He looked at me quizzically a moment and then said, "You're a friend of that Farringay fellow, are you?"

"We know each other."

"Does his daddy really own a horse farm in Maryland?"

"Is there anything funny about what happened to Actaeon and Nile Queen?" I countered.

"Why do you suppose Glass's dog Tusker was carved up last night? You were there, you said." Under his heavy lids, his eyes might have been amused.

"Talking about Glass, what's behind his run of bad luck at Windemere?"

Yates took a deep draw on his cigar and exhaled the smoke from his nostrils. "You certainly are a man of many questions, son. Maybe sometime we may want to take in each other's laundry, but I don't think today's the day. And if and when the day comes, I think I'd rather do it in my office than in my old friend's home."

I nodded. By the windows Dorcas seemed to be having trouble maintaining amicable relations among the three suitors clustered around her. She turned from a glowering Lawler to a sardonic Farringay, and then to a haughty Glass, and then back to Lawler again, as Sandy Braddock stood nearby, watching with evident enjoyment. Finally, as Lawler turned to Glass with clenched fists, Dorcas slid between them and drew them across the room and out the door, with Farringay trailing behind. A few moments later I heard the sound of "I Dreamt I Dwelt in Marble Halls," played with dogged accuracy on the drawing-room piano.

" 'Music hath charms—' " Yates suggested, smiling.

"They do say that," I answered. I looked from Miss Rhoda, happily gossiping with two elderly ladies, to Judge Caleb, frowning judiciously over the comments of an irascible neighbor, to Sandy Braddock, studying his glass with a vacant smile, the fingers of his left hand pressed against his ribs, and decided I was unlikely to get any information from any of them. The prospect of joining the foursome at the piano was also uninviting.

"Mr. Yates," I said, "I don't think my chances of learning anything from you today are any better than they are of learning anything from the McAuliffes. What do you think?"

He thought a moment. "I'd rate 'em about the same."

"Well, in that case I'll be heading back to Lexington. Tomorrow's a working day, and time, tide, and editors wait for no man."

Judge McAuliffe was, surprisingly, kind enough to offer me the use of a horse, so after making my good-byes to Miss Rhoda, Sandy, and the musical four, I walked to the barn, where Lomas Fugate directed a stablehand to saddle me a pretty little dappled mare.

As I hauled myself into the saddle I asked Fugate casually, "No more trouble with any of the horses, I hope?"

He scowled. "Not so's you'd notice it. Why?"

"Just interested. Friend of the family. Give my regards to your charming daughter." I saluted him with a wave and trotted from the barn and down the wide drive, flanked by pin oaks and tulip poplars, to the Lexington road.

7

A Private Showing

I spent the afternoon in my room at the hotel working over my notes, trying to concoct a feature article on the Lexington racing season that would satisfy Otto Hochmuth, my editor—although for me to satisfy Otto Hochmuth with anything short of my own incapacitation, dismemberment, or ultimate demise was highly unlikely.

Certainly it was unlikely on the strength of the material I had to work with. I gave it up and treated myself to three fingers from my traveling bottle before going downstairs for an early dinner in the hotel dining room.

I ignored the French dishes and treated myself to sautéed lamb fries, grits soufflé, black-eyed peas, and spoon bread—dishes that can only be dreamed of north of the Ohio River—and anchored them with a wedge of chess pie and three cups of black chicory coffee. By the end of the meal I had cheerfully concluded that the Kirkargyle story would never shape up and I was glad of it, because now I would be free to concentrate on more promising material. I felt a brief twinge of regret that I would probably never learn the final word on Kirkargyle's troubles, Miss Rhoda's mythological intuitions, or Jack Farringay's romantic and financial ambitions, but assured myself that I would soon discover even more interesting questions to take their place.

After dinner I strolled along Main Street as far as Broadway, paused to inspect the playbill at the opera house, and then wandered back along Second Street to Gratz Park, where I found a bench and sat watching the high-stepping horses and opulent carriages that bustled along the surrounding streets. It was a lovely soft Kentucky dusk, lingering over the city as if reluctant to leave the Bluegrass for the harsher geography of the west. As the sky slowly darkened and the first stars appeared, the serenity of the evening reinforced the comfortable fullness of my belly, and I found myself amused at the idea that any agency in this beneficent community could intentionally cause the mutilation or murder of a valuable racehorse, whether for natural or supernatural reasons. *Why, it would be like Bedouins killing their camels*, I thought, *or Hindu vegetarians eating their sacred cows.*

No question about it, the whole Kirkargyle business was a mare's nest.

I went back to my room, read the evening paper, made myself a nightcap, and went to bed.

The next day I was at the Fair Grounds track twenty minutes before the first race, feeling healthy in body and confident in mind. My colleague Cocanougher tried to interest me in some allegedly inside information at prevailing rates, but I responded with a patronizing refusal. In my sanguine mood I was confident an exciting new story would appear momentarily.

The only one of the Kirkargyle people in the McAuliffe box was Sandy Braddock. When I passed by on my way to the paddock before the third race, he stopped me with a wave of his hand and a proffered flask. His face was flushed and his grin was loose. "Get over here, Moretti. You don't want to see me drink alone, do you?"

Even though I had given up on the Kirkargyle story, I thought it might be inconsiderate to refuse such an invitation. His whiskey was eight-year-old bonded bourbon, and went down as mildly as mother's milk. He asked me to watch the remaining races with him, and I spent the next two hours pleasantly chatting and sipping and jotting down notes in an increasingly large and awkward script.

After the last race I began to thank him for his hospitality, but he said impatiently, "Hush up, Moretti. We've got us some serious drinking to do." He took my arm and drew me with him through the departing crowd. When I protested that I had a story to write and file, he said, "Don't worry—I'm paying for it," as if that settled the matter. Which, in a sense, it did. Five minutes later we were ensconced at the bar of a dark little saloon in a third-rate hotel called the Wabash, across from the Southern Railway station, and Sandy Braddock was reciting "Bannockburn" with gestures.

He was a relentless drinker, with remarkable staying power. Just when he seemed on the verge of collapse, he would restore his energy with a pickled pig's foot or a chunk of summer sausage from the free lunch counter, and continue drinking with gusto. We moved from the Wabash to another two or three saloons whose names I forget. Around eight o'clock we had dinner at a German restaurant—schnitzel and cabbage and potato pancakes, washed down with tankards of lager—and then Sandy decided that we would have brandy at his studio. Disregarding my woozy protests, he pulled me into a cab and gave the driver an address on West High Street.

We stopped before an unassuming two-story building, and Braddock led the way to a rickety stairway that ran up the side of the house to the second floor. He paused at the door to fish a key from his pocket, then opened it with a flourish and beckoned me in.

We entered into a darkness that smelled of turpentine and mustiness and a sweet, corrupt odor suggesting an Oriental bazaar. I stood still, not wanting to risk bumping into the furniture, while Sandy struck a match and lit a lamp with a ruby-red chimney. Carrying it with him, he moved through the long room lighting other lamps until the whole space was visible. The apartment was a single room that occupied the entire second floor of the building, unpartitioned except for the beaverboard walls that boxed in a toilet and bathtub. The end that we had entered contained a shabby sofa, two overstuffed chairs, and a long table piled high with books, newspapers, pipe rack, humidor, decanters, and a brandy snifter. An unmade bed sat in the middle of the forty-foot oblong, and at the far end, beyond the bathroom, a kitchen sink was flanked by a stove and an icebox. There was a dirty shirt on the bed, dirty socks on the floor, and dirty dishes in the sink.

My host waved me to one of the chairs, sloshed brandy into the snifter, and handed it to me, then rinsed out another glass at the sink and filled it for himself. "Confusion to the enemy," he said, taking a deep drink and falling backward into the other chair. I raised my glass to acknowledge the toast. It was sticky in my fingers.

In the dim red light from the table lamp Braddock's lumpy face had a two-dimensional quality, like an illustration on a Parisian poster. He sat slumped in his seat, his eyes fixed on his glass in his left hand, his right hand resting heavily on his thigh. He was silent so long I thought he had forgotten my presence. I said, "Nice place. Do you do much painting here?"

He looked at me blankly for a moment. "Painting?" He shook his head slowly and looked back at his glass. "Who says I do any painting? It's a damn lie. Haven't painted since—haven't painted in years."

I glanced at a stack of canvases in the corner beyond the icebox and the easel leaning beside them, and smelled the undeniable smells of oil paint, linseed oil, and turpentine in the air. "Too bad," I said. "I have the highest admiration for painters."

"You do, do you? I don't." He frowned at me. "You involved in the late unpleasantness, friend?"

" 'Fraid not. I was eight years old when the war ended."

"Your loss. A colossal experience. Much more fulfill-

ing than picture painting. I had the privilege, sir." He
raised his brandy. "To General Joseph Wheeler, God bless
him. And to the pride and glory of the Confederate cavalry." He drank.

"Against Sherman, in Georgia?"

"Against Sherman's bummers, yes. The off-scourings
of the human race. Thieves, rapists, degenerates—not
hardly the kind of force you'd expect to win a great moral
confrontation. And that's what it was, wasn't it?" He
paused for a moment, then added simply, "We did what
we could."

"You and Amory Glass?" I suggested.

"Me and Amory Glass." He shifted restlessly in his
chair. "Amory was a corporal, but after Atlanta he was
brevetted a lieutenant. I was a private, but they made me
a sergeant. There were plenty of vacancies, you see." I
nodded. "By November the troop was down to a dozen
men. We were living off dried persimmons. The horses
were so weak they couldn't hold a gallop for more than a
minute or two. Every night two or three of them lay down
and didn't get up the next morning.

"And Sherman had sixty thousand men. Sixty thousand
infantry, and Kilpatrick's troopers to burn houses and poison wells, chop down orchards and slaughter livestock and
leave them lying there to rot. Oh, that Kilpatrick—he was
a man that needed killing if anybody ever did.

"We were trying to get him that last day. And by God,
we almost did." He took a swallow of brandy, and when
he spoke again, his words came faster. "It was near Mil-
len, where the prison was, and General Wheeler found out
that Kilpatrick was spending the night in a farmhouse
there. It was our troop that got the job of going in after
him. Amory was in charge, and I was sergeant, and there
was six other boys in the detail.

"Little Kil was there all right, but he heard us coming
and got out a window before we could get to him. He
rallied his bluebellies and come back after us. We were
outnumbered three to one, and all of Sherman's cavalry

was about five minutes away, so there was nothing to do but skedaddle.

"That was when our luck ran out. Glass's horse went down, and I reined in and dragged him up behind me. Just then I was hit in the arm—felt like a red-hot iron going through it. I would have fallen off if Glass hadn't held on to me.

"With us double-mounted like that, old Glenna couldn't keep up with the rest of the troop, and the Yankees were coming closer and closer. I figured the only chance we'd have would be if I could get off the road without the Yanks seeing where we'd gone. So at the first turn I swung off to the right, into the trees. By the time they came up, we were back off the road fifty feet or so, and they went by us in the dark."

He fell silent, his eyes focused on a scene far beyond the walls of the apartment, perhaps the vision of trees dimly seen in the darkness, himself swaying on a shuddering horse, his arm throbbing in pain, as the clatter of pursuing horsemen peaked and receded on the road behind him. I waited for him to resume. After a moment he shook himself and drained his glass. "Thirsty work," he said, and poured himself another drink.

"There was no percentage in going back to the road, so we tried to lead Glenna through the woods," he resumed. "But I couldn't do it—I was losing too much blood. I passed out. When I came to, Amory had put a tourniquet on my arm, and it was almost dawn, and we could see we were on the edge of a field, and there was a farmhouse about a hundred yards away.

"We watched the house for an hour to be sure there were no Yankees inside. When Amory figured it was safe, he left me and Glenna in the woods and ducked across the field to the house. I saw him go in the back door—" He stopped in midsentence, his mouth open and his eyes focused on some distant scene. After a long moment he shook his head and said, "What the hell are we talking about? You want a drink?"

"I'm doing fine. Glass went in the back door—"

He lowered his head and raised his gloved hand from his thigh, turning it palm down and them palm up again, as though he were studying it. When he looked back at me, I could feel his pain. "I guess Old Amory made a mistake. There were Yankees in the house—Yankee bummers, deserters. Amory barged in and interrupted them.

"I heard shooting, and then pretty soon a half-dozen Yanks came out, one of them carrying a pair of silver candlesticks, another one lugging a grandfather clock, all of them with some truck or other. The one in charge got a horse and a wagon out of the barn to load the stuff in, and then packed the rest of them aboard and took off down the road. By the time they were gone, there was smoke coming out of the house.

"When I got there the front of the house was all in flames. I went in through the kitchen. The smoke burned my eyes, and I reckon I was weak from loss of blood. I fell down a lot. I got as far as the dining room, and that was far enough. Amory was there, lying on his back, with half his face blown off. There was a girl a few feet away, fifteen or sixteen she looked like, with her skirts up around her neck and her drawers pulled off and her legs spread out. Her face was swollen and her tongue—well, she'd been strangled. And in the doorway to the hall was an old man, seventy or so. He was holding an old cavalry saber in his hand, probably had brought it back with him from Mexico. His skull was stove in like a busted egg.

"The fire was moving fast. I tried to drag Amory out of there, but with only one hand and weak as I was, it couldn't be done. It was all I could do to get myself out. I lay on the ground till I got my strength back, and the house went up like a damn bonfire. And after a while I went back into the woods again. I stayed there the rest of the day and the next night. The day after that some kids found me and took me home. An old doc came by and carved off my arm, and after a month or so I got my strength back enough to travel. There didn't seem much point in trying to catch up with Wheeler's cavalry, what with my condition and the Confederacy's condition, so I came on back to Kirkargyle. And told Rhoda what had happened to her fiancé.''

''She didn't hold you responsible for that?''

He grinned mirthlessly. ''Oh, my stepsister isn't all that different from the rest of her sex. Of course she held me responsible. He was gone and I was there, wasn't I? Or at least most of me was there.'' He paused as if considering an excursion into self-pity, then rejected it with a snort. ''The devil of it is, the drinking's slowing down, Moretti. Bottoms up, damn it—'' He emptied his glass and reached for mine impatiently. ''The night's a pup.''

We continued drinking, Braddock with a brutal steadiness and I more judiciously. But I have never had a head for brandy, and before long I found I couldn't close my eyes without the room tilting beneath me. I opened the door and sat on the outside steps, taking deep breaths. Behind me I heard Braddock's irregular steps as he moved around the kitchen area looking for another bottle. ''Man can't walk on one leg,'' I heard him say, and then glass clinked against glass. ''Wha' 'bout you?'' he called. ''You walkin' on one leg? Or drinkin' with one arm? No problem drinkin' with one arm. Very graceful. Do it all the time. Watch.'' I glanced over my shoulder to see him raise his glass and drain it. He stood motionless for a long moment, and then shook with a sudden violent spasm. Dropping the glass to splinter on the floor, he stumbled into the bathroom and began to vomit into the toilet bowl.

I sat listening for a while and felt an incongruous pang of hunger. I rose and went to the icebox to find something to eat. There wasn't much except half a loaf of bread and a chunk of cheddar cheese. I broke off pieces of each and made myself a sandwich, which I washed down with tap water. Sandy was still retching in the bathroom. ''Anything I can do?'' I called. His answer was a groan.

I carried my sandwich to the stack of canvases in the corner and picked up the one on top, tilting it to catch the lamplight. It was an unfinished sketch of a city on fire. The buildings, which were homes and a church and a city hall, were rendered in choppy black lines, almost as if they had been drawn by a child. But the flames that swept about them, jagged whorls and tongues of yellow and orange and crimson and blue, were so realistic they looked as if they would be hot to the touch. Human figures twisted in the fire, realistically drawn in their agony, but, like the buildings, rendered in black and white, as though the color of life had already been burnt away. It was a malevolent picture, and as drunk as I was, I shuddered as I stared at it.

The next canvas was also unfinished. It consisted of three sketches of a nude woman, standing, kneeling, and seated on a stool. In each sketch the woman's face was invisible, because she was turned away from the artist or because her arm or shoulder intervened. Her hair, arms, and legs were barely suggested; only from the shoulder to the knees did the body suggest three-dimensionality, with the modeling of the torso in the sharpest relief. Breast and belly were sensuously realized. As I looked at the picture I felt a sudden flush of physical desire combined with moral revulsion, as though I had caught myself peeping at my little sister naked in her bath. Guiltily I set the canvas aside.

The next picture, which was a completed oil, was a landscape at night. Under a sliver of moon glinting through dark clouds, a mansion stood in fog-shrouded fields. It was abandoned, a ruin—a chimney had collapsed, shards of broken glass glinted in the dark windows, the driveway under the porte cochere was clogged with underbrush— and yet it seemed somehow to possess a sinister vitality, as though it were poised and waiting.

It was, I realized instantly, Kirkargyle—Kirkargyle accurately portrayed as it would appear after catastrophe, Kirkargyle in a time beyond some future horror.

"You bastard, put those down! I'll break your goddamn head!"

I looked up to see Sandy Braddock glaring wildly at me, teeth clenched, arm drawn back for a blow. I dropped the canvases and raised my open hands. "Wait a minute! I'm sorry but—I was interested in your work, that's all!"

"Who told you you could poke around here?"

"I just happened to see them. They're very good, very unusual. . . ."

His arm swung forward, knocking my hands aside. It was like being struck with a ball bat. I stumbled backward, a sense of acute danger penetrating my muzzy brain. Braddock stepped after me, his arm poised for a reverse blow, his face a blind mask of fury. "Sandy, wait!" I shouted. "It's your friend, Paddy Moretti! Just here to have a bit of a drink!"

"I know who you are," he said. "You poke around. Poke, poke, poke. Stirring up trouble, sticking your fingers into things that don't concern you." He swayed on his heels, glowering, and suddenly shouted, "Bastard!"

"I won't argue the point," I said.

He lowered his arm slowly, and the fury on his face turned to sadness. "Poor Moretti. Keep poke, poke, poking around, you'll poke yourself to death. Pitiful. Big New York newspaperman poking himself to death because he couldn't keep his fingers out of things. Wouldn't listen to what an old country boy told him."

"I'll listen, Sandy." I leaned forward. "Want to tell me about the pictures? I really do like them." I touched him on the shoulder, which was a mistake. He leaped back and his eyes glared wildly; then, when I was expecting another attack, he burst into tears.

"Want to go home," he gasped. "Want to go to Kirkargyle. Take me back home, please? Please?" He reached toward me, and I could smell the vomit on his breath. Instinctively I stepped away.

"Tonight? It's late, Sandy. It's a long drive. Why don't you sleep here, and I'll go back to the hotel—"

"No! Want to go back home! You come, too, Moretti.

We'll get a buggy.'' He smiled cunningly. ''Take a bottle along—have a drink on the way!''

It was a ridiculous idea, and even though I couldn't argue him out of it, I expected him to sink into unconsciousness long before we could put it into operation. But I underestimated him; half an hour later we were sharing the seat of a rented buggy and heading out of town on the deserted Frankfort pike. Only after we were beyond the limits of Lexington did his chin sink to his chest and his breathing change to snores.

He continued to sleep as we passed the empty tollhouse where Sean Carmody had fought his lonely battle against the Regulators. The wooden turnstile pole lay beside the road, and the house had an abandoned look to it, as if it had been empty for years. I felt a sudden chill, and Sandy mumbled in his sleep, and even the horse between the shafts gave a nervous whicker.

The bed I had shared with Farringay was empty, and I was grateful. I expected to dive into sleep as soon as my body touched the sheets, but instead found myself perversely restless, my mind continuing to turn over the episodes and personalities connected with the McAuliffes and Kirkargyle. It did no good to remember I had given up on the story; the story would not allow itself to be given up on. I thought about Dorcas and her suitors, Sandy and his paintings, Rhoda and her fantasies, Caleb and his declining fortunes. When I had run through all the people, I started on the animals, Actaeon, Nile Queen, Uranus, and Glass's Tusker. And what were the other horses Farringay had pointed out in the stable? Saladin, Thunderer, Sebastian, Bonne Jeanne . . .

Somewhere in the house a clock chimed, a door closed, a floorboard creaked.

I turned my pillow over looking for a cooler spot, and suddenly felt a shivery sense of *déjà vu*—I had lived this moment before, here, in this room, in this very bed. I had turned my pillow just this way, stretched my legs and kicked my sheet and filled my lungs just so. I sat up, my nerves as tense as taut wires.

I remembered. It had been like this the night Uranus had been gelded. The same stillness, the same heavy sense of foreboding . . . the only difference was that then something had awakened me, and tonight I hadn't been able to sleep at all.

I stood up and moved to the open window. The moon had set, and the stars were hidden behind the clouds. The trees stirred restlessly, and an owl hooted in the distance. I remembered the painting I had seen earlier, of a mansion deserted and in ruins, yet charged with an aura of evil. Not Kirkargyle as it was now, of course—but not entirely different, either.

I drew a deep breath. Was there a smell of smoke in the air?

Bonne Jeanne. *Jeanne*—as in Jeanne d'Arc.

Something terrible was happening in the stables, something as terrible as what had happened to Uranus, or maybe worse. Without any conscious decision I found myself pulling on my shirt and trousers and thrusting my feet into my shoes. I hurried through the dark hall and down the front stairs, across the foyer and out onto the porch.

From the side of the house I could see a faint ruddiness that barely silhouetted the nearest horse barn. I began to run toward it. As I came nearer, the path in front of me became clearer—it looked as if it were washed in red light. A flicker of flame appeared at one corner of the barn.

I could hear the screams of terrified horses.

As I drew nearer, gasping for breath and stumbling over the uneven ground, something passed between me and the fire—for a second the twisting scarlet worm was blotted from view and the blackness in front of me became complete. At that moment my ankle turned under me, and I thudded to my knees. I saved myself from sprawling flat by catching my weight on my hands. And at that moment, as I rested on all fours in the dirt, something crashed against my head. For a moment the night was a Fourth of

July celebration of pinwheels and Roman candles, and then the darkness swallowed everything.

I couldn't have been unconscious for more than a minute or so. When I opened my eyes the flames on the barn roof were only a little wider and higher than before, the horses were still screaming, and no one else was visible. I struggled groggily to my feet and continued toward the stable door. I was tugging at it when another man joined me, and together we swung it open. It was Jack Farringay.

The inside of the barn was a flickering chiaroscuro of red and black, noisy with the roaring crackle of the fire and the terror of the horses, suffocating with the smoke of burning wood and hay. The fire centered outside Bonne Jeanne's stall halfway back. By its light we could see a crumpled figure lying on the floor just inside the door. Farringay ran toward the fire and I bent over the injured man.

It was Lomas Fugate, and his skull was—as Sandy Braddock had phrased it a few hours before, in a different context—stove in like a busted egg. The face was ghastly—eyes rolled back, mouth agape, clotting blood gleaming wetly over the brutal features. I seized him by the ankles and snaked him through the door, his head bouncing along the packed dirt floor. Leaving him outside, I dashed back inside to help Jack.

He had the door to Bonne Jeanne's stall open and was trying to drag her out past a pile of burning straw. "Help me—push!" he cried, and I got behind the terrified mare and threw my weight against her rump while he tugged on her rope bridle. With a shuddering leap she sprang past the flames and out of the stall, knocking Jack to one side, and bolted out the stable door.

We were dragging open the next stall door when two stablehands appeared, and soon there were half a dozen of us to bring out the rest of the horses. In five minutes they were all out, tossing their heads and rolling their eyes in the firelight, as a column of flame and smoke and whirling sparks rose from the blackened skeleton of the barn.

Judge Caleb McAuliffe, his nightshirt carelessly stuffed into his trousers waistband, appeared as the stable roof collapsed. He was followed closely by his daughter Dorcas and Sandy Braddock, both obviously fresh from their beds, although Sandy looked quite the opposite of fresh. Judge Caleb seemed in a daze as he stared down at the body of Lomas Fugate; his stern features had become those of a weak and vacillating man, and his hands fluttered aimlessly at his sides. Dorcas took command, directing the restabling of the horses and the carrying of Fugate's body to his home. In contrast to her father and her uncle, she was energetic and decisive.

A horse galloped into the firelight, and Emmett Lawler pulled up and dismounted. "I saw the glow from my window and came to see if I could help. My God! How many horses did you lose?"

"We got them all out, thanks to Jack and Mr. Moretti here," Dorcas answered. "But the awful thing is—"

A stablehand appeared at her elbow. "Excuse me, Miss Dorcas, but you and the Judge better come quick. In the shed there."

"What? All right." She brushed a strand of hair from her forehead impatiently. "Come on, Father," she said, taking the old man's arm and drawing him with her. "Let's see what else is in store for us." The rest of us followed her to an outbuilding where another hand stood beside an open door.

Inside, barely visible in the dying firelight, sprawled the unconscious form of a man. An empty bottle lay beside him, and the sharp reek of whiskey cut through the smell of burnt wood and hay. His mouth was open, and his breath came out in a liquid snore.

"There's your murderer," Jack Farringay said grimly.

"Murderer?" Lawler repeated in surprise. "What do you mean, murderer?"

"The man who killed Lomas Fugate, Mr. Lawler," Dorcas said. "The man who set fire to the barn. Sleeping it off. Sean Carmody."

8

A Roll of the Dice

When the sheriff arrived at Kirkargyle four hours later, he reached the same conclusion—that Sean Carmody had been interrupted by Lomas Fugate in the act of setting fire to the stable and had killed him during the subsequent struggle. His wife Molly had died the day before, and the distraught man had been heard to swear revenge against Judge McAuliffe in the name of his motherless children. No doubt he had been crazy drunk when he started the fire, and after disposing of Fugate had felt the need for another drink, which had been enough to render him unconscious. It all seemed clear enough, even though Carmody denied it. The sheriff took him away.

I walked back to the house with Jack Farringay. "It's interesting that the fire seemed to have started next to Bonne Jeanne's stall," I said.

Farringay covered a yawn. "Is it?"

"You think that Sean Carmody knows 'Bonne Jeanne' stands for Joan of Arc? It seems unlikely to me."

He glanced at me quizzically. "Ah, you're a deep one, Bunky. To tell you the truth, I hadn't thought about it one way or another."

"Well, if he did know, it's crazy enough—but if he didn't, it makes no sense at all. It couldn't be an accident the fire started by her stall. Somebody planned for Joan to be burned at the stake. If it was Carmody, then he had to know what Bonne Jeanne stands for.''

''You're riding Miss Rhoda's poetic inevitability hobbyhorse, eh?'' He smiled patronizingly. ''You have the mind of a romancer, Moretti. Carmody had every reason to burn down the stable, or at least he thought he did. The poor wretch blamed the Regulators for the death of his wife, and Judge McAuliffe for the Regulators. Maybe he was right. Anyway, he came out here and did the dirty, popped the interfering Mr. Fugate on the skull, and then went nappy-bye in the shed and got caught red-handed. End of story.''

''What made him start the fire by Bonne Jeanne's stall?''

''Who says he did? You just assume it was started there. It could have been started anywhere.'' He shook his head. ''You're barking up the wrong tree. If there's a story here for you at all, which appears increasingly doubtful, it's about the plain bad luck that's bedeviled a famous racing stable. Luck,'' he added comfortably, ''which may be about to change.''

''Oh?'' I glanced at him quickly, and he raised his chin and presented me with his matinee-idol profile. ''Apropos of that, I couldn't help noticing you weren't in bed when I rolled in last night.''

''I wasn't, was I? How very observant of you. You know, Moretti, I like you. I want you to know that whenever you come back to Kentucky, you'll have a friend at Kirkargyle.''

''You can guarantee that?''

''Would I say it if I had any doubt?''

Breakfast was a perfunctory affair, with little conversation. More than ever before, I felt like an outsider. Judge McAuliffe took a cup of coffee into his armory and closed the door; Miss Rhoda twittered a little about some obscure nuance of bluegrass society and lapsed into silence; Farringay and Emmett Lawler sat flanking Dorcas, each ignoring the other's presence as she answered them both distractedly; and Sandy Braddock, his lumpy face as moist and white as bread dough, stared into his coffee cup as if it contained the only meaning in life.

I made my good-byes as soon as I could. As I waited on the porch for a horse to be brought around from the stable, Dorcas emerged from the front door, alone.

"Will we see you again before you go back to New York, Mr. Moretti?" she asked. I said I doubted it—I expected to be on the train as soon as the meet ended on Saturday afternoon. "Oh, what a shame," she said. "I'm afraid the memories you'll take with you will be very unpleasant. I wish you could have been here at a happier time."

"I'm grateful to have had the chance to meet you under any conditions, Miss McAuliffe."

She flashed me a sudden smile. "Maybe you'll be paying Jack a visit here one day."

"Any reason that brings me back will be welcome," I answered.

She regarded me thoughtfully. "Forgive me, Mr. Moretti, but I can't help noticing that you're a little less than enthusiastic in pressing your friend's suit. Or am I doing you an injustice?"

"I wouldn't presume to advise a colleen like yourself on an affair of the heart, Miss McAuliffe. I can only say that my envy of Jack Farringay is fearsome."

"You don't need to blarney me. What I need is support. I need someone to tell me I'm not an idiot. Everything is such a terrible mess here—all the trouble with the horses, and this awful thing with Lomas Fugate last night. Daddy's scared, I know he is, and Sandy just keeps drinking and drinking, and Mr. Lawler's always hanging around, and Carroll Glass never takes anything seriously, and you know what Aunt Rhoda's like—" She put her hand on my arm, and an expression of entreaty crossed her lovely face. "Don't you see, I have to know I'm right about Jack. I'm behaving shamelessly, but—can you just tell me what I need to hear?"

I thought to myself that there is very little justice in this world. "Jack Farringay is one of the most remarkable men I've ever known," I said carefully. " 'Resourceful' is the word that springs to mind. Never at a loss, never one to throw in the sponge—people who get to know Jack never forget him, you can be sure."

She peered into my eyes for a moment, then shook her head. "That's not what I'm asking."

"I'm sorry."

She was silent a moment, then abruptly changed the subject. "Thank heavens Bonne Jeanne will be all right for the sale. I don't know what we'd do if she had been injured."

"The sale?"

"The bloodstock sale. Next week. We're selling Bonne Jeanne, didn't you know?"

I said I hadn't heard a sale was scheduled. She explained that the regular annual Thoroughbred auction was to be held the following weekend, and that Kirkargyle planned a consignment of more than a dozen stallions, mares, and weanlings, headed by Bonne Jeanne. "Of course she's worth as much as the others combined," Dorcas said. "What she'll bring in will keep us going over the summer. When I think what it would have meant if she had been hurt last night—" She shook her head. "But the jinx didn't happen. That business of Aunt Rhoda's, about the destiny of certain names, it didn't come true with Bonne Jeanne. So it was all coincidence. Wasn't it?"

"At least there's no supernatural inevitability about it," I amended. I looked admiringly into her fine brown eyes, then let my gaze move slowly down her hollowed cheek, past her full pink lips and rounded chin and smooth throat, to rest briefly at the V of her neckline before returning to her eyes again. "I wouldn't worry my pretty head about it, Miss McAuliffe. I'm sure everything will work out just fine for you and—whoever."

"Dorcas, please. And I'll call you Paddy." Impulsively

she took my hand and squeezed it. "As an old friend of Whoever, you deserve to be on a first-name basis."

I felt a surge of aversion to Jack Farringay which I succeeded in concealing. I put my other hand on top of hers, thinking what a satisfactory sandwich it made. "I thank you kindly for the compliment, Dorcas. I wish I could stay here in Lexington long enough to take advantage of it."

"Oh, but you'll be back one day. And then the three of us can have a real get-together, and you and I can really get acquainted." She allowed her hand to remain between mine a moment while she smiled into my eyes, then withdrew it deftly as a stableboy leading a horse appeared at the edge of the porch.

Damn Farringay for an unscrupulous thieving bunco artist with no more common decency than a Belfast butt-peddler, I thought bitterly as I pulled myself up into the saddle. I waved good-bye to the lovely young woman on the porch and turned the chestnut gelding's head toward Lexington.

I didn't return to Kirkargyle or see any of the McAuliffes again before I left the Bluegrass. I covered the last days' races, filed my stories at the telegraph office, ate and drank moderately, and in due course found myself in a Chesapeake & Ohio parlor car heading for Washington and New York, trying to dispel a sense of approaching doom with a glass of bourbon and water.

There was no point in refusing to face facts. My work in Lexington had not been of stellar magnitude. The story I had counted on to pacify Hochmuth had run like water through my fingers, and no other story of equal promise had appeared to take its place. It was returning to the arena without my shield, and with an empty scabbard at my hip. And who would be there to give the thumbs-up signal, with me lying on my back in the sand and the kraut tinker's foot on my neck? Nobody, that was who. I groaned and took a pull at my glass.

"Oh, it can't be as bad as that, Moretti," said a dry voice on my right.

I turned to see an elderly gentleman sitting beside me. He had silver hair, a high, narrow brow, and a patrician profile. His eyes regarded me ironically, and his thin-lipped mouth curled up at one corner. He looked like a man who might be capable of ruthlessness or compassion, as circumstances warranted, but never, never, of dishonesty. His looks were deceiving.

"It can and it is," I answered coldly. "C. Hamilton Yarnell, I do believe. Before you waste your time, let me assure you I have no money, no wealthy friends, no influence with any judges, and no intention of buying you a drink. I have problems enough without enmeshing myself in confidence games."

"Moretti, my friend, if I were working the marks, I wouldn't have spoken to you. You may relax; I'm at liberty. Until we arrive in Gotham, my only concern is finding decent food and drink and a little companionable conversation." He fished a gleaming leather cigar case from his breast pocket, popped it open, and offered it to me. "Havana. You found them tolerable, as I remember."

The last time I had seen Hamilton Yarnell was at the railroad station in Cogswell, Kansas, at the conclusion of an episode that had also served as my introduction to Jack Farringay. Since it had involved considerable danger to life and limb, not to mention a brouhaha in a bordello and a stint in jail, I wasn't anxious to renew the relationship. On the other hand, it was a long, dull ride to New York. I took the cigar.

Yarnell was a superb raconteur, and since I was reasonably sure there was nothing I had that he wanted, I settled back and listened as he touched on some of the high points of his recent career.

We had been talking and drinking for an hour or so when he said, in answer to a question, "Conscience? You're asking me about a guilty conscience? Moretti, if there's anything you should know by now, it's that you can't cheat an honest man—other than fleecing feebs, I mean. Every mark has larceny in his heart—he wouldn't be messing with you if he hadn't. He thinks he's a shoo-in for a sure thing, and he's willing to take it out of somebody else's hide, and tell himself afterward the bozo had it coming. That's the nature of the beast, Moretti—Mr. Bates, of the species *homo sap*. The boob from which all blessings flow.''

I asked if he wasn't doing the same thing he accused the mark of—justifying his own crookedness by exaggerating the venality of his victim. He snorted delicately through his aquiline nose. ''Listen. I was working out of a big store in Little Rock, pulling the wire and the rag. Harry Horseapple set it up, and I was handling Inside, and the Brown-Nose Kid was roping for me. Did you ever meet the Kid, Moretti?'' I shook my head. ''A steady man, the Kid,'' Yarnell mused, considering the tip of his cigar. ''Until he got on the needle. That's what killed him, the poor yap.'' He shrugged. ''Anyway, the Kid brought in this sucker, and we set him up for the rag, since he had these delusions of financial genius. He ran a bucket shop, was what he did. Specialized in selling stocks that sounded as safe as church to widows and orphans. A real son of a bitch. I still remember his name—Frederick Lawler Emmett.''

I lowered my glass from my mouth. ''Lawler? Emmett? What did he look like?''

''Heavy-set, shoulders out to here, bushy eyebrows, face like a slice of rare roast beef. A pompous bastard—he enjoyed looking down on people.''

''How old was he?''

''Oh, early thirties, I'd say. Too young to take himself as seriously as he did.''

''How long ago was this?''

''Seven, eight years. He'd be about forty now.'' He looked at me curiously. ''What's the matter? You think you know him?''

''Tell me what happened.''

Yarnell leaned back in his chair, stretching his legs into the narrow aisle, and made a church steeple of his fingers, resting on his snowy shirtfront. "Well, Moretti, this Mr. Bates was the highest type of mark—just half-smart enough to convince himself that anything bad that happened couldn't possibly be due to him being outsmarted. He had to believe it was a one-time-only act of God. I clipped him for a big score three times. Each time he came back with a new roll a few months later and wanted to get back in the action again. I'd probably be tapping him right now if the bunco squad hadn't nailed him for his stock swindling."

"Did they send him up?"

"Not Brother Emmett. This is the guy you thought I was exaggerating the venality of, remember? He didn't spend a night behind bars. He turned state's evidence and gave the DA his two partners on a platter, and threw in a crooked lawyer and an abortionist for makeweights. By the time he got off the stand you would have thought the state owed him a medal."

"Then he left town?"

"Had to. He was okay with the law, but nobody was going to invest any money with him. He moved north, I understand, taking a considerable amount of loose change along." He shot me a sudden penetrating glance. "To some place like Kentucky, maybe? Would that be the reason for your sudden interest?"

"Ummm? Oh, merely making conversation. I'm always fascinated by the doings of your fraternity, Yarnell. Like What's-his-name, your old partner back in Kansas—Farrenholt? Fibbleframp? Festergay? The old memory's not what it once was, I fear. Anyway, that fellow. Heard from him recently?" I turned guileless eyes toward him as I sipped my drink.

"Farringay," he said carefully. "As I think you have reason to remember. Come off it, Moretti. The last time I heard anything about Jack Farringay, he was working the wrestle-store grift in Louisville—which is also in Kentucky, if I remember right." He leaned forward, resting his elbows on the razor-edged pleats of his trousers. "All right. We've horsed around enough. What's the office?"

"Office?" I repeated blankly. "That must be another of those picturesque expressions you people are so fond of." I emptied my glass and pointed to his. "You're in need of sustenance, Yarnell, and this time the honors are on me."

He knew very well I was holding out on him, but he couldn't get me to admit it. After another hour we carried our drinks into the diner and got a table. Traveling on trains always sharpens my appetite, and I ordered a dozen oysters, a rare beefsteak, and a wedge of Camembert with crackers. Yarnell had a shrimp cocktail, mutton chops, and a strawberry tart, and we shared a bottle of Burgundy and followed it with coffee and brandy. After an hour of eating and drinking we sprawled back in our chairs, marvelously sated, and lit two more of Yarnell's excellent cigars.

The waiter presented the check. Yarnell glanced at the total and pursed his lips. "Feel lucky, Moretti?" he asked.

"What did you have in mind?" I replied cautiously.

He picked up two sugar cubes from the silver bowl on the table and rolled them between his slender fingers. "I'll shoot you for the check. Galloping dominoes. How about it?" He drew a fountain pen from his breast pocket and uncapped it.

I hesitated. The prospect of pocketing the cost of an expensive dinner was appealing to a man under the shadow of approaching editorial wrath, and if I had to pony up for both meals, how much worse off would I be? On the other hand, what I knew about C. Hamilton Yarnell was not reassuring.

He smiled and handed me the sugar cubes. "You think I'd cheat you over the cost of a trifling dinner, Moretti? Here, see for yourself. They're perfectly ordinary sugar cubes. If you don't like them, here, choose two more." He pushed the bowl across the table to me.

"No, no." I handed the cubes back to him. "Mark them up."

Carefully he placed spots on the faces of the cubes, ones opposite sixes, twos opposite fives, threes opposite fours, and held them out for my inspection. I took them in my hand, hefted them, and gave them back. "They look fine to me," I said. "Roll 'em."

He capped his pen and replaced it in his pocket with a flourish. Then he cupped the dice in both hands, rattled them vigorously, kissed the knuckles of his right hand, and rolled the cubes out on the tablecloth. The points totaled seven. He picked up the dice and offered them to me.

I took them with a presentiment of defeat, rattled them with empty bravado, and cast them on the table. Snake eyes.

"Ah, too bad, Moretti. I hate to see you lose, old man— I know how hard you newspapermen work for your miserable salaries. Would you like another go at it, double or nothing?"

I have never considered myself a brilliant thinker, but I am not quite the village idiot. I shook my head. "No thanks. I think I'll quit when I'm only moderately behind."

"Suit yourself, friend." Smiling sympathetically, he ground the marked sugar cubes together and deposited the resultant grayish powder in his empty coffee cup. "I've enjoyed our time together, but I think I'll retire now, if you don't mind. Tomorrow promises to be a busy day." He rose, gave me a courteous nod, and left the dining car, every inch a distinguished and upright gentleman.

I paid the check and made my way to my upper berth, where I lay for an hour listening to the clattering of the wheels, the keening of the whistle, and the night sounds of my neighbors, before I finally fell asleep.

I didn't see Yarnell again until the train was pulling into Washington. He and I were both waiting beside our valises in the vestibule of a Pullman car. He greeted me with a remote smile and glanced away. I moved close to him.

"Just tell me one thing, Yarnell. Do you always carry a pair of loaded sugar cubes with you?"

"Ummm?" His expression was tolerantly questioning.

"You pulled a switch. After I looked at the cubes, you palmed them and rolled another pair, the loaded ones. You got your natural, then you switched them again and gave me the straight ones to shoot. Or was it a third pair you passed me, another loaded pair that was set to come up craps?"

He regarded me in silence for a moment while he decided on his answer. Then he smiled artlessly, his bright blue eyes crinkling at the corners and his fine white teeth gleaming. "No, there's only one loaded pair, Paddy. In case of a tie we roll again, so one loaded pair is all you need. Besides, it would be too tricky handling three pair at once."

"Now that I know the bitter truth, I don't suppose—" I suggested.

"You know better than that."

I nodded. The train came to a grinding halt and the conductor clanged open the hinged panel at the top of the steps. Outside, steam hissed and redcaps shuffled expectantly, awaiting luggage. Passengers surged forward. Before we were separated, I touched Yarnell's arm. "The thing that gets me is, it's so damn *foresighted*!"

He gave me a final glance before starting down the iron steps. "Not really," he said in a kindly voice. "You'd be surprised how many bowls of sugar cubes you find on the tables of America."

9

The Glamour of Gotham

I left Washington for New York on the Pennsylvania Railroad and did not see Yarnell again. I arrived in Penn Station a little after noon, and went directly to my rooming house on Bleecker Street, just east of Sixth Avenue. My landlady, Mrs. Gaugherty, was shaking a dust mop on the front stoop when I arrived. Her lips tightened as she saw me.

"Mr. Moretti, is it?" she demanded, striking an assertive posture, with her large feet spread and one red fist on an ample hip. "It's so long since I've had a glimpse of you I find me memory is unreliable. Living somewhere out west now, are you? And back now to pack up your possessions? Or do you want to leave them here as a permanent museum?"

"If it's the back rent you're worried about, Mrs. Gaugherty, I can assure you you'll have it this very day. It's merely a matter of checking in at the office and picking up the money that's coming to me." I smiled reassuringly and tried to step around her. She moved to block my passage.

"And don't be rushing past me like I was contagious. Checking in at the office, is it? And how do you know they won't hand you a pink slip instead of a paycheck?

These are hard times, Mr. Moretti, and I have me own bills to pay, and much as I'd enjoy to let you live rent-free for the rest of your days, cruel necessity declares otherwise. So I have to insist, Mr. Moretti—it's the back rent by the end of the week, or it's out on the sidewalk with you.'' She drew a deep breath, and then, having delivered the ultimatum required of her, she relented a trifle. ''Sure, and I don't want to sound unfeeling, Paddy—but if you'd pay more attention to your work and less to your drinking and cardplaying, you might get yourself ahead of the game for once.''

I gave her solid arms a squeeze. ''Ah, that's the truth, Mrs. Gaugherty, and it's like my own mother you are for saying it! And it's my firmest resolution—to change my trifling ways and give my employer the dedication I owe him, to put my foot on the ladder of success, and to repay the trust of dear Christian friends like you!''

Hope and suspicion contested across her wide Irish face. ''You could be so much more than you are, you know.''

''Ah, don't I know, indeed!'' I tried another step around her. ''And this is the beginning of it—you just see if it isn't.''

She moved reluctantly to one side. ''And you'll call a halt to the card games, and the drinking, and running around with those hooligan friends of yours?''

''Haven't I said so? And do you think I would lie to the second mother in me life?'' I got my hand on the front doorknob and then turned for a final look at her worried face. ''And don't give another thought to that back-rent business! You'll see! In the new order of things, it will be as the snows of yesteryear!''

Clem Harber sipped his whiskey thoughtfully. ''Give me two cards,'' he said. ''Off the top of the deck, if you please, Moretti.''

''For shame.'' I dealt him two cards and glanced inquiringly at the next player, Pomerance of the *World*, who was holding his cards against his round belly as though he had gas pains.

"I'll play these," Pomerance said in a defensive tone.

"I'm delighted to hear it." I turned to the worried face of Bertram McAnly on Pomerance's left. "How about you, Bert? What can I do for you?" I spoke in a warm, supportive tone; since McAnly was present at the table only because the other players, myself included, considered him to be a veritable milch cow at poker, we were careful to treat him with the utmost kindness.

"I—I'll take three cards. No, wait a minute. I want two—just deal me two." McAnly gnawed his underlip with his protruding front teeth. He threw two cards facedown on the table and I dealt him two more to replace them. Then hastily he discarded a third card. "I mean I want three—give me another one." I added another card to the two in front of him, and he clutched them eagerly. I exchanged a quick glance with the other players at the table and said, "I expect you're making the wise play, Bertram."

In addition to Harber, Pomerance, McAnly, and myself, the others in attendance were Eddie Gans of the *Evening Post*, Harve Tallboy of the *Herald*, and Dutch Egan, who worked for Richard K. Fox on the *Police Gazette*. We were playing in the back room of Wimple's Saloon, around the corner from police headquarters on Mulberry Street. A free lunch tray was set up in the corner, beside bottles of Scotch, rye, and bourbon. Aside from McAnly, each of us was ahead or behind a dollar or two. I calculated "Bert the Barnacle" was already down at least twenty.

I dealt two cards to Tallboy and threw down a single card from my own hand and replaced it. "And one for the dealer. That's all it takes, gentlemen."

Clem Harber regarded me over his cards. "For your sake, I hope so, Moretti. Seeing as how you seem unlikely to have any paycheck to count on for a while."

"Please. I am still gainfully employed. My discussion with Mr. Hochmuth this afternoon represented a simple airing of opinion—there was no discussion whatever of terminating employment.''

McAnly leaped into the discussion as if he were happy to take his mind off poker playing. ''It didn't sound that way to me. Or anyone else in the room, I bet. It sounded to me like you were one inch from—'' He drew a finger across his throat, made a gurgling sound, and grinned around the table. ''So if any of you fellows are looking for a job reporting horse races . . .''

What a diseased little rabbit the man is, I thought. *How very satisfying to accept his financial contribution.* ''You misunderstand our relationship, Bertram. Mr. Hochmuth and I are outgoing types who enjoy a vigorous exchange of ideas, but underneath we have the greatest respect for each other.'' I inspected my cards and resisted the urge to place them in ascending order. ''I believe you are the opener, Brother Gans.''

Gans and Dutch Egan folded. Harber bet two dollars, Pomerance raised a dollar, and McAnly agonized for half a minute before seeing the raise. Tallboy folded and poured himself another drink. I saw the raise. Harber threw me an inscrutable glance and said, ''I'll see it,'' and tossed another dollar on the table. Pomerance did the same.

McAnly looked warily from Harber to Pomerance and then to me. ''Nobody's very confident, is what I think,'' he said with a sudden smirk. ''Here—let's get rid of the ribbon clerks.'' He counted out five dollars and tossed it into the pot, and sat back in his chair with his arms folded.

I frowned and pursed my lips as I considered my cards. ''Impetuous though it may seem,'' I said, ''I have to raise you ten dollars.''

''Fold,'' said Clem Harber.

''Fold,'' said potbellied Pomerance.

''Wait a minute,'' McAnly yelped. ''You passed the first time around, Moretti!''

''So I did. One of my cards was misplaced.'' I gave him an apologetic smile. ''I hope I didn't lead you astray. Even with''—I made a quick mental addition—''eleven of your dollars already in the pot, maybe you should drop out, Bertram. I wouldn't want to see you hurt. It's not as if you were an experienced poker player, like these rounders here. No point in throwing good money after bad." I paused. "Of course, I may be bluffing."

Gans offered Harber a pickled pig's foot, and Pomerance joined Tallboy at the improvised bar. Dutch Egan studied the curly black hairs on the back of his left hand. McAnly glared at his cards, and then me, and then at his cards again. "It's ten dollars to call, Bertram," I said gently.

His mouth opened and closed over his buckteeth. He looked around the table for help in his decision, but all eyes were otherwise engaged. He turned back to me wildly. "Ten dollars!" he cried. "All right! I think you're bluffing! Let's see 'em!" He threw a crumpled sawbuck on the pile.

I turned my cards over. "It's just a straight, Bertram. Nine high."

He expelled his breath in an explosive puff and threw down his cards. He had three jacks; probably he had begun with a pair, and had kept them along with an ace kicker, then thought better of it and thrown away the ace and replaced it with another jack. Too bad. If he hadn't drawn that third card, he wouldn't have had enough strength to stay in the game. I felt a twinge of pity for the boob, which I sternly repressed as I drew in my money.

All of us grew healthy at McAnly's expense that evening, but I fared the best, which was only simple justice, since my prospects of continued employment at *The Spirit of the Times* seemed more tenuous than ever before. Bert the Barnacle was picked as clean as a boardinghouse turkey before eleven o'clock, and departed the scene with ill-humored comments. The rest of us immediately agreed to reduce the bet-and-raise limit to a dollar, allowing us to concentrate on drinking and conversation.

I told them about Yarnell's unscrupulous swindle with the loaded sugar cubes. "I tell you, to a fellow who believes in the inherent goodness of man, it came as a considerable shock.''

Clem Harber's eyes moved around the room as if in search of a sugar bowl. "I can believe it," he said. "It's a lucky thing you didn't mention it in front of McAnly. There's no telling what profound disillusionment it might have caused." He glanced back at me thoughtfully. "Yarnell, you said his name was? Would that be the same Yarnell who was involved in that Kansas business, when those fight-store sharpies fleeced the owner's nephew?''

"The very same." Harber and I had both been assigned by the owner of *The Spirit of the Times*, Frederick Follinsbee Monk III, to seek out the perpetrators of the confidence game in question, and Harber was familiar with the details of the case. "Odd that you should ask. Remember another of the grifters was named Jack Farringay?''

Harber nodded. "The matinee-idol one. The one that almost plugged you.''

"Yes. By a remarkable coincidence, I've been seeing a good deal of him during the last week. We've been in bed together, as a matter of fact.''

Dutch Egan looked up from his glass. "Finally decided to give up on women, hey?''

"As roommates. In an ancestral mansion in the Bluegrass, while witnessing the unfolding of a supernatural curse, or something along those lines." I picked up the cards in front of me and began sorting them. "Murder—vigilante mobs—castrated horses—flaming stables—a beautiful heiress surrounded by fortune hunters—who dealt this disaster, anyhow?''

Gans and Pomerance exchanged resigned glances, and Tallboy tossed his hand on the table. "All right, Moretti, tell us about it." He rose to make himself another drink.

I told them most of what had happened since I had spotted Farringay at the Lexington Fair Grounds. They listened with varying degrees of interest. When I finished, Pomerance shook his head and said in dismissal, "No focus. There's nothing there, Moretti. Let's play cards.''

"I don't know," said Gans as he idly dug wax from one ear with his little finger. "I sort of like the crazy old lady. You don't suppose she did the job on old Uranus, do you? Sneaking around with a sickle in her hand, getting even with life for taking her boyfriend away thirty years ago?"

Tallboy yawned and looked at his watch. "Nothing—no story, and now no poker game either, not if I'm going to get to work on time tomorrow. Next time you bring a sheep to one of our games, Moretti, let the rest of us share in the shearing, all right?"

Clem Harber pulled down on his remarkably elastic upper lip and regarded me moodily. "I'm afraid I agree with them, Paddy. There's just no story. A bunch of pieces, but nothing to hold them together. Hochmuth's not going to waste a column inch on it, no matter how you dress it up."

I turned to Dutch Egan. "How about a *Police Gazette* feature, Dutch? Would Fox buy it? It's got everything he likes—rich people, torture, sex, blood, mystery—"

Egan shook his head. "Not the way it is now. Not unless you can tell who did what to who, and why. You know that, Moretti. Fox likes things neat, and this thing is an unmade bed."

They were right. The Kirkargyle story was stillborn, and I was naked to my enemies. I had a powerful premonition that the next day at the paper would be my last, that the only reason Hochmuth hadn't fired me today was that he wanted to savor the anticipation for another twenty-four hours. I poured myself a drink and counted my night's winnings.

Tallboy left, taking Gans and Pomerance with him. Clem Harber, who was an insomniac, and Dutch Egan, who worked on a weekly newspaper with a deadline two days off, stayed for a final glass. The busboy, a toothless Bowery veteran in a red striped undershirt and a filthy white apron, appeared and carried away the free lunch; he was warned off before he could remove the whiskey. Harber tried to promote a rummy game and, when that failed, began to construct a tower of playing cards. Dutch Egan put his sizable feet on the table and folded his hands behind his head.

"You know, Paddy," he mused, "the Kentucky business of yours could make a passable *PG* story if it was to work itself out in any kind of reasonable shape. It's the kind of thing King Richard likes. Put an ending on it and he'd be willing to pay."

I spread my hands. "What am I supposed to do? Hire the Pinkertons?"

"Think logically. Avoid red herrings. Go to the heart of the matter. Crime is almost always simpler than you expect." His voice took on the orotund self-satisfaction of a professional lecturing amateurs. "I remember one case we featured, in which a woman was found murdered in her bedroom. There were five orange pips on the bedside table, a sheet of paper in the wastebasket bearing the mysterious word 'GROC,' which means 'revenge' in an obscure Balkan dialect, and a wet spot on the carpet for which no explanation could be found. The woman had been stabbed to death with a stilettolike weapon which had disappeared. After initial bafflement, the investigation officers discovered—"

"—that she'd been in bed eating an orange and starting a grocery list when her lover arrived," Clem Harber said, balancing one card precariously on three others. "The lover being the family iceman, he set his block of ice down on the rug and hopped in beside her. Then her husband came back and nailed her with her inamorato's ice pick. Husband and iceman both hastily decamped. *Sic transit gloria mundi.*" The tower of cards collapsed, and Harber swore.

"Um, yes," said Egan, somewhat deflated. "There were subtleties, but you've got it mostly right.. The point is, simplicity is the key. Look for the basic passions— jealousy, greed, fear, lust, hatred. Look for the obvious suspect. Look for the straight line that is the shortest distance between two points. Look—"

"Look for a new job, Moretti," Harber finished dryly.

"It boils down to that," I said. "That terrible man is going to throw me away like yesterday's newspaper, after I've given him the best years of my life. And nobody will ever know what's really happening at Kirkargyle." I made my way to the whiskey and freshened my drink, which I raised in a toast. "Here's to Bert the Barnacle! I wonder if I can make a career out of him?"

The next day I sat slumped at my desk all morning, trying to keep my head out of Otto Hochmuth's line of sight. McAnly, whose desk was just inboard of mine, commented on my posture and added bitterly, "Don't think you can hide, Moretti. Your poker-playing skills won't help you now."

"If the man gives me my walking papers, I'll put in a good word for you before I go, Bertram. I'll tell him you represent all the qualities I value most highly in the journalistic profession."

He blanched. "God, don't do that! I mean, I couldn't let you put yourself out for me."

I stretched out my arm and patted his shoulder. "It's the least I can do, and a small reward indeed for years of staunch comradeship. It will ease the pain of leaving to know that you're still here, still carrying the Moretti colors, as it were. No, don't try to thank me." I glanced past his appalled features and saw the unappetizing face of Otto Hochmuth turned in my direction; as our eyes met, he raised a bony finger and crooked it. "Well, it appears I'm to have my chance right now—it's himself that wants to see me."

Ignoring McAnly's bleat of entreaty, I walked across the busy editorial room. Hochmuth, his green eyeshade turning his skin the color of wet putty, looked up at me. "Mr. Moretti," he said in his dry, uninflected voice, "since we have been out of touch for the past fortnight, I wonder if you could bring me up to date on your interests."

"Sure and it'll be a pleasure, sir. What was it you wanted to know?"

"What are you feelings about the current Sino-Japanese conflict? Do you feel the Japanese have a right to intervene in Korea, or are you sympathetic to the traditional hegemony of the Celestial Empire in the area?"

"Why—to tell you the truth, Mr. Hochmuth, I haven't given it all that much thought."

"Oh?" He assumed an expression of mild surprise. "Well, would you choose to cover the fighting in P'yong-yang personally, or would you prefer to pursue your duties in Port Arthur, under the assumption it will soon become the eye of the hurricane, so to speak?"

"I'm not sure I have a firm opinion on that," I said carefully. "Would you mind telling me why you're asking?"

"Why, since you have apparently given up the profession of sportswriting, I thought you might be considering a career as a war correspondent. Perhaps Mr. Bennett or Mr. Dana has a job that would suit you. Or, what about working as roving political editor for *Harper's Weekly*? I understand they are very generous on travel expenses."

I looked at my shoes. "You're upset with me."

"Me? Upset? Why would I be upset, Mr. Moretti? Because you spent two weeks in Kentucky, eating and drinking in your usual Epicurean manner, and failed to deliver the story you were assigned to report?" His buttonhole of a mouth opened and closed primly. "Because the copy you sent in could have been supplied by any cub reporter in the country who is currently overpaid at five dollars a week?"

"It's true I didn't discover all I was hoping to from the McAuliffes. You're entirely in the right of it there, Mr. Hochmuth."

"I also understand there were certain perhaps newsworthy occurrences at the Kirkargyle stable while you were present in Lexington. However, I have waited in vain for any explanation of their significance. Is it any wonder, Mr.

Moretti, that I question whether you are altogether happy in your work?''

I began a long-deferred mental search for choice expletives and appropriate terms of abuse as I asked, "Are you telling me I'm fired, then?"

Hochmuth regarded me with stoic disappointment. "No, I am not, sir. Such an action is beyond my powers at the present moment. Apparently The Owner feels some sense of obligation to you because of your efforts on his nephew's behalf, and therefore insists that you be offered another chance. *Another* is the operative word, Mr. Moretti. The word is singular in number. It has no connotation of repetition. Do you understand?"

I abandoned the search for the perfect pejorative phrase with mixed feelings. "Indeed I do. And I thank you and Mr. Monk for behaving so understandingly, although it's no more than I would have expected of the both of yez."

Hochmuth winced slightly at the brogue. "Your expectations may not prove as accurate in the future. You may return to your duties, Mr. Moretti. For as long as they continue." He bent his head over the copy paper on his desk, and for a moment I saw his face through his green isinglass visor. He looked like something swimming on the ocean floor.

McAnly watched me as I returned to my desk. He could hardly wait till I was seated before he demanded, "Did he give you any notice, or just tell you to get out? And you can whistle for any recommendation, I'll bet."

I looked at him with raised eyebrows. "What in the world are you babbling about, Bertram? Mr. Hochmuth and I were discussing the state of the racing business, and he took the opportunity to pass along a compliment or two from The Owner, which modesty prevents me from repeating."

He gaped. "He didn't fire you? After what he said yesterday?"

"What a question. Mr. Hochmuth and I understand each other perfectly. I only hope, Bertram, that you and he will achieve an equally rewarding relationship during your tenure here." And to signify an end to the conversation I picked up a galley proof and began studying it.

During the rest of the summer I remained in the New York area, except for a week each in Philadelphia and Baltimore. I was kept busy covering meets at Morris Park, Brighton Beach, Sheepshead, Gravesend, and a clutch of new tracks that had recently opened in New Jersey, and paid little attention to racing in other parts of the country.

I did spend some time with the results of the August meet at Churchill Downs, however, and noted that Kirkargyle's Sebastian was the winner of a major stakes race, with a time that nearly tied the track record. Then three weeks later Sebastian won again, against a highly esteemed speed horse that had previously won a dozen purses.

Aha, I thought, *the fortunes of the McAuliffes have taken a turn for the better. And maybe the fortunes of Jack Farringay as well.*

Then in September came the Buford Stakes at Lexington, $25,000 added, and a field of the finest horses in the United States, including both Sebastian and Sir Gawain, the horse he had beaten the previous month, now with another major victory to his credit. Hochmuth decided the race should be covered by a personal correspondent.

"We're sending you back because of your relationship with the McAuliffes, for whatever that's worth," he told me. "Consider it an opportunity to expunge a failure from your record."

"Yes, sir."

"Your expense account will be analyzed by experts."

"Yes, sir."

"In addition to descriptions of the races, we expect a behind-the-scenes feature on Kirkargyle and the effect of the Buford Stakes on its future. This feature will be written from the point of view of the horse-racing business, with no excursions into murders, superstitions, perversions, vendettas, or hexes. Understood?''

"Yes, sir." I swallowed, smiled, and added, "Thank you."

Three days later I was on a train back to Lexington.

10

The Statue in the Courthouse Square

"**I** don't believe it. The bad penny is back again. Damn it, Moretti, you rascal, have a drink." Grinning broadly and obviously well on the way for so early in the day, Sandy Braddock thrust his flask in my face.

It was just after the second race, and there was a long afternoon before me. I shook my head. "Later. There are those who have to work for a living."

"Here?" He pantomimed apprehension, glancing over his shoulder with a hunted expression. "People like that are a threat to all of us. I better have a drink." He took a quick swallow and grunted with satisfaction. "Well, you can chew on a chicken leg at least. Come on and renew old acquaintances."

The McAuliffe box was full. Grouped around a large picnic basket were the Judge, his daughter, and her three suitors. Dorcas McAuliffe, radiant in a straw picture hat that contrasted with her gleaming auburn hair and made her eyes as meltingly attractive as two chocolate opera cremes, was gazing up into Jack Farringay's face as Emmett Lawler talked to the back of her hat, and Carroll Glass gazed pensively over the track.

Judge McAuliffe saw me first, as I ducked under the iron bar that enclosed the box. His face froze in an expression of disapproval, and he quickly glanced away, pretending ignorance of my arrival. A moment later Farringay saw me. The sudden anger that twisted his features passed so quickly I almost doubted it had been there at all. He thrust out his hand and gave me a firmly sincere grip. "Well, old *chou*, you just couldn't keep away from us, could you? Welcome back to the Bluegrass." He turned to Dorcas. "Look who's come back to pay his respects, my dear." His tone was noticeably proprietary.

Dorcas smiled radiantly. "Why, how good to see you again! Back for a nice long visit?" She tucked one hand under Farringay's elbow and glanced up at him. "Jack would enjoy that, I know."

"I hope so." I looked past her at Emmett Lawler. "And how are you, Mr. Emmett"—I paused, then continued— "Lawler?" I smiled innocently and offered him my hand, which he ignored. I touched Carroll Glass on the shoulder, and he turned to look at me blankly. We exchanged nods, and he resumed his station at the rail, staring over the track. I sought Caleb McAuliffe's eye, but he continued to avoid mine.

Sandy pressed a chicken drumstick into my hand and offered his flask again. I took a bite of chicken. "So— what's the newest on the Curse of Kirkargyle?" I asked as I chewed.

Dorcas answered. "If there ever was a curse, it's gone now. Bonne Jeanne sold for even more than we had hoped, and Sebastian's been winning purses every time he runs, and the other horses are doing well, too, and—" She shot a glance at Farringay, and her cheeks colored. "And everything's just perfect!" she concluded positively.

I said I was delighted to hear it. "And that man Carmody—has he gone on trial yet?"

"Next week—finally," Dorcas said. "I'm sorry for the poor man, but I don't see what good it does to delay these things."

"Of course, when he's found guilty, it'll cut down on

our mail considerably,'' Sandy Braddock said, unscrewing the cap of his flask.

"Oh?" I inquired.

Caleb turned to glare at his stepbrother and appeared to be about to speak until he thought better of it. Dorcas sighed, Farringay tightened his lips, and Emmett Lawler pulled his head down between his broad shoulders. Carroll Glass continued to stare over the track's infield.

Sandy smacked his lips and recapped his flask. "We've had quite an epidemic of poison-pen letters this summer, Moretti. Dorcas and I admit we've each gotten one. Caleb and Rhoda ain't saying, but I'd put money on it they have, too. I don't know about the three musketeers here"—his gesture included Farringay, Lawler, and Glass—"but I wouldn't be surprised if they were on the list. And who knows who else?"

Judge McAuliffe chose to break his silence. "Damn foolishness!" he snorted. Farringay shrugged his well-tailored shoulders, and Lawler abruptly turned his back to Braddock.

"Letters?" I repeated. "What kind of letters?"

"Barely literate letters, for starters. Dorcas's and mine were, anyway. Of course, maybe they were supposed to look that way. Mine started out something like this: 'You know Carmody never killed Lomas Fugate. Why don't you tell the truth? Is it 'cause you never told the truth about what happened to your friend Amory Glass in that Georgia farmhouse? No wonder you ain't been nothing but a drunk ever since.' " He grimaced. "Vigorous prose style."

I couldn't help glancing at Dorcas, and she saved me embarrassment by speaking first. "Mine was equally ungrammatical. Something about that awful accident two years ago—'Ain't one killing enough for you? You're a real McAuliffe, all right!' It was along those lines." She shook her head as Farringay moved to put his arm around her. "It's not important; it's only stupid and malicious. But I just don't understand anybody sending it."

Braddock gazed sympathetically at her for a moment before demanding from the others in the box, "Anybody else get a letter he wants to tell us about? No? I would have hoped for more mutual trust in our happy group."

The bugle calling the next race cut through the hubbub in the stands, and the conversation ceased. The race was a predictable affair, and afterward, as I made notes, Dorcas and Farringay put their heads together, and Lawler engaged Judge Caleb in what appeared to be a weighty discussion. Carroll Glass came past me on his way out of the box.

"I hope you're having more luck here today than you did at Kimbro's barn," I said to him. "That business with your dog Tusker—that was a terrible thing."

"What? Oh, my dog. Why? Why should you care?" His handsome features registered dislike. "It was an Irishman who cheated him out of his win."

"I'm only Irish on my mother's side, and she disapproved of gambling on general principles. I was wondering, Mr. Glass, if you got one of those letters Braddock was talking about?"

"Why would I get one? I'm no kin to the McAuliffes, and the way it looks, I never will be." He pushed past me and ducked under the box rail.

I put my notebook in my pocket and moved next to Farringay. "Ah, Jack, you'll never guess what happened to me on the train back to New York," I said.

He glanced at me unwillingly as Dorcas said, "Oh? What?"

"I'm afraid I fell among thieves—or one thief for sure. A scalawag named Yarnell, J. Hamilton Yarnell. An amusing fellow who taught me a neat little swindle with two sugar cubes." I recounted my costly experience in the C&O dining car, emphasizing its comic aspects as I watched Farringay's face and the back of Lawler's neck. Farringay's face was composed; Lawler's neck seemed to swell and darken over his tight white collar.

"Why, the idea!" Dorcas cried when I had finished.

"Do you suppose he just travels around on trains cheating people with sugar cubes?"

"Oh, no. From what I gathered, he practices a number of different confidence games. One called the rag, if I'm not mistaken; it involves setting up a fake stockbroker's office and convincing the victim he can take advantage of inside information to make a killing. Apparently this Yarnell was very clever at it—or else his marks were very stupid." I paused, then resumed: "Another one of his swindles involved something called a fight store. I never got all the details, but the setup was in a small town in Kansas."

"Kansas? Really? I never knew the people out there were worth cheating," said Farringay with a curl of his lip.

"You'd be surprised where a man like Yarnell will go to make a killing," I said.

"I guess you meet every different type of person in your work, Paddy—it must be fascinating." To Farringay's raised eyebrows, Dorcas explained, "Oh, Paddy and I are on a first-name basis now, ever since his last visit to Kirkargyle. Aren't we, Paddy?" I bowed. Farringay looked back at me coolly.

"How cozy. I think I'll take a stroll to the paddock and look over the next entries. Care to join me, Moretti?"

We left the box and started down the busy aisle, he leading. "All right, you can spare me any more surprises," he said over his shoulder. "What's this about Yarnell?"

"Just what I said. An accidental meeting on the train."

"What did he say about me?"

"Nothing—only that he understood you were in Kentucky someplace. I pretended I'd forgotten your name, but I don't think he believed me."

He slowed down and I came up beside him. He threw a companionable arm around my shoulders. "Moretti, it's good to see your ugly Irish mug again. I never thought I'd say it, but I'm glad you came back to the Bluegrass."

"I never thought you'd say it either, Jack."

He chuckled. "We've had our little misunderstandings, but I hope you know I consider you a true friend. I want you to know you can trust me just as far as I trust you—and that's a considerable ways, *amigo*."

"I know that, Jack."

"As you can see, things have been going very well here, Paddy. Going well for me, and that means"—he gave my shoulders a squeeze—"going well for my friends. The course of true love is running smoothly, and the fortunes of Kirkargyle are in the ascendancy. I think it's no violation of confidence to tell an old crony that we may look forward to orange blossoms before the end of the year."

"Congratulations."

He waved a hand. "I'm the luckiest man in the world, and the least deserving. But one thing I guarantee, Paddy—I'll do everything possible to protect Dorcas from any unhappiness." He raised his chin sternly.

"Such as having old acquaintances like Yarnell appear with their hands out."

"Exactly. We're men of the world. We understand the importance of shielding the fair sex from the grosser aspects of life. There are things they would never understand." He shook his head. "When I think of how Dorcas would feel if she heard some of the stories—"

"All right," I snapped, suddenly tired of his verbal minuet. "If Yarnell comes here, he didn't learn it from me. I'm not going to spill the beans about you. As far as I'm concerned, our original agreement still stands. You help me get a story and I'll clam up about your unsavory past, and may God forgive me."

He gave my shoulders a final squeeze and dropped his arm. "You're a friend to count on, Moretti," he said simply.

"Then bring me up to date. Nothing more on the jinx, I gather. Bonne Jeanne brought a good price, Sebastian's winning big, and the rest of the stable's also in the black."

Farringay nodded. "What about these letters Sandy was talking about? Who would want to send them?"

"Some friend of Carmody's?"

"What about the toll road and the Regulators?"

"What about them? That lawyer, Yates, has been stirring up trouble, but nothing has come of it. Too many big people are paying good money to break the toll-road company."

"Like Caleb?"

"So they say. Although now you mention it, there's a rumor that Yates has a mystery witness who's willing to testify in Frankfort—somebody who can pinpoint where the money's coming from." He shrugged. "But there are always rumors like that."

We had reached the paddock and joined the other spectators watching the entrants in the next race parade around the oval. I looked for the Kirkargyle colors, but they were not represented. "Who do you like?" I asked.

"No preference. Unless they're Kirkargyle stock, it's a matter of indifference to me. I'm not a gambler, you know."

"I know," I said thoughtfully.

We watched the handsome animals prancing past, skittish and vain. Across the paddock I saw Cocanougher of the *Lexington Herald*. He raised his hand and then pantomimed tossing down a drink. I nodded agreement.

Farringay stirred restlessly beside me, shifting his weight from one elbow to the other on the paddock rail. "Moretti, how long are you planning to stay in Lexington?"

"Until after the Buford Stakes. I'll leave on Sunday, I expect." I shot him a glance. "Why? Is that too long?"

"Too long? You misunderstand me, old friend. It's grand having you here. The only thing I meant was that it must be a strain on you, having to watch what you say all the time, never being free to relax and reminisce . . . I'll bet you can't wait to file your story and decamp."

"Au contraire," I said comfortably. "It'll be a terrible

wrench, leaving your intended bride without ever letting my hair down with her. I feel we'd have so much to talk about, once we started exchanging confidences.'' His face hardened, and I continued, "No, Jack, it's all right. We made an agreement and I'll stick to it. But I do like the girl.''

He looked at me levelly. "And so do I, Paddy. Believe me. This is straight goods. I'd do anything for Dorcas—anything in the world.''

I nodded. "All right, I believe you. And I didn't sic Yarnell on you, Jack. If he appears on the scene, don't blame me.''

"Fair enough.'' We watched the horses circle the paddock for a few seconds more and then returned to the McAuliffe box, where Farringay imparted his personal recommendations on the coming race to an admiring Dorcas, a sullen Lawler, a preoccupied Glass, a tight-lipped Caleb, and a loose-mouthed Braddock. I excused myself and headed for the clubhouse.

I pursued my trade the rest of the afternoon, and six o'clock found me with Cocanougher and two companions of racing's fourth estate in a saloon named Wanny's, sitting beside a window overlooking the courthouse square. One of the companions, a Cincinnati German named Weir, raised his glass in a toast to the huge equestrian figure in the yard outside. "To the bloody Rebel, whoever he may be.''

"Please. The gentleman's name is John Hunt Morgan,'' Cocanougher said. "The Thunderbolt of the Confederacy. A Lexington native. Astride his faithful mare Black Bess.''

The other companion, a pinch-faced bespectacled fellow named Sneed, peered at the statue. "Goddamnedest mare I've ever seen. She's hung like a bull.''

Weir agreed. "No wonder the damn Rebels lost the war, with cavalrymen that couldn't tell a stallion from a mare.''

Cocanougher frowned. "No, Morgan could tell. There's every reason to believe Morgan could. It's the sculptor who couldn't.''

"A sculptor of equestrian statues who was unaware of the fine distinction between male and female anatomy?" I asked.

"On second thought, he probably did know. That is, he would have known if he'd *known*. Known that Black Bess was a mare, that is."

"You're saying he assumed it was a stallion because its name was Bess?" Sneed demanded. "Most Besses in his experience had been males? That sculptor must have had himself some life."

"No, what I'm saying is that he probably didn't know *anything* about the damn horse, not its name, not its sex, not *anything*."

"Then why did he make it a male—and such a fully endowed male?" I asked.

"Because he was sculpting a war-horse, for Christ's sake!" Cocanougher took a deep swallow of whiskey. "He knew he was making a statue of a cavalry general, so naturally he assumed the horse would be male."

"Naturally?" echoed Sneed.

"Typical. No wonder the Rebels lost the war," Weir repeated. "Imagine cavalrymen not knowing the difference between stallions and mares."

Ignoring Weir, I said to Cocanougher, "What Sneed means is why would anybody assume a war-horse is necessarily male? Surely a combative nature is not solely the prerogative of the male gender. If my experience has taught me anything—" I paused to allow the waitress to deposit a fresh supply of drinks on the table, then resumed, "If my experience has taught me anything—"

"Jesus, Moretti, let's not get into what your experience has taught you," Sneed interrupted. "What I want to know is, what happened when the statue was unveiled? I mean, here is this thirty-foot-high monster towering over everybody's heads, the most famous war hero in the city's history riding his equally famous horse Black Bess, and everybody stares up at balls like you'd see outside a pawn shop? What happened?"

Cocanougher drank his whiskey deliberately. "Nothing," he answered, wiping his mouth with the back of his hand.

"Nothing?" Sneed stared incredulously.

"Nothing. This is Lexington, Kentucky, the Athens of the Midwest, my friend. This town is *genteel*. Which means that the hundreds of gentlemen present instantly decided not to call attention to the offending organs for fear of embarrassing their ladies, and the ladies simultaneously decided not to notice them for fear of showing an unseemly interest in sexual matters."

I nodded. "Very genteel indeed. No doubt saved the ceremony from degenerating into farce. But why didn't somebody arrange for modification later? In the interest of historical accuracy, if nothing else?"

Cocanougher shrugged. "Why bother? It might have called attention to something already successfully ignored. And how important is historical accuracy, anyway?"

Marveling, I said, "And this is the horse-breeding capital of the United States."

"When in Athens, do as the Athenians do," Cocanougher said, raising his glass in a toast.

"No wonder they lost the damned war." Weir was now noticeably the worse for wear.

We drank and talked for another hour, and then ate supper. Afterward, Cocanougher, in his role of our Lexington guide, suggested an evening's entertainment at the famous bagnio operated by Belle Breezing.

"In case Black Bess gave you the idea that we're sexually ambiguous down here, I think Belle's establishment will put that idea to rest." Smiling proudly, he motioned us to rise. "Shall we proceed, gentlemen?"

11

A Hell of a Way
to Run a Whorehouse

It is perhaps paradoxical that one should spend part of his first visit to a famous bawdy house brooding over the lost loves of a lifetime. The only way I can explain it is that it is a very manageable form of self-loathing, since release is immediately at hand. And also because one is half-Irish and half-Italian.

I sat in the ornate parlor, in an armchair made of red plush and the horns of Texas longhorn steers—a gift to "Miss Belle" from one of her southwestern customers, I assumed—and thought about a very proper lady named Alison and a very improper lady named Kate and a woman named Marya who rejected the title of "lady" and everything it stood for. It was very pleasant, in a bittersweet way. I sipped very good champagne and told myself I was probably too straightforward and open a person to be markedly successful with the opposite sex.

In between remembering amorous disappointments I watched the comings and goings of the customers of the house. They were the most distinguished-looking gentlemen you would see outside the United States Senate, bearded and sideburned dignitaries who were obviously civic leaders, and mustachioed gallants who would have been at home in a naval wardroom or the clubhouse at

Saratoga. They conversed comfortably with one another as they waited to go upstairs, sipping their drinks and eyeing the decorously clad women seated on the settees around them.

Remembering Cocanougher's story, I thought, *And to think they wouldn't notice the balls on a mare.*

"Miss Belle" Breezing had greeted us when we were shown into the drawing room. She was a small woman, almost tiny, with a heavy crown of mahogany-brown hair piled on top of her head. Her face would have been lovely in a conventional way except for her decisive mouth and the emphatic dark brows that arched over her glittering brown eyes. Her figure was slender and well formed, beautifully set off by a modish evening gown of rose and ivory. She was perhaps in her midthirties, but looked five years younger.

"Mr. Cocanougher, how very nice," she said, extending her hand to him. "We are always delighted to entertain members of the press." She acknowledged his introduction of Weir and Sneed, and then turned her eyes to me. "Mr. Moretti, it is always a pleasure to welcome a gentleman from New York to the provinces."

I bowed over her hand. "It's New York that becomes provincial by comparison, Miss Belle."

She smiled, dimpling one cheek. "I shall tell our ladies they must watch out for you, sir. You are a dangerous man." Disengaging her hand, she waved over a white-jacketed waiter carrying a tray of champagne glasses. "Please refresh yourselves, gentlemen. If you care for anything stronger, Phylas will take your order. And now, if you will excuse me—" Her eyes held mine for a moment before she turned away and left the room.

Cocanougher and Sneed immediately struck up conversations with two young women on a nearby sofa, and Weir sank into an armchair and regarded his glass owlishly. I carried my champagne into the parlor and occupied the aforementioned longhorn lounger, which was more comfortable than it sounds.

I had been mentally leafing through my memory book for ten minutes when the first of a chain of new arrivals caught my attention. It was Carroll Glass, face flushed, hair mussed, cravat loosely tied, and an unfocused look in his eyes. He didn't notice me through the doorway of the parlor, and passed immediately from my line of sight.

It couldn't have been more than five minutes later that his rival Emmett Lawler arrived, in the company of another gentleman who looked like a successful merchant. They stopped just inside the drawing room to chat with Miss Belle, Lawler assuming the heavy aura of self-importance that seemed his only escape from sullenness. Miss Belle didn't spend long with them; I got the impression she found the conversation heavy going. A moment later the two men moved past the parlor doorway and out of my sight.

I finished my glass of champagne and took another from the attentive Phylas. A string quartet began playing in the next room—oddly enough their first selection was "I Dreamt I Dwelt in Marble Halls," causing me to switch my thoughts of lost loves to Dorcas McAuliffe, although she hardly fitted the category.

Time passed as I sipped the cool, dry, effervescent wine. I found I was unwilling to hasten either the recollecting or the drinking. The surroundings were tasteful, the music soothing, the murmuring voices of courtly men and coquettish women in the drawing room promised satisfaction at some future time. It was nice to know it was out there for me, whenever I might want it.

I glanced away from the door toward an oil painting on the adjacent wall. It was the portrait of a young woman sitting in a swing by a blooming magnolia tree. Although she was simply and chastely dressed in a high-necked white blouse and dark skirt, there was a vibrant sensuality suggested by her body that reminded me of another I had seen recently, although I could not remember where.

It was, recognizably, Belle Breezing. A Belle Breezing ten years younger, but hardly either less worldly or more beautiful than she was today. Her gleaming dark eyes held mine as I raised my glass to her. "To you, dark lady," I said softly.

"Shame on you, Bunky—toasting the shadow while the substance waits in the next room. But I agree with you— Belle was a good-looking piece back then. Still isn't so bad, as a matter of fact, if you don't mind a certain hardness."

Jack Farringay had entered the parlor while I had been absorbed in the portrait. He was sportily dressed in a blazer and a tattersall vest, and a black forelock curled down his forehead in studied casualness. He grinned, showing perfect white teeth, and snagged a glass of champagne from a passing Phylas. "Or have you already been upstairs and are now regrouping for another engagement?"

"Just enjoying a moment of quiet reflection, Jack." I waved to a chair. "Join me. And tell me what's going on here—a meeting of the Dorcas McAuliffe Admirers Association?"

He raised his eyebrows inquiringly as he sat down. I told him that he had been preceded by both Carroll Glass and Emmett Lawler. He chuckled. "Poor wretches are obviously driven by their aching frustration. I feel for them."

"And what's your excuse?"

He regarded me guilelessly. "Why, I'm too considerate a chap to force my crude male appetites on the lady I care for—not until we share the legal marriage bed. I'm sure no gentleman would feel otherwise."

"Are you sure no lady would feel otherwise?"

He shrugged. "All I know, Moretti, is that it seems judicious to wait. And that's all the conversation we're going to have about the lady in question while we're in this establishment." He lit a slender black cigarillo and exhaled a cloud of smoke that smelled faintly of perique and rum. "So you fancy Belle's looks, do you? Fat lot of good it'll do you. Unless you change your name to Billy Maburn.''

"Who?''

"Billy Maburn—her partner, procurer, protector, adviser, confidant, lover, and God knows what besides. He takes up so much space in her life there's no room for anyone else. That's what the girls say, anyway. So I wouldn't waste any more time mooning over her portrait, Bunky. Get up and circulate. I'll even advise you on the relative merits of the merchandise.''

I remained in my chair. "In a minute. Tell me something, Jack. Belle's pretty young to own a showplace like this. Who put up the money—this Maburn?''

"No, apparently it's all hers. And made on her back, the hard way. Belle's a local girl, comes from the slum area they call Irishtown—no offense, old horse. She was on the streets at fifteen. A couple of years later she was the star attraction at the Mary Todd Lincoln house.''

"What?'' I cried.

He chuckled. "You heard me. The house Mary Todd grew up in, where Honest Abe came visiting his in-laws before the war. By the 1870s it had become the number-one riding academy in Lexington. And our Belle was the prime filly. They used to wait in line for her.''

I thought again about the statue of Black Bess.

"The only one who ever got it for free was Billy Maburn,'' Jack went on. "Belle saved every penny she earned and opened her own crib on Upper Street while she was still in her early twenties. And since then word has it that she's never put her butt on the block to anybody, no matter what price was offered.'' He smiled cynically. "You can believe that or not, depending on your faith in human nature. But in any case she's certainly out of *your* price range, Moretti.''

I sighed. "So it would appear.'' I raised my glass to the woman in the portrait. "To what might have been,'' I said, and emptied it. "All right, Jack, I'm off and running. You may advise me." I started to rise from my chair and then stopped.

C. Hamilton Yarnell was entering the parlor.

He smiled in greeting as casually as if he'd seen us both only that afternoon. "Ah, well met, lads!" he called. "This establishment must live up to its advance billing if I find you two connoisseurs in residence!"

Perhaps the alcohol was beginning to reach me, but I felt no surprise at all in his arrival. It seemed the most natural thing in the world. I raised my hand. "Hey—got your sugar cubes?"

Farringay's reaction was less spontaneous. His eyes narrowed slightly, and his handsome face suddenly appeared to be carved from wood. He withdrew the cigarillo from his mouth and expelled a perfect smoke ring. Then he said, "Cheers, Hamilton. What a nice surprise. Just passing through, are you?"

"Well, I don't know. Something friend Paddy let drop on the train suggested you might be prowling these parts, Jack. So I thought it might be nice to drop by and cut up old touches, so to speak. How fortunate to have such a salubrious setting for it!" He lounged against the marble mantel, the very picture of worldly condescension.

Farringay remained silent a moment, and then, with his eyes fixed on Yarnell, said, "Paddy, I wonder if you'd mind leaving the two of us alone. We seem to have some catching up to do."

I rose to my feet with dignity. "Far be it from me to intrude on male conversations in a bordello. I shall find more sympathetic companions elsewhere—even if have to struggle along without the benefit of your considerable experience, Jack." I waited to see what effect this Parthian shot would have, and when I saw it had none, I left the parlor.

The drawing room presented a lively scene. The string quartet was sawing away on "Sweet and Low," the indefatigable Phylas was working in double harness with another white-jacketed waiter to see that everyone was well supplied with champagne and hors d'oeuvres, a dozen distinguished-looking customers were displaying their *gravitas* to one another and to Madame Breezing, who indicated her admiration as she moved from group to group, four or five young ladies in décolleté gowns sat around a table, viewing stereopticon slides or leafing through magazines, and in a corner of the room outside the traffic pattern, my colleague Weir was sleeping, head on chest, eyes closed, lips vibrating gently as he snored. Lawler and his friend were eyeing the girls surreptitiously, as if preparing to make their selections. Neither Cocanougher nor Sneed was present.

I had just substituted a new glass for my empty one when a voice behind me boomed, "My God, Moretti, don't you ever go anyplace where I'm not?"

I turned as Sandy Braddock's hand descended on my shoulder. It was not his black-gloved one, but it still struck with unpleasant force. He was smiling, but his eyes were angry; it was as if he were unsure of his own reaction to finding me here. I said pacifically, "What is it they say about great minds traveling in the same plane, or groove, or whatever? Will you join me in a glass?"

He ordered bourbon from Phylas, who immediately left to fill his order. He waited impatiently for the waiter's return, and when the drink was brought, he half emptied the glass in a single swallow, standing with his eyes closed and his head thrown back, as though performing a solemn rite.

He turned to me; he was still smiling, but now his eyes were sad. "Well, since I can't seem to get away from you, I might as well accept it. But damn it, Moretti, you show precious little variety in your choice of entertainment. Your liver must be in terrible shape."

"This time there are girls around," I said.

"So there are," he noted, as if half-surprised. "That does make a difference." He surveyed the women in the room thoughtfully. "Charming. Not one of them with enough brains or character to fill a thimble, of course.

Except for Belle.'' He shot me a look. ''You've met our hostess?'' I told him that I had enjoyed that pleasure. ''A remarkable woman,'' he continued. ''She could have accomplished anything she set her mind to. It's our gain that this''—he gestured to include the room—''is what she set her mind to.'' He paused, then added softly, ''Or our loss.''

He asked who had brought me to Belle's, and I pointed out Weir in his chair and identified his two absent colleagues.

''I didn't reckon it was *him*,'' he said with a jerk of his head toward Lawler. ''But where's your right bower Farringay today?''

''In the parlor, with an old friend he ran into here tonight. You know, it's a remarkable thing about Belle's—I have a feeling if you drop in here three or four times you'll meet everybody you've ever known. Mothers and the clergy excepted, naturally.''

We emptied our glasses, and Phylas brought us new ones. The quartet played ''When You and I Were Young, Maggie,'' and followed it with ''The Rosary.'' I contemplated the girls sitting around the table through a rosy haze, thinking that if I were to make a choice I had better do it soon.

Then a number of things happened at the same time.

Farringay and Yarnell emerged from the parlor arm in arm, conversing easily, with every appearance of cordiality. Yarnell glanced across the room at Lawler, who saw him at the same moment. Lawler stiffened, splashing liquor on the rug and causing his companion to stare at him in surprise. Yarnell nodded pleasantly, and Farringay's lips turned up in a sneer.

Simultaneously the door to the rear of the house, through which Phylas and the other servants passed on their way to the kitchen and wine cellar, burst open to reveal Cocanougher, disheveled and trouserless, struggling in the grip of a massive black man dressed in a tuxedo. Sneed, fully dressed but barefoot, capered beside the black man, raining ineffectual blows on his chest and shoulders. "Let go of me, you ape!" Cocanougher yelled. "I'm a paying customer!"

"Ain't no call to disturb the folks out front now," the bouncer said reasonably. "You come on—we'll leave by the back door." He gave emphasis to his words by lifting Cocanougher a foot off the ground and drawing him back toward the kitchen.

"Give him his pants!" Sneed hollered, pummeling away furiously. "You can't throw a man out without his pants! That's a hell of a way to run a whorehouse!"

As the two reporters disappeared behind the swinging door, my eye was caught by a movement on the curved stairway in the hall. Carroll Glass, in his shirtsleeves and carrying his jacket, was descending the steps briskly, undeterred by the woman clinging to his arm and trying to prevent his departure. His face was set in stony resolution, hers in tearful entreaty. It was a moment before I recognized her: Marybee Fugate.

Her dress looked as if she had tugged it on hastily, and her carrot-red hair was down around her shoulders. Weeping had swollen her eyes and blotched her lovely face, and her bosom was heaving with her labored breathing. She cried, "Oh, please—" and then Glass shook her loose, and she sank down on the steps as he hurried along the hall to the street door and slammed it behind him.

The rest of the guests in the drawing room were still keeping an eye on the kitchen door in hopes of a reappearance by Cocanougher, Sneed, and the bouncer, and I was the only one who witnessed the scene on the stairs. I hurried up the staircase and, taking her arm gently, raised her to her feet. "It's all right, don't cry. No man's worth crying over, *macushla*. What you need is a little drink and a sympathetic shoulder. Come on, now." These inane words seemed to have a quieting effect on her, and she allowed me to lead her into the empty parlor and ensconce her on a settee. I took my seat beside her and held her hand in both of mine.

"Now then. Remember me? Paddy Moretti? Of course you do! I'm your greatest admirer. I saw you at Kirkargyle, and you asked me about New York. And I watched you making the boys jump through hoops at the dogfight at Kimbro's barn, and I thought to meself, 'Ah, there's a girl for a man with eyes in his head.' And here you are at Miss Belle's, and I can hardly believe me good fortune."

This blarney had the stabilizing effect I hoped for. She stopped crying and regarded me uncertainly. "What do you want? Did you come here to find me?"

"And why does a man come to Miss Belle's, if it's not in the hope of finding a charmer like you?" Phylas's face peered around the doorjamb and I waved him in. "Here, have a taste of champagne to keep out the chill." I handed her a glass and took one myself. "Here's to you, and your very promising new career, and no tears about it."

Her green eyes narrowed slightly as she regarded me over the rim of her glass. "Oh, yeah, I remember you. You work for that horse-race newspaper." She lowered her voice. "You seen what happened on the stairs?"

"With Glass? Yes—but I don't think anyone else did. What was the matter with the man?"

I could see her preparing to lie to me, so before she could get started I said coolly, "Did he get tired of having his little playmate servicing half the male population of Lexington?"

Her face began to crumple again. She pressed her hands against her shapely breasts, as if to reassure herself they were still as desirable an asset as they had been. "He loves me—he does! He just don't know it yet. But he's going to come back and take me away, you just see if he don't! And then he's going to marry me!"

I shook my head. "Carroll Glass, marry a girl in a house? A blue blood like him? You know better than that!" I leaned toward her and took the glass from her hands. "Did he put you in here, Marybee? So he would have something nice waiting when he came to Lexington?"

She looked at me in hurt surprise. "No! He didn't have

nothing to do with it! It was—Maw kicked me out after Paw was killed, and I didn't have nowhere to go, and afterward Miss Belle let me come here!''

"Your maw kicked you out, Marybee? How come? Why would she do something like that?'' She looked down, her lower lip trembling. I leaned closer and tried a wild guess. "Because you were going to have a baby, Marybee?'' She looked up, wide-eyed, ready to lie again. "No, it's all right. These things happen.'' I squeezed her hand. "Whose was it? Glass's?''

"No!'' she cried.

"Then whose?''

"I—I can't—''

"Now, child, what in the world are you doing downstairs looking like that?'' asked a honeyed voice from the doorway. I looked up to see Miss Belle observing us, her lips smiling but her fine eyes glittering with irritation. "I declare, everything is at sixes and sevens tonight! Now you just get back upstairs, missy, and try to get yourself together! You're enough to give a gentleman a fright!''

Marybee withdrew her hand from mine and rose to her feet. "Yes'm,'' she said meekly, and took a step toward the door.

"Wait a minute!'' I moved after her. "Why don't I come up with you?''

Miss Belle slipped between us. "Oh, please, Mr. Moretti—I simply couldn't allow one of my young ladies to receive a caller while she was looking less than her best. Later, when Marybee has had a chance to put things right—of course!'' Marybee rounded the corner and disappeared as the madam slipped her hand under my arm and gave it a squeeze. "But meanwhile, if you can put up with me for a moment, I'd like you to give me your opinion on a new brand of bourbon I'm considering for our cellar.''

We went back into the drawing room, and Miss Belle dispatched Phylas for the bourbon. I noticed that Weir was gone from the armchair, and Lawler and his friend were also no longer in evidence. Farringay and Yarnell were sitting with two girls on the settee, looking through a stack of stereopticon slides and joking with one another in the most genial manner. Sandy Braddock stood with three other gentlemen, but seemed not to be listening to their conversation. The string quartet was playing "Drink to Me Only with Thine Eyes."

Phylas arrived with two glasses of neat bourbon, one the current house brand and the other the new one under consideration. I compared them, sniffing their bouquets, rolling them around on my tongue, and studying the way they beaded on the glass.

"They're both wonderful," I said.

"Pshaw, you haven't tasted enough yet to have an opinion," Miss Belle said, signaling Phylas.

I could feel the alcohol begin swirling gently in my brain. I tried to focus my eyes on my hostess, who seemed to have developed blurred edges. "Tell me, Miss Belle, how did you happen to take Marybee in here?"

She raised her handsome dark eyebrows. "I beg your pardon?"

"How did you happen to take her in? I realize it's gauche as the devil of me to ask, but who arranged for it? And was she pregnant then, or was she past it?"

All trace of coquettishness disappeared. "Mr. Moretti, this is your first visit to my establishment, so I won't judge you as harshly as your question deserves. I will simply remind you that the personal histories of my young ladies are their own affair, and that no gentleman in this house pries into subjects which are none of his business. I know you will take my words to heart."

I felt like I was being dressed down by my fourth-grade teacher for a particularly heinous offense, and it didn't help that there appeared to be two of her doing it. I hung my head. "I'm sorry. 'Tis what you'd expect from a newspaperman, you're thinking. And you're right, for that's the kind of hounds we are. Lewd fellows of the baser sort, as the Good Book says."

Miss Belle smiled forgivingly. "Well, we'll say no more about it, Mr. Moretti. Here's Phylas with two more samples for your comparison. Now take your time, and give me your most considered opinion."

I took a glass in each hand and raised the first one to my lips. Miss Belle beamed approvingly. I took a mouthful and held it in my mouth for a few moments before swallowing it.

"Was it Carroll Glass?" I asked.

Miss Belle's smile disappeared, and her lips tightened to a thin white line. "Good evening, Mr. Moretti," she snapped, and turned on her heel.

I found an empty chair and sat down with my two tumblers of bourbon. I sipped on one and then the other, judiciously. *Must decide which is better—awful job, but somebody has to do it,* I thought. *Miss Belle expects every man to do his duty. One way or another.*

Time passed. I must have dozed off in my chair, and when I awoke I saw that the two tumblers in my hands were empty. The quartet was playing "Humoresque," and it sounded as if they were at the far end of a long, long hall. I felt the rush of apprehension one always feels when a part of his life has passed without registering on his memory. I looked around quickly. I saw no faces I recognized; one bearded dignitary regarded me briefly with distaste and then turned away. Belle was not present. There were only two girls on the settee; one was yawning and the other was inspecting her fingernails. Neither was Marybee.

Marybee. Suddenly I remembered. *Where's Marybee? Didn't she come down? You've got a question or two to answer, my girl.*

I set my two glasses on the deep-piled rug and stood up carefully. Nobody seemed to be paying any attention to me. Placing one foot in front of the other with deliberation, I made my way across the drawing room, past the parlor door, and into the hall. The sound of the music and conversation receded, and the quiet in the hallway seemed

to roar distantly, like a seashell held up to the ear. I began
to walk up the stairs, steadying myself on the smooth walnut banister. At the top was a wide dark hallway extending
the length of the house, past seven or eight doors, all
closed. Small, nondescript sounds came from behind some
of the doors.

Halfway down the hall a young black woman dozed behind a table stacked with snowy towels. She continued to
sleep until I stopped in front of her and cleared my throat.
Then she opened her eyes wide. "What you want, mister?" she asked apprehensively.

"Marybee. Which room is she in?"

"You ain't supposed to be up here alone." She stood
up and drew away from me, as if preparing herself to
sound the alarm. I fumbled quickly for my wallet, ex-
tracted a bill, and thrust it at her. It was a five, causing
her eyes to widen even more.

"I'm a friend of hers. She asked me to come up. She's
not busy, is she?" The maid shook her head. "Then take
this, and tell me what room she's in." She made no move
to take the bill, so I pushed it into her hand and closed
her fingers over it. "It's all right, damn it! What room?"

She pointed silently to the second door to the left, across
the hall. I walked to it and hesitated with my hand on the
knob, listening for sounds within. From the corner of my
eye I could see the maid standing behind her table, staring,
the bill heedlessly clenched in her hand.

I turned the knob and pushed the door ajar. "Marybee?" I whispered hoarsely. There was no reply. I opened
the door wider and stepped inside, closing it behind me.

She was lying on a canopied bed. A pink satin comforter with silver butterflies was turned back under her,
and a frilly white pillow was behind her head. Her carrot-
red hair was braided and wrapped around her head in a
crown, and the rouge on her cheeks and lips stood out
against the blue-white pallor of her skin. Her eyes bulged,
and there were purple marks on her throat.

I must have stood by the door, frozen, for half a minute.

It was as if I were swimming upward through dark fathoms of drunkenness, until my head finally burst out into fresh air. I took a deep, shuddering breath and crossed to the bed. I leaned over her, my ear close to her mouth and one hand on her breastbone. I could detect no sign of life. "Marybee," I cried, "Marybee, wake up! Damn it, Marybee, tell me who did it!"

"All right, you son of a bitch," said a cold voice behind me, "straighten up real slow and keep your hands where I can see them, or you're a dead man, so help me God."

12

Of Miracles and Martyrs

He was a slight man, with narrow shoulders and a sunken chest, small thin hands and feet, a narrow, blade-like face. The face might have been handsome if it hadn't been so deeply lined; his brow was corrugated by three parallel grooves, and two others ran down over his cheekbones, connecting the web of wrinkles around his eyes with the deeper slashes that bracketed his mouth. What could be seen of the mouth under a drooping mustache looked cruel, but the eyes were tired.

He was pointing a derringer pistol at my chest, and it was rock-steady. "Now just what have you been doing to her, mister?" he asked in a light, flat voice.

I raised my hands and stepped away from the bed. "I found her like this! I haven't been in here a minute! Ask the girl outside!"

There was a bustling sound of silks and satins, and Miss Belle appeared beside the man in the doorway. "All right, Billy," she said crisply. "Keep him covered." She moved to the bed and bent over Marybee. After a few moments she straightened. "She's not dead, thank the Lord. Close enough, though." She withdrew a small vial from her bodice, unstoppered it, and passed it back and forth under the unconscious girl's nose. "That's right—take a deep breath, now." Marybee snorted weakly and rolled her head on the pillow. "Good." Miss Belle put the smelling salts away and chafed the girl's wrists briskly. "You're going to be fine, honey. You just rest now, hear?" She straightened. "Billy, tell that girl to come in here."

The maid appeared in the doorway, her eyes like saucers. "Annadora, I want you to tap on all the doors and tell the gentlemen very quietly that we've had a little trouble, and they might want to leave right away. Understand? Just that—nothing else." The black girl nodded. "Then go next door to Dr. Crislow's, and ask him if he could step over here on a professional matter. And Annadora—don't make a fuss." The maid nodded again and disappeared.

The man called Billy gestured at my chest with his pistol. "What about him?"

Belle looked at me in cold appraisal. "Yes, what about you, Mr. Moretti? Here you are, red-handed, so to speak. I thought reporters asked people questions, but you seem to prefer silencing them instead."

"Miss Belle, I swear she was like this when I found her. I wasn't in the room alone with her for more than a minute—you can ask the girl at the table in the hall."

Belle studied me a moment, then nodded. "I know it. I saw you leave the drawing room. I thought you were too drunk to climb the stairs." She glanced at the slight man. "You can put the gun away, Billy. I don't think Mr. Moretti plans anything violent."

Almost regretfully he slid the deadly little toy into his vest pocket. "Then who did it?" he asked.

"Someone who thinks he was successful, and has now almost certainly left the establishment."

I could hear bedroom doors opening and closing, and footsteps hurrying down the carpeted staircase. "Or if he hasn't yet, he soon will have," I said.

Belle raised her handsome brows. "As soon as Dr. Crislow arrives, Mr. Moretti, Mr. Maburn will notify a member of the police department that a small difficulty has arisen. That officer, who is noted for his discretion, will come and question any of the young ladies who may have information, including Marybee, if she is up to it. That will conclude our responsibility; any further action is up to the authorities. Now I suggest you join the other gentlemen who are beating a hasty retreat down the stairs."

"How would it be if I hung around until Marybee is questioned? I'd stay out of the way—" I stopped as Billy Maburn's small hand moved from his hide to a new position next to his vest pocket. Belle checked his movement with a touch to the wrist.

"I'd hate to have to ask Dromio to escort you from the house, Mr. Moretti. I think you saw him helping your friend Cocanougher from the premises a while ago?"

The recollection of the enormous tuxedo-clad bouncer, and of my colleague, hapless, helpless, and trouserless in his clutches, silenced me. I bowed to Miss Belle, nodded to her friend, and made my way out of the room and out of the house.

I slept until nearly noon, and woke up, not surprisingly, with a throbbing headache. Putting one foot on the floor caused such discomfort that I quickly pulled it back onto the mattress. Obviously, getting out of bed was something to be approached with great care. Meanwhile, the best thing to do was to reorganize the facts about *l'affaire McAuliffe* in light of last night's events. With eyelids closed against the abrasive light that seeped through the curtained window, I tried to make some kind of order of the chaos.

Who had tried to kill Marybee? Did she know herself, and if she did, would she tell anyone? Would Miss Belle let her? Was there any way I could find out? It seemed unlikely—I had a strong suspicion that any information of potential value that came Belle Breezing's way would be as closely guarded as assets in a bank vault.

Who had brought Marybee to Belle's? The same person

who had gotten her pregnant? What had happened to the baby?

I remembered the evening before as a series of clearly seen moments separated by murkiness. One image that stood out was the portrait of Belle Breezing, chastely dressed, but communicating an almost palpable sexuality. Why did it seem important? Another was Yarnell's appearance in the parlor, and Farringay's, and later Lawler's reaction to it. Why was Yarnell in Lexington? Because of Farringay? Or Lawler? Or both?

I thought about horses. Specifically, about Uranus and Black Bess, and their problems with male generative organs—the first without a pair he needed, the second with a pair she didn't. And about Sebastian, the golden promise of Kirkargyle, whose fleetness had already eased the financial problems of the McAuliffes, and whose victory in the Buford Stakes could turn the family fortunes around.

Sebastian. What is it about his name that worries me?

I tried my foot on the floor again. It seemed possible, but when I raised my head from the pillow the sharp increase of the pressure inside persuaded me to lay it back down.

What about Carmody? Did he kill Fugate? And the anonymous letters Sandy Braddock and Dorcas had received—who wrote them, and why?

Who killed Carroll Glass's dog?

I thought about what Dutch Egan had said in the back room of Wimple's Saloon on Mulberry Street: Crime is almost always simpler than you expect—look for the basic passions, jealousy, greed, fear, lust, hatred. . . .

But which one of them, I asked myself, *since there's enough of each to damn a churchful of Christian martyrs?*

This was the second-to-last day of the Lexington Summer Meet. Tomorrow would be the Buford Stakes, and afterward I would have no excuse to remain in the Bluegrass. Whatever I was going to find out, for use in *The Spirit of the Times* or the *Police Gazette* or my personal memoirs, had to be found out in the next thirty-odd hours.

For the third time I put my foot on the floor, and this time brooked no argument.

It was too late for breakfast in the hotel dining room, but I prevailed on the waiter to take an order for angels on horseback, served with a bottle of Louisiana hot sauce and a pot of black coffee. There is something about eating oysters when one has a hangover—it's as though you were saying to Nature, "Do your worst, madam; there is no havoc you can wreak worse than what I have already wrought on myself. This will prove it, and the road to redemption is open before me." In any case, it seems to work.

The law office of Birdwhistle & Yates was half a block from the hotel. I asked the clerk in the stuffy waiting room to announce me to Willis Yates, and sat down in an uncomfortable oak chair and leafed through a dog-eared copy of *McClure's*.

Yates didn't keep me waiting long. When I apologized for arriving without an appointment, he waved my words away. "Not doing any work anyway—might as well chew the fat with you. Tell you the truth, I was about ready to close up shop and sneak out to the Fair Grounds and deplete my bank account." He leaned back in his swivel chair and folded his bony arms behind his head. "What can I do for you, Mr. Moretti?"

"Remember back this spring at Kirkargyle, when you said that maybe someday we might want to take in each other's laundry, but that wasn't the day for it?"

He nodded, and a faint grin crossed his turkey-gobbler features. "I remember. And you think maybe today is?"

"Would you tell me about the Regulators and the toll roads, Mr. Yates? Now that we're not imposing on Judge McAuliffe's hospitality?"

He pursed his lips. "Maybe I might—if you'll contribute a *soupçon* of candor to the conversation yourself." I said I would tell him whatever I could. "Good enough. About the toll roads: they're a lost cause, have been for years. They serve no economic purpose, they strangle commerce, and the way people gad about nowadays, they've become an inconvenience to the common man. It's only a matter of a year or two till the legislature passes the laws that will put them out of business.''

"A victory of the public will?" I asked.

"The public will? Mr. Moretti, let me explain something to you about Kentucky politics. People don't vote the same way down here as they do up north. Up there they vote according to where their self-interest lies, or where they think it lies. Down here they vote the same way they bet on horses—they vote for the man they think will win the race. If they guess right, that's all the satisfaction they need—they don't expect any politician to do a damn thing for them anyway. They go back home congratulating themselves on their shrewd judgment, and get their pockets picked for another four years.''

"They'd vote for a man they didn't want, if they thought he had the best chance of winning?" I asked doubtfully.

"Certainly! Because they don't really want any of them. All politicians are politicians, just like all horses are horses. You don't bet on a horse because you like his character. You bet on him because you think he'll win. Politics is marvelous in Kentucky, Mr. Moretti. It exactly meets expectations.''

I digested this for a moment. "Then why, after fifty years, is the legislature going to outlaw toll roads, Mr. Yates?''

"Because the times have changed. They've become anachronisms. They're irrelevant; they don't belong anymore; they don't work. It's a matter of economic inevitability—it has nothing whatever to do with public will.'' Studying my expression, he sighed. "You just don't understand, do you? Politics in Kentucky is a not-very-important spectator sport. Life-and-death matters are decided in a different arena. Just like the toll-road question will have been decided before the legislature ever acts on it. It's the way things are.'' He regarded me sympathetically, like a teacher with a student who will never understand the problem. "Don't worry about it. The point is, Caleb McAuliffe had already won. He didn't need the Regulators. All he needed was to wait."

"And if he'd waited, Mrs. Carmody would be alive today?"

"I didn't say that. Hell, lightning might have struck her, for all I know. But it's damn unlikely she would have been brained by bullies." He groped in his pocket and produced a half-smoked panatela, which he relit, creating an evil miasma that caused the oysters in my stomach to react. "Can't offer you one," he explained politely. "I just have the one to last me till dinner. My doc's got me rationed."

I assured him I didn't mind at all. "Why couldn't Judge McAuliffe wait?" I asked.

"Caleb McAuliffe's a weak man, Mr. Moretti. I say that as an old friend of his. Furthermore, he's the most unfortunate kind of weak man, which is one who wants to show everybody how strong he is. His wife Elizabeth knew how to handle him, but since she died there's been nobody to tell him not to make an ass of himself trying to be a man of destiny. He's a poor manager, and he's had some bad luck, and the worse things got the more determined he was to turn Kirkargyle around. Which made him putty in the hands of anyone who took the trouble to use him."

"Such as certain of his family, or his neighbors?"

He shrugged. "Maybe." He inhaled deeply, then took the cigar from his mouth and ground out the coals in an ashtray. After inspecting the butt, he replaced it in his pocket. "Got to make it last. All right, my turn. About your friend Farringay: did he really descend from a long line of Maryland aristocrats?"

I answered carefully, "My limited knowledge of Jack's family background would incline me to doubt it."

"What is he, an ordinary fortune hunter?"

"I wouldn't call him an ordinary anything."

"Come on, Moretti, fair's fair. Is he a crook?"

I sighed. "To tell you the truth, he's had his problems

with the law once or twice. And I'm afraid that's all I can tell you about it, Mr. Yates.''

"I expect I can find out anything I need through a police inquiry. All right, what's your relationship with Sandy Braddock?''

I blinked. "With Braddock? I don't have any, aside from drinking with him a time or two.''

"He didn't have any reason for bringing you into the house?''

"Nothing more than my own charming personality. And maybe what I might write about Kirkargyle for the paper. My turn again. Tell me about Carroll Glass.''

He spread his hands. "What's there to tell? He's a cliché—the spoiled son of the wealthy squire, doing his best to go from riches to rags in one generation. Now that he's running the place himself, he'll probably succeed.''

"I hear he's had considerable bad luck. Could it have been arranged?''

"I have no idea. He's not the most popular man with some of his neighbors. The ladies like him, though.''

"Not Dorcas McAuliffe. At least, not enough.''

"For which Caleb is thankful, if for nothing else. Are you going to do a story on Kirkargyle?''

"It may depend to a large extent on what you're telling me right now, Mr. Yates. What about Carmody's trial? And have you heard about the anonymous letters the McAuliffes have been getting?''

He grinned. "Everybody in Lexington has heard about the anonymous letters. They wouldn't be as well known if they had been printed in the paper. You'd think somebody was taking a personal interest in publicizing them.''

"Why?''

"Maybe to help Carmody. Maybe because somebody thinks it's time certain facts came out.''

"Are you defending Carmody, Mr. Yates?''

"Not personally. Of course I'm on retainer from the Bluegrass-Capitol Toll Road, and as his employer they have an interest in the case.'' He took out his cigar butt, looked at it speculatively, and after an inner debate put it back in his pocket. "From what I hear, Carmody's chances for acquittal are very good. Better than Caleb McAuliffe's for coming out with his reputation intact."

"There's evidence connecting him with the Regulators that killed Carmody's wife?"

"So I understand. I'm not sure it's admissible—but that doesn't mean the jury won't have heard all about it before they reach a verdict. Things like that get around." He snorted. "The goddamned fool. Wanted to be A Man To Be Reckoned With. Look where it got him."

We sat in silence for a few moments, each with his own thoughts. I felt a sinking sensation which was either hopelessness or the aftereffects of my previous evening's excesses. I couldn't think of any more questions to ask.

I stood up. "It was good of you to take time to see me." We shook hands—his was dry and ropy, like vines in the late summer. We made polite farewells, and I started from the room. At the door I turned. "Does the name 'Sebastian' mean anything special to you?" I asked.

"Only that I have ten dollars riding on him in the Buford tomorrow," he answered.

As I stepped out onto Main Street a church bell was tolling twelve o'clock. I had an hour before I needed to be at the track, so I walked across Gratz Park to Transylvania University, and into the medical hall, where the Lexington Public Library was located. A pleasant-faced little woman asked if there was anything she could do for me.

"Yes, ma'am. Let me see the best book you have on mythology."

She found me the *Wonder Book* and *Tanglewood Tales* and, as I was paging through it, brought me a great tome called *The Dictionary of Classical Antiquities*, which was almost as heavy as she was.

In neither book could I find any mention of a Sebastian.

I returned the books to her with thanks, and went outside and hailed a cab that took me to the Fair Grounds. The crowd inside the gate was smaller than usual, due to the absence of any major races on the day's card—people were saving their money for the Buford Stakes the next day. The McAuliffe box was empty, as were many others. I made my usual rounds and came up with few newsworthy items. After the third race Cocanougher arrived belatedly at the betting ring. His face was the color of liverwurst except for the area around his right eye, which was mustard and burgundy.

I gave him a fraternal clap on the shoulder. "Say, you look good enough to eat. You must have remarkable recuperative powers."

He clung to his equilibrium with difficulty and regarded me with distaste. "You Judas. Didn't you see that great ape manhandling me? Didn't you see him actually throwing me out of that foul brothel, and nobody saying a word against it? What kind of a friend are you?"

"The kind of friend that didn't want to follow you out the same way. Anyway, it's just as well you left when you did. There was a little trouble later—I mean real trouble."

"You mean the little whore somebody tried to strangle? Hell, she didn't even die! Look at this eye of mine, Moretti!"

"You know about that?"

"Certainly I know about it. Just because I'm maimed by aborigines doesn't mean I stop being a newspaperman. A contact at police headquarters passed the word this morning. I heard about it when I came in to the office." He touched his cheekbone gingerly. "I tried an eye patch, but it wasn't big enough. Looked like it had a purple border."

"Do they have any idea who did it to the girl?"

"Beats me. The lid's on. Belle pays for protection, and she gets it. I wish I had protection. Cannibals don't savage people who have protection. Or who have loyal friends to help them." He shot me an indignant look.

"Do you know who the girl is?" I asked.

"Just some apprentice chippie—isn't she?" His expression became suspicious. "Isn't she, Moretti?"

I widened my eyes. "Why, I presume so. I'm a stranger in town. That's why I bring my questions to you. Which reminds me—what do you think about the advance betting on the Buford tomorrow? Do you expect the odds on Sebastian to get better, or worse?"

I kept the conversation on horse racing until we separated a few minutes later. The question of prevailing rates didn't arise, since neither of us had much interest in the hair of the dog that afternoon.

The day wore on slowly. There were no surprises, no dramatic reversals that could fan the interest of a newspaper reader or increase the forbearance of a newspaper editor. I made my notes automatically as my mind kept returning to the McAuliffes and the situation at Kirkargyle. At the end of the eighth race I slipped my notebook in my pocket and left the grounds, just as happy to see no one I knew.

I had dinner alone at the hotel, Kentucky River catfish and hush puppies, accompanied by a good Moselle and finished off with pecan pie, but I didn't pay it the attention it deserved.

A phrase kept echoing in my mind.

Poetic inevitability.

If there was a time for it to make itself manifest again in the affairs of the McAuliffes, this was it. Tomorrow, when Sebastian ran in the Buford Stakes, the future of Kirkargyle ran with him. If Sebastian won, the stable was safe, the jinx was broken, Caleb was again A Man To Be Reckoned With, Dorcas was solidly an heiress, Sandy could drink himself to death without fear of losing his credit in Lexington's saloons. But if Sebastian lost, if something happened to him . . .

I finished my coffee, refused a second cup, and left the dining room and the hotel. Dusk had fallen over the city; the sky in the west still glowed with livid colors reminiscent of Cocanougher's eye, but more appropriate to the time and place; the rest of the sky had darkened to a cool slate gray, and the first stars of the evening were poised at the edge of visibility. I walked toward the park, breathing deeply, and when I got there I circled it twice before I found an empty bench and sat down.

I remembered the other time I had enjoyed the gathering night on a bench here in the park—on a Sunday evening in the spring, the day following the dogfight at Kimbro's barn. The situation at Kirkargyle and my feelings about it were quite different now from what they had been then: at that time the family's fortunes were spiraling downward, and now they were recovering handsomely, and yet my uneasiness about them was as acute—no, *more* acute—now than it had been then. Instead of the serenity I had felt that mild spring evening, I was experiencing the same anxiety, the same sense of foreboding that had driven me to the stable the nights of Uranus's mutilation and Fugate's murder.

Because it's not over. Last night at Belle's proves it. Somehow.

I was too restless to remain seated. I stood up abruptly and began walking toward the Phoenix Hotel. At the next corner was a Catholic church. On an impulse I went in.

A young priest was coming toward me up the aisle. He smiled and nodded.

"Father," I said, "what does the name Sebastian mean to you?"

He stared at me blankly. "I beg your pardon?"

"Sebastian. The name Sebastian. What does it make you think of?"

"Why—Saint Sebastian, I guess. I can't remember hearing the name anywhere else. Why?"

"Tell me about Saint Sebastian, Father."

He drew back from me slightly, as though to guard against irrational behavior. "I hardly remember. He was a soldier, I think—yes, an officer of the Roman guard, under one of the emperors. He was a Christian, and made many converts among the troops under him. The emperor heard about it and ordered him to stop. When he wouldn't, he was bound to a stake and shot with arrows."

"With arrows?" Suddenly a picture appeared in my mind—a handsome young man hanging limply from the ropes that held him erect, a half-dozen arrows protruding from bloody wounds in his naked torso.

"Yes. You may have seen a painting of it—it was a popular subject with artists during the Renaissance. The soldiers left him for dead, but a woman took him away for burial. She found there was still a spark of life in him and nursed him back to health. As soon as he was well, he went and confronted the emperor, who ordered him executed again, this time by being beaten to death with rods."

"And did the same thing happen?"

He smiled wryly. "Even miracles have their limits. No, this time he was really dead. But he appeared to another woman in a dream, telling her where to find his body and where to bury it. She did as she was told, and it was on that spot that a church was later built in his honor." Apparently concluding that I was unlikely to become violent, he leaned toward me. "Now, do you want to tell me why you're so interested in a fifteen-hundred-year-old martyr?"

I was already moving toward the door. "Poetic inevitablility, Father," I flung over my shoulder.

Outside I waved down an empty hack and jumped into the seat. "The Fair Grounds—but take me out back, to the stables. And see how fast you can get there."

The driver, scenting a tip, whipped up his horse and sent us clattering down Broadway. Traffic was light, but even so we drew more than our share of outraged looks and shouted curses. We made the twenty-odd blocks in half as many minutes. When the driver reined up at the stables, I tossed him two silver dollars as I stepped down. Some men were enjoying a smoke by the nearest stable door. "Sebastian—Kirkargyle—where is he?" I called to them.

One of them pointed to the next stable down the lane. "Down at the far end. You got business there, mister?"

"I've got business." I started walking briskly, but broke

into a trot almost at once. *There's no point in running,* I told myself, *five minutes isn't going to make any difference.* Nevertheless, I ran.

I turned in at the end of the second stable and pulled open one of the double doors. Inside, the darkness was damp and heavy and smelled of horse. I stood still, listening to the breathing, stirring, creaking, rustling, jingling, to the breaking of wind and the spatter of urine against wet straw. Close by me a horse whinnied in irritation or fear.

"Hello—can anybody hear me?" I called. "Anybody got a light? If you can hear me, give a shout!"

The only reply was an increase in horse noises. The darkness remained inpenetrable.

I felt in my pocket for matches, found a half dozen, and struck one. In the sudden flare huge black shadows surged away, then regrouped and moved in closer again. Two more horses whinnied in alarm—and I thought I saw something peculiar just beyond my feet.

Before the match went out I found a kerosene lamp hanging from a nail in an overhead beam. I turned up the wick and lit it with a second match, and suddenly the space around me was a luminous island in an ocean of blackness.

The light lapped over the figure on the floor.

It was a man lying on his back, with his head, or what was left of it, close to the door of the nearest stall. He was a burly man, broad-shouldered and thick-necked, dressed in what had once been a handsome suit but was now soaked in blood almost to the waist. Only a small part of the face was visible—I stared at it for ten seconds before I realized it was what remained of Emmett Lawler.

I tore my eyes away and looked at what was clutched in the dead man's hand.

It was an arrow—and its point was shiny with blood.

Suddenly a horse neighed close at hand, and I looked up into a pair of bulging eyes even with mine and only a foot away. The horse was in the stall beside which Lawler lay, and as I stared at him he reared up on his hind legs and pawed toward me with his front hooves. As I pulled back from him I saw the long bloody gash down his neck.

I raised the lantern to illuminate myself as much as possible and said as reassuringly as I could, "It's all right, Sebastian—I won't hurt you. Settle down, now. Good boy." He tossed his head, eyes rolling, and whinnied again. I put my hand on his neck, being careful to keep away from the raw wound, and he shuddered but allowed me to stroke him. After a few moments he began to gentle down.

"Well, is the wretch dead?" asked a voice behind me in a conversational tone. "I should imagine he is—he doesn't look exactly sprightly."

Startled, I spun around to face Jack Farringay, who was looking down at Lawler's body with an expression of mild distaste. "Jack! What are you doing here?" I cried.

"Oh, protecting my property, you might say." He prodded the corpse's arm with his toe, causing the arrow to move and its bloody head to gleam in the lamplight. "Easy enough to see what happened, isn't it?"

"Is it?"

He smiled condescendingly. "Feller sneaked in with an arrow and tried to kill Sebastian with it. Sebastian spooked and bashed his brains out with his hooves. Seems clear enough to me." In the yellow glare of the kerosene lamp his face was as coolly arrogant as an Egyptian death mask.

"Why stab the horse with an arrow? Why not use a bow?"

He shrugged without interest. "Maybe because he didn't have one? Too conspicuous to carry? I don't know, Bunky. Excuse me." He moved to the stall door and inspected Sebastian's head, neck, shoulders, and chest as the horse eyed him nervously. "The gash looks worse than it is, and there isn't any other damage. No reason I can see he can't race tomorrow."

"Wait a minute. There's a man dead on the floor. The

horse killed him. You think the stewards aren't going to want to hold a hearing about that?''

"Purely routine, I should think." He ran one hand up the horse's mane and scratched him between the ears. "What do you say, old boy? You're not about to let them sideline you, are you?"

"Now wait a minute, Jack! I can understand your proprietary interest, even though it seems a little premature, but there are legal considerations here! Lawler's dead, killed by a horse he was trying to kill! The horse has a foot-long slice out of its neck! Thousands of people have money bet on that horse, and thousands more have money bet against him! The track has its reputation for honest racing to uphold! If you think that in less than eighteen hours from now—"

Another voice spoke behind me. "That's exactly what he thinks, Moretti—and just exactly what I think: in less than eighteen hours the Buford Stakes will be won by Kirkargyle's Sebastian, to the considerable financial advantage of some of us. If in the process we choose to run a horse with a scratch on his neck, whose business is it but our own?" Sandy Braddock stepped into the light, his blue eyes gleaming, his sturdy body bent forward. "Listen to me. There are no problems here unless we choose to make them."

I looked from one to the other of them in disbelief. "Nobody's even called a doctor yet, and you say there are no problems?" When neither responded, I went on, "All right, we won't talk problems. We'll talk answers. Lawler's the answer. It was Lawler that killed Lomas Fugate, and tried to strangle his daughter Marybee last night, and gelded Uranus and set fire to Bonne Jeanne's stall and somehow managed to put dogs on Actaeon and copperheads on Nile Queen, and cut Carroll Glass's dog Tusker's throat, for God's sake—" I paused to draw breath. "You're saying Lawler's the answer to all of it?"

"We can dot the *i*'s and cross the *t*'s later, but for now, yes, that's what we're saying. It's over, and we can straighten it out at our leisure, and there's no reason to make a fuss about it when the doctor gets here," Braddock said. "Agreed, Farringay?"

"Oh, certainly. Agreed." He looked at me inquiringly. "You too, Paddy?"

"But—I—" I felt a sudden helplessness. *It's running through my fingers again, and there's nothing I can do to stop it,* I thought. *Hopeless.* "Hell, I guess so. Go call a doctor, Jack. At least he can look at the poor bastard before rigor mortis sets in."

13

A Rainy Night's Farewell

It was a long night. Regardless of what Farringay had thought, the authorities considered the situation a little more than "routine." The police who came began with two patrolmen and continued through a sergeant, a lieutenant, and the chief himself. Medical personnel included a doctor, a coroner, and a veterinarian. The chief steward of the track arrived well after midnight, and Caleb McAuliffe came an hour later.

By the time we had told our story of the night's events and what had led up to them three times, Jack and Sandy and I were performing like an operatic trio. The explanation we offered was as follows:

Emmett Lawler, a man with an unsavory past as a bucket-shop operator, had moved to Lexington and bought a horse farm. As his fortunes improved, he had hoped to combine his Folly Hill with the McAuliffes' Kirkargyle through marriage to Dorcas McAuliffe. Caleb McAuliffe, undergoing financial reverses, was not unmindful of the advantages of such a merger, but was unwilling to try to influence his daughter in her choice of a husband. Lawler decided to apply financial pressure. After Rhoda McAuliffe's bizarre explanation of a pair of unusual but perfectly natural accidents as "poetic inevitability," he planned a series of additional "accidents" that would ultimately force the McAuliffes to accept his merger-by-marriage or face bankruptcy.

Working through the corrupted Lomas Fugate, Lawler arranged for the castration of Uranus and the immolation of Bonne Jeanne. However, something happened the night of the stable fire—we may never know what—that caused the conspirators to fall out; Lawler killed Fugate and left his body to be consumed in the fire, and the drunken and unconscious Carmody to be blamed for it.

Then the McAuliffes' luck turned; Bonne Jeanne brought an excellent price in the bloodstock sale, and Sebastian began winning races. Lawler felt he had to act again if he were to see his plan succeed, and this time he had to do the work himself. He decided to strike before Sebastian could win another purse, and to use a method that would continue the "poetic inevitability" theme.

The result of his bungled attempt was his own death under the hooves of the terrified horse.

Braddock and Farringay and I told this story so confidently that it was accepted without serious question. When the veterinarian stated that in his opinion Sebastian was perfectly capable of running in the Buford Stakes, the chief steward agreed to allow the race as scheduled.

At three-thirty A.M. I walked wearily along Broadway toward my hotel.

Jack Farringay walked beside me, his arm linked in mine. He whistled a chorus of "Aura Lee" through his teeth and glanced at me from the corner of his eye. "We are still enjoying our meeting of the minds, are we not, Bunky?" he asked.

"Who tried to strangle Marybee Fugate? Lawler?"

"Who else? Obviously he was afraid she knew her father had been his partner in the Uranus business, and that he had killed him the night of the fire."

"Who got her pregnant?"

"Don't look at me, old boy. I've had other fishes to fry."

"Who's been writing the anonymous letters?"

"Carmody's lawyer?" He masked a yawn with his fingers.

"Who killed Glass's dog?"

"The old woman who lived in the shoe? Oedipus Rex? How would I know? Moretti, you worry me. You seem unwilling to accept success. You have your story, complete with a murderer who is also the owner of a horse farm. I would hate to think that you would refuse such a neat package because of one or two trivial questions." He turned and gave me a sincere and earnest look. "I have enjoyed our relationship while you were here, but to be absolutely frank, I have been looking forward to our exchange of comradely handclasps as you climb into your Pullman car headed for New York. I hope I can count on that immediately after the Buford Stakes."

"Those are my plans," I said.

"Good, good. And of course you depart with our arrangement intact: you with all the information I can channel your way, and I with your assurance of silence on certain unfortunate events in my past. True?"

"Those are my plans," I repeated.

His eyes narrowed. He opened his mouth, then closed it again without speaking. We walked the remaining half block to Main Street in silence. At the corner, where I was to turn and he was to continue on to the livery stable, he said, "Until tomorrow, Moretti. Until Sebastian solves all our problems."

Maybe all your *problems, Jack,* I thought. *But not all of mine.*

The next day was cloudy and cool, offering the possibility of rain. I wondered how that would affect Sebastian's chances—as I remembered, he had never won a race in mud, but I had no idea if he had ever lost one under the same conditions.

The stands at the Fair Grounds were packed. It was difficult to push a path along the aisles, and by the time I got to the McAuliffe box the second race was over. Except for the late lamented Lawler, the occupants of the box were the same as the first time I had visited it: Judge Caleb, Sandy Braddock, and Dorcas, coping with Carroll Glass and Jack Farringay. They greeted me at varying climatic levels: Dorcas, sunny and warm; Sandy, blustery; Jack, dryly cool; Glass, remote and chilly; Caleb, arctic. No one mentioned Lawler's death, and I didn't either, although I inquired about Sebastian's condition.

"Never better," Braddock answered. "They put a watch on him this morning—I'd tell you what he did, but you'd never believe me."

"How'll he handle a muddy track?" I asked.

He glanced upward. "It's not going to rain, but it wouldn't make any difference if it did. Sebastian's going to win walking away. Take my advice, Moretti—bet your bankroll on him."

"I'm sure Mr. Moretti doesn't need your advice to place a wager, Alexander," Caleb McAuliffe said acidly.

"Oh, don't worry," Sandy retorted. "They don't pay newspapermen much. Moretti could bet his year's salary on Sebastian and it wouldn't lower the odds a hair."

This was so painfully true it defied comment. I took out my notebook and flipped through the pages, frowning in concentration. Sandy opened the picnic hamper and rooted inside, emerging with a thigh. Dorcas and Jack conversed in low voices, and Glass stared morosely over the stands.

Then a voice from the aisle hailed Caleb, and the Squire of Kirkargyle's face lit up with genuine pleasure. "Why, Mr. DeLeon, how are you, sir?" he cried. "Come join us! I insist! We've plenty of room, and I want you to meet my daughter and my brother. Come in, sir!"

A man in a well-cut white linen suit and a panama hat stepped agilely over the bar and entered our box. It was C. Hamilton Yarnell. McAuliffe introduced him to the rest of us, obviously proud of his new acquaintance. "Mr. DeLeon's from New Orleans," he informed us. "He's in the oil business. Mr. DeLeon is a personal friend of John D. Rockefeller.''

Yarnell brushed the words aside with slender fingers. '' 'Colleague' might describe the relationship mo' accurately, Judge McAuliffe. John D. calls very few men 'friend.' '' He bowed over Dorcas's hand, the expression on his patrician face a nice synthesis of respect and frank admiration, and exchanged manly handclasps with Braddock and Glass.

''Mr. Moretti? Don't I recognize that name? Yo' ah not related to the well-known racin' columnist of *The Spirit of the Times*, by chance?'' he said as he squeezed my hand.

''Not by chance—nothing could be more predictable,'' I answered. ''Don't I know you, Mr. DeLeon? Didn't we have a conversation in a dining car once, over sugar cubes?''

''I'm afraid not. I certainly would remember if we had. I rarely meet any of you fascinatin' folks from the spo'tin' world.''

''Mr. DeLeon is in the Bluegrass on business,'' McAuliffe said. ''It was by purest chance I happened to meet him. It wouldn't happen again in a thousand years—''

I never learned what chance occurrence Yarnell had contrived to meet Judge Caleb, for just then the bugle summoned the horses to the gate for the third race, and afterward the two men were too deeply involved in conversation to offer me any further opportunity. When I mentioned the subject later to Farringay, he gave me a blank stare. ''I'm afraid I don't know anything about Mr. DeLeon, Moretti, except that he certainly seems like a cultivated and charming gentleman.''

''You two snakes got together in Belle's parlor, eh? Sort of a mutual 'don't tread on me' association? But if you let him clip the Judge, aren't you ultimately going to pay it out of your own pocket? I should think that might interfere with your live-and-let-live philosophy a tad.''

He looked away as if he had exhausted any possible interest I might offer. "Moretti," he said softly, "screw."

I left the box shortly afterward and didn't come back until just before the Buford Stakes. The sky was still threatening but the track was dry. Dorcas reached her hand to mine and gave it an impulsive squeeze. "Oh, Paddy, isn't it exciting? Sebastian just has to win! It means so much to us! I mean, to Kirkargyle!" Farringay smiled tightly; his eyes were like the eyes of a gambler as he prepares to see a bet and raise. Carroll Glass sat with his feet up on the railing, cleaning his fingernails with a small pearl-faced penknife. I leaned against the rail facing him. "What's your best prognostication, Mr. Glass?"

He looked up sullenly from under a lock of blond hair that fell across his brows. "If that means who am I betting on, I'm not."

"Oh? No faith in the great Sebastian?"

He shrugged. "He's all right. He'll probably win."

"Then why not win along with him?"

"If it's any of your business, Mr. Moretti, because I don't see how Sebastian's winning will help to make me a happy man. And also because I don't have the money to make it worthwhile."

"Carroll, I swear you're getting to be an old stick-in-the-mud," Dorcas turned from Farringay to complain. "You're no fun at all anymore. You'll be sorry when Sebastian wins."

Glass smiled bitterly. "You can be sure of that."

I moved to a seat beside Sandy Braddock. "Any last-minute comments?" I asked.

He turned bloodshot eyes toward me. "About what?" His breath smelled like a half-empty whiskey barrel. I explained I meant about the race. He shook his heavy head slowly. "I'm not going to write your story for you. Think up your own comments. Want a drink?"

I refused, and glanced toward Judge Caleb McAuliffe. He was still deep in animated conversation with Yarnell.

I was debating whether or not to approach them when the bugle announced the Buford Stakes.

The crowd came to its feet as the horses proceeded single file from the paddock toward the starting gate. There were seven horses in the line; Sebastian was third, and the other favored horse, a rangy roan named MacTavish, was last. Sebastian was giving his jockey a little trouble, tossing his head, curvetting, and dancing sideways, but it looked more like high spirits than rebelliousness. I studied his throat through my binoculars; no wound was visible, but the hair was darkened as though by an ointment of some kind.

Sebastian's fractiousness continued as the horses lined up for the start, which he delayed by a minute or two. His position was fourth from the rail, two places outboard of MacTavish. The moment he was finally in place, the starter gave his signal. The other horses burst from the gate in unison, leaving Sebastian standing as if surprised by the unexpected suddenness of it all. By the time he started to run he was five lengths behind the crowd.

"Oh, no!" Dorcas wailed. Caleb swore uncharacteristically, and the sudden tensing of Farringay's body belied the bland smile on his face. A great groan burst from the crowd.

Sebastian remained in last place through the first turn and into the backstretch. Then, his head straining forward and his neck almost parallel with the ground, he began to move up. He passed one horse, then another, then a third, and by the time he reached the three-quarter pole he was neck and neck with the number-two horse, and passing.

They came out of the turn with Sebastian two lengths behind MacTavish, and it was as if the front runner suddenly realized his victory was in jeopardy. The big roan stretched his legs and for fifty yards Sebastian was unable to close the gap by even an inch. "Oh, run, run, please! Oh, please, Sebastian!" Dorcas prayed as she pounded her hands on the rail. Then the Kirkargyle stallion was only one length behind, and then the two horses were head-to-head, and the finish line was only yards away.

This is the time for it, I thought. *For the curse of the McAuliffes, for the arrow to cut Sebastian down.* Suddenly I was so sure of coming disaster I felt I was carved from ice, unable to move, rooted where I stood as a witness to the final demonstration of poetic inevitability. *Now he will fall.*

But he didn't, of course. With a final desperate thrust Sebastian drove his nose six inches in front of McTavish's flaring nostrils, and crossed the finish line clearly the winner.

Kirkargyle was saved. The McAuliffe jinx was broken. The crowd went wild.

Five hours later the rain had come, slow, steady, and drenching, promising to last all night. The streets of Lexington gleamed wetly under the streetlights, and the few horses and carriages on the streets splashed through deep puddles. It was almost time for me to leave.

I had said good-bye to the McAuliffes after a radiant Dorcas and a smugly modest Caleb had joined Sebastian and his jockey in the winner's circle for the victory presentation. My leave-taking was hardly noticed in the general excitement. I nodded to Farringay and to Yarnell, who were standing apart from each other in the circle of onlookers. Farringay smiled slightly, and Yarnell said, "Yo' servant, suh," in a Delta accent. Then my eyes met Sandy's. His brows rose as if in inquiry for a moment, then he made an abrupt gesture with his black-gloved hand.

Leaving the Fair Grounds just as the rain started, I trotted four blocks to the telegraph station, arriving soaked to the skin. It took me an hour to compose my dispatch. I began with

Only hours after surviving a murderous attack in his stall, a gallant Sebastian today won the celebrated

Buford Stakes for his Kirkargyle Stable, in one of the
season's most dramatic and hard-fought races.

Mystery surrounds the role of horse owner Emmett
Lawler, whose dead body was found on the stable
floor outside Sebastian's stall late last night. . . .

I alternated paragraphs describing the race and the
death scene, and included an abbreviated version of the
Farringay-Braddock-Moretti theory of Lawler's activities
and the Kirkargyle jinx, to give Hochmuth something to
blue-pencil. Then I handed the sheets to the telegrapher
and headed into the rain again.

At the hotel I packed my bag and paid my bill. The
clerk at the desk told me the train for Washington and New
York was due to arrive at ten-twenty. I had supper in the
hotel restaurant, and afterward sat down with a magazine
in the lobby. The clock on the wall read eight-ten when I
gave up the struggle and went to the cabstand outside.

We splashed through empty streets. The night air had a
yeasty smell.

"Want me to wait, sir?" the driver asked when we arrived. I shook my head, turned up my collar and seized
my Gladstone, and hurried up the exposed stairway to the
second floor.

Sandy Braddock opened the door at the first knock. He
was in his shirtsleeves, with his collar off and his hairy
chest showing through his open shirt. "Moretti," he said
without surprise. "Come for a stirrup cup?"

"I wanted to look at a picture," I said.

He nodded and stepped back, allowing me to enter. The
apartment smelled even gamier than I remembered, odors
of turpentine and brandy and tobacco lying in layers over
other more corrupt smells, like some spoiled *pousse-café*.
I walked into the long dark room, pausing to set my valise
on the sofa, and continuing toward the stack of canvases
by the icebox at the back. I heard Sandy close the door
behind me. An easel was standing near the windows, with

a partly finished canvas upon it. I paid it no attention. The picture I wanted to see was on the top of the stack. I held it up to catch the light from a coal-oil lamp.

"These weren't the original sketches for the portrait of Miss Belle, were they?" I asked.

"Of course not. I did this ten years later," Sandy said behind me.

I nodded. "But you saw them with the same eyes. Sensual eyes. Lover's eyes. The breasts, the belly, that inviting downward slope between the legs, almost beckoning—I recognized the style when I saw Belle's portrait, even the clothes she was wearing didn't hide it, but I couldn't remember where I had seen it before."

"But now you do."

"Yes." I pointed to one of the nude sketches on the canvas. "Who was your model when you painted this, Sandy?"

"Don't you know?"

"Yes. Marybee. She was your model, and a lot else besides. Did you seduce her, or the other way around?"

He stood motionless, his feet wide apart, his artificial hand resting in his real one. "A little of both, I imagine. It flattered her that she excited me. And she did, oh God she did. Especially after I taught her a few things. You have no idea, Moretti. . . ." His tone was conversational; he could have been talking about the weather as he described a few of the specialties he and Marybee had perfected.

"But then she found she was pregnant," I interrupted.

"Yes, that was an unpleasant development." He paused and smiled grimly. "I wonder who the father was. Could have been me, I suppose."

"Who did Marybee say it was?"

"Oh, Carroll Glass, naturally. The bold cavalier, *sans peur et sans reproche*. The matinee idol. To her poor-white tastes, he represented the beau ideal. A shotgun wedding to him would have been the end of a storybook romance." He began to slap his artificial hand into the palm of the other. "Are you sure you want to hear all this, Moretti?"

"I have to."

"Of course her father had other ideas. When he found out she was pregnant he made her tell him the names of all her lovers—a time-consuming task, I imagine. When he learned that I was a member of the illustrious group, he saw an opportunity far beyond a forced marriage to a wastrel like Glass. He saw a chance to join the Fugates to the McAuliffes of Kirkargyle!" He punctuated his words by slapping his black-gloved hand into his naked palm with a sound like a pistol shot.

"But Fugate was being paid by Emmett Lawler to bankrupt Kirkargyle. Wasn't he? That's the way we told it to the police."

"That's right. He did Lawler's dirty work for him on Uranus, and would have on Bonne Jeanne, too—" He paused.

"—if you hadn't finished him off first," I concluded.

He stared at me, his mouth curved in a tight smile. "What makes you think you're going to catch that train east tonight, Moretti?"

"The eternal optimism of the Irish, or maybe the Italians. What happened at Bonne Jeanne's stall that night, Sandy?" I felt easier turning the conversation away from me, somehow.

"Fugate asked me to meet him there. He told me he knew I was the father of Marybee's baby. He said if I married her he'd make sure no more accidents happened, that Kirkargyle would come back to what it had been. If I wouldn't, he'd sue me in the courts and drag the McAuliffe name through the mud, and the accidents would keep on until there wasn't any Kirkargyle left.

"I told him it was ridiculous, to sue and be damned. He didn't like that. He held up the lamp and threatened to throw it into Bonne Jeanne's stall. He despised me, a cripple and a drunk. What could I do?" He paused, staring at me wildly, and raised his artificial arm in the air. "I showed him what I could do. I brained the bastard!'' The arm hissed through the air and crashed against the back of a kitchen chair, which disintegrated under the blow like a handful of dry straw. He was silent a moment, then went on in a calmer voice, ''He went down like he was pole-axed. I tried to grab the lamp from him as he fell, but it got away from me and broke just outside the stall. The fire started to spread so fast I couldn't stop it. I—I pan-icked.''

Like you did once outside a Georgia farmhouse, when your friend Amory Glass was inside? I thought. It was a question that would never be answered. Instead I said, ''It was you who ran into me in the dark outside the stable.''

''I didn't want to be the first one there. Later, when you and Farringay were getting the horses out, I came back. There was nothing I could have done by myself anyway.'' His voice ended on an uncertain note.

''What about Carmody?''

''As God is my judge, I didn't know he was there! He must have sneaked in before I met Fugate, and then passed out in that shed!''

''And once he was arrested, all you could think of to help him was to start an anonymous-letter campaign, and publicize it all over town. Beginning with yourself, of course, so nobody would suspect you of writing the let-ters.'' *And choosing the death of Amory Glass to write about—was that some sort of expiation?*

I forced myself to keep my eyes from straying to the artificial arm that rested heavily on the shattered chair back. ''That was a generous act, Sandy,'' I said. ''I can sympathize with that.''

He smiled mockingly, and then his expression changed to a grimace of pain. He swayed on his feet and drove the fingers of his good hand into his belly, grunting as though from a massive blow. For a moment I thought he was going to fall, and instinctively put my hand out toward him, but he took a step backward. He dropped his hand to his side, straightened, and said, "Sure you don't want to change your mind about that drink? I'm having one."

I said I'd have a short one. He opened a cabinet door and took out a quart of bourbon, poured me three fingers, and took a full glass himself. He drank half of it, shuddered, and said, "Ah, blessed anodyne!" I took a sip from my glass, watching him over the rim. He set his drink on the table beside him and once again rested his gloved hand in his ungloved one. His eyes moved to the sketches of Marybee in the nude, her face hidden in each pose.

"She was a selfish little bitch, but I tried to take care of her," he said. "After Fugate's death her mother threw her out of the house. I got Belle Breezing to take her in. Belle didn't want to, but I persuaded her"—he smiled crookedly—"for auld lang syne. She got her house physician to do the abortion. The little fool would have been all right if she hadn't tried to get her hooks into Carroll Glass again."

"You didn't try to kill her, did you, Sandy?"

"No, I told you, I was trying to take care of her. In spite of everything, I—no, it was Lawler. He saw you talking to her on the stairs, saw you take her into the parlor. So did Belle; so did I. Belle sent her back upstairs, but Lawler had no idea what she might tell you, now that you knew where to find her. Maybe she knew her father had been on his payroll, doing his butcher's work for him. He couldn't take a chance on that coming out. So he snuck up after her. The towel girl was asleep—"

"Why didn't he finish the job once he'd started?"

He shrugged. "Maybe someone in the hall outside, voices, a hand on the doorknob, who knows? He was a yellow bastard. He convinced himself she was dead so he could get out of the room fast. Too bad for him."

His ungloved hand had moved up his side again and was now pressing rhythmically against his diaphragm. He seemed unaware of it. "I really had too many things against him then: forcing his attentions on Dorcas, trying to bankrupt Kirkargyle, strangling Marybee—I knew he was bound to make his attempt on Sebastian last night, before the Buford Stakes. I figured that since Fugate was dead, he'd have to do it himself. I was waiting for him in the stable.''

"I know."

He registered surprise. "How?"

"The bow. There had to have been one. Lawler would never have chosen to stab Sebastian with an arrow when he could have shot him with a bow instead—it would have meant getting too close to those hooves. So someone else had to have been there, and taken the bow with him when he left. Why? So it would look as if the reason Lawler's skull was crushed was because he had gotten too close to Sebastian when he tried to stab him. No one would look for any other explanation.''

He nodded his head. "My congratulations, Moretti."

"I suppose the bow's around here somewhere?"

"Under the bed. I was going to put it back in Caleb's armory, but I haven't had a chance. I hated scratching Sebastian's neck. Had to do it, though. 'Oh, what a tangled web we weave when first we practice to deceive!' Not Bobbie Burns, unfortunately, but the next best thing—Scott.'' He grimaced again, and his fingers pressed convulsively into his side. "Anodyne," he said, and drained his glass. Then, setting it down, he raised his artificial arm to shoulder height. "Now you think I'm going to let you walk out of here, Moretti?''

My heart was pounding. I forced myself to breathe evenly and even managed a small smile. "Yes, I do. I wouldn't have come unless I was sure of it.''

"Why?"

"You're not a murderer, Sandy. You're a gentleman who's killed a couple of people who deserved killing. What you did, you did to protect your people, your clan, your land. Your friend Burns said it—'Wha will be a traitor knave wha can fill a coward's grave; wha sae base as be a slave—let him turn, and flee!' You didn't flee, Sandy. You stayed and did what had to be done. And now you'd never stain your honor by committing a dishonorable act, and that's what killing me would be. Because I've done nothing to deserve it, and you can't pretend to yourself I have!''

I delivered this foolishness as sincerely as I've ever said anything in my life. He stared at me for an almost interminable moment, his black glove suspended in the air even with my head. Then he slowly lowered his arm to his side.

"You're a reporter," he said dully. "You'll want to write about all this."

"I'm a racing reporter," I corrected. "My editor only cares about horse-racing news. That's all they ever take from me at *The Spirit of the Times*."

He licked his lips. "If you could promise, if I could be sure you wouldn't print anything about me, for—" He stopped in midsentence. His eyes were as imploring as a collie's.

I finished his question for him. "For how long?"

"Did you see the canvas on the easel, Moretti?" I shook my head. "Look at it," he said. I moved to the picture, which was dimly illuminated in the reddish lamplight. "Until then," he said.

It was an oil painting of a man lying in a coffin. It was Sandy. His eyes were closed, and there was a peaceful smile on his face. He was wearing a black broadcloth suit of old-fashioned cut, and his hands were crossed on his breast. The hand underneath was flesh and blood, the one on top was ingeniously constructed of metal and wire and leather. It was hard to be sure in the dim light, but I thought there was dried blood painted on the artificial hand.

"Until then," he repeated.

"How long is that?"

"The doctor says no more than a month. I'm all rotten inside. I can't stand a half hour of it without whiskey. Just a month, Moretti! If you'll give me your word as a gentleman you'll hold off on the story for a month—"

I moved slowly past the easel and toward the front door.

I felt like an inexperienced lumberjack walking on floating logs. "Sure, you've got my word for it, or may the devil take me for an Orangeman. A full month, Sandy." I passed the lamp with the ruby-red chimney crowded between books on the long table; passed the two overstuffed chairs; picked up my Gladstone where I had dropped it on the sofa. I could hear Braddock moving heavily behind me. When I had my hand on the doorknob I turned to face him. "Then it's good-bye, Sandy. I doubt if we'll see one another in this world again—"

He put his black-gloved hand on my shoulder. It was as heavy as mortal sin. "One thing I don't understand, Moretti. What happened to Glass's dog Tusker at Kimbro's barn?"

Knowing what I knew about Farringay, and suspecting what I suspected about his standby plan to develop a dog-fight store in case his matrimonial plans fell through, I was fairly certain that he was responsible for the dog's death; perhaps he had selected Glass for his partner and was attempting to coerce him into agreement. In any case, it didn't seem to be information to which Sandy Braddock was entitled.

"I haven't a thought in me head about it," I said, and stepped out into the rainy night.

The Washington train was twenty minutes late, which was lucky, since I barely made it. I found my berth, which was already made up for the night. Changing into my pajamas, I climbed into it with my notebook, pencil, and traveling bottle; I wanted to get all the facts on paper as soon as possible, before I forgot any details.

I'll wait the month I promised, Sandy, I thought. *The story will still be just as good.*

With any luck Farringay won't have married Dorcas yet, and Yarnell won't have gotten his harpoon too deep into Judge McAuliffe. So I'll be able to square accounts with both of them.

I uncorked my bottle, took a healthy swallow, licked

my pencil point, and held my pencil poised over the blank page. Outside the window, the rolling bluegrass meadows lay sodden under pregnant gray clouds.

Odd that Sandy would have assumed I'd write his family history for a horse-race newspaper, I thought. *I told him my editor wouldn't take anything from me but racing news.*

He's lucky he won't be here to see it when it runs in the Police Gazette.

Author's Note

The lovely and talented Belle Breezing, who was the model for Margaret Mitchell's "Belle Watling" in *Gone With the Wind*, operated her Lexington establishment (called by *Time* magazine "the most orderly of disorderly houses") from 1891 to 1917. At one time prior to that, she had in fact worked in a bordello operated in what is now known as the Mary Todd Lincoln house—a fact perhaps relished by some of Lexington's Confederate Dames. Various authorities spell her last name "Brezing," "Breazing," and "Breezing"; I prefer the last, because the airiness seems appropriate.

Belle's relationship with Billy Maburn is a matter of record, unlike any relationship she may have had with other characters in this book. She is buried under an eight-foot shaft in Lexington's Calvary Cemetery, which bears the inscription, "Blessed be the Pure in Heart."

I must admit to one anachronism: the equestrian statue of General John Hunt Morgan was not installed in the courthouse square until 1911. I would be more embarrassed about it than I am if I hadn't found a precedent—in *The Ides of March*, Thornton Wilder moves an important historical event, the profaning of the rites of the Good Goddess by Clodius Pulcher, from 62 to 45 B.C. As far as

I know, Wilder never bothered to justify his action; the reason I did it is because Lexington's attitude toward Black Bess's genital superfluities seems wonderfully typical of values that have long existed in the Bluegrass (and still exist, judging from the fact that the city resolutely refuses to notice when every year the organs in question are painted a vibrant Day-Glo orange by blithe spirits from the university). Anyway, the statue *could* have been erected in the nineties, couldn't it?

The struggle of the landed interests against the toll road operators ended in victory around the turn of the century, opening the way for the construction of a marvelous network of interurban trains connecting Lexington with Frankfort and other Bluegrass cities—a system which we can see now, when it is too late, was the most efficient and economical form of mass transportation this country ever produced. Too bad.

J.S.

About the Author

JAMES SHERBURNE, a well-known historical novelist, has turned to mysteries with the acclaimed Paddy Moretti series, the first three volumes of which became Detective Book Club selections. He lives in Midway, Kentucky.